Helen McCabe was born and educated in Worcester. She began her career as a librarian, but later became an English teacher.

She is now a full-time novelist and scriptwriter. A member of MENSA, Helen lists her main interests as literature, history and the paranormal, the latter being a constant inspiration in her creative life.

Her 19th century "dream" novel, *TWO FOR A LIE*, was well-received and *RAVEN'S MILL* is a worthy successor.

Also by Helen McCabe

TWO FOR A LIE
TEMPESTUOUS SANDS
TIDES OF LOVE
WIND OF CHANGE

Helen McCabe

Raven's
Mill

Peacock Publishing Ltd

1997

Raven's Mill

Published by Peacock Publishing Ltd
3, St. Mary's Street
Worcester WR1 1HA, England

ISBN 0-9525404-1-X

Cover illustration © Angela O'Riordan 1997
Cover design: Excalibur Graphics 1997

British Library cataloguing-in-print data has been applied for

Typeset in New Century Schoolbook 10pt

Printed in Malta by Interprint Ltd.

When beautiful Lydia Annesley returns to Upwych from London at the age of eighteen to take her rightful place as heiress to a salt fortune, she discovers that her business rival, handsome Caleb Vyne, master of sinister Raven's Mill, appears to have other ideas concerning her future.

AUTHOR'S NOTE

There has been salt in Worcestershire since Roman times and, at the end of the first century, the Evesham Chronicle, written by monks, records the name of Upwich as the site of a salt house which yielded two bushels of salt a year.

By the nineteenth century, brine masters had become powerful men striving in competition with their rivals in the town which had become a thriving industrial centre, producing up to 120,000 tons of salt annually.

The river Salwarpe, which is now a sleepy stream, was also of much importance but the notion that the mill or the court ever housed a Vyne or a Stretton is wholly fictitious.

Worcester, 1997

To

Caroline, Philip and Lucy

ACKNOWLEDGEMENTS

I offer special thanks to my friend and fellow author, Dee Wyatt, who has been closely involved with the preparation of this book. Her input, both in advice and additions has been invaluable. Also to the following; Sue Sallis for her continued support; Tim Wood, whose legal advice regarding the trial has been of great help, and to Hereford & Worcester County Library service for providing historical records.

Chapter 1

"Did you sleep well, aunt?" asked Lydia.

"Well enough, my dear." Elizabeth Annesley sighed, spreading her hands to the welcoming glow of the coal fire in the grate of the sitting-room. "But when one reaches my age," she added, "a strange bed is an uncomfortable companion and I will not be sorry to be back in Upwych." Then Lydia's elderly aunt looked up from the dancing flames and glanced fondly at her niece. "I saw your trunk and hatbox in the hall when I came downstairs. Is everything ready for the journey?"

"Almost." Lydia needed to add just a few personal possessions.

"Then we will leave as soon as the hired carriage arrives whether your stepfather has come home or not."

A small troubled frown puckered the girl's fine brow. "He's home, aunt. I heard him in the night."

Elizabeth Annesley moved forward to pat the small hand of her niece affectionately. The pale shrewd eyes of the older woman were lit with such a genuine warmth that Lydia knew instinctively the observation was spontaneous. It seemed she much admired the courage of the green-eyed, chestnut-haired girl standing so stiffly before her.

"Don't look so distressed, dear. Life at Upwych will be very different from your life here in London, but you will find much warmth and solace there, I'm sure."

"Yes, aunt." Lydia hoped so with all her heart. Suddenly, Aunt Elizabeth looked very sad.

"You are so like your poor, dear mama," she observed softly. "Such a face your mother possessed, like the Madonna." Then the old lady chuckled. "But you're like Bertram, too. You have his eyes, and, I sense, a little of his spirit - a true Annesley."

Those same eyes smiled candidly back, green like emeralds, eyelashes strikingly long, and her eyebrows dark, darker than her hair.

"Thank you, aunt. Come, I have prepared breakfast in the dining-room."

Lydia led the way along the wide tiled hall, immensely touched by her elderly relative's compliments. When her aunt had arrived late yesterday afternoon, she had been afraid that she might be disappointed and, as she had held her hand in greeting, she wondered if Aunt Elizabeth had noticed that it was not quite as smooth as it should have been for a young lady of her social standing.

Now, as they walked along the corridor together, discoursing on the whims of the chilly autumn weather, Lydia instinctively curled up her hands as if to hide the offending palms; despite having spent the morning trying to soften them with glycerine and witch hazel cream. It had been an impossible task. Her daily turns at sweeping and dusting, and the arduous task of hearth blacking, had left their indelible, calloused marks.

Lydia found herself warming to the plump, fussy lady by her side. This was the first time they'd had an opportunity to converse at any length, for when she had arrived yesterday her aunt had been tired and had retired early.

But, now, Lydia felt she had a friend. Except that her relative's references to her parents had shaken her a little. She had only a slight remembrance of her father but the recent loss of her mother had been hard to bear.

Lydia sighed inwardly. It had been hard enough making ends meet before but, now, in the few months that had passed since her mother had gone from them, her step-father's rash investments had swallowed up most of what little money had been left, making domestic life far from easy. She had been forced to dismiss the servants long ago.

Lydia led her aunt into the dining-room, glad that she had taken more care than usual with her dress. She wondered, too, whether the elegant old lady had noticed that her unhooped skirt was lacking in circumference by many an inch compared to those worn by the fashionable ladies of the day; that her petticoats, peeping below the green cambric dress, were plain; and that the same green cambric dress was untouched by even a wisp of lace? But, if she had noticed, the lady had given no sign.

Her aunt glanced around with approval at the pleasant decor of the dining-room; at its square mahogany table and the hard, upright chairs placed around in a prim line. "A handsome room," she commented approvingly.

Then Lydia saw how her eyes were drawn to the picture on the wall, a landscape of hills and bright open skies reflected in a gleaming river. As her aunt examined it, she remembered her mother's delight the day she had brought it home as a gift for her birthday. Was it only ten short months ago?

Remembering, Lydia's gaze drifted to the vase of flowers on the small table by the window, and thought again of the daffodils she had placed on her parent's grave. They would be withered now, the loving words, so carefully written, washed out by rain and only the smudged card left to tell of her love and grief.

The familiar stab of pain forced her eyes back to the lady gracing her dining-room, as she tried to control her tears.

"What a striking picture!" Aunt Elizabeth's gentle voice broke into her silent thoughts and made her start and, when Lydia nodded, she commented softly, "What a talented artist!" She adjusted her lorgnette to peer more closely at the painting. "I must confess I've never seen this artist's work before, but he shows great talent - I rather think the young man will go far."

"It . . . it belonged to my mother. It's lovely, isn't it?"

"Indeed it is. I will arrange for it to be brought to Upwych along with the rest of your things."

Elizabeth Annesley turned away from the painting and placed an affectionate hand on Lydia's arm. "And you, my dear, you too are lovely. So like your dear mother, yet with my family's eyes."

Lydia allowed herself to believe that, although she couldn't possibly be as beautiful as her mother, she shared, at least, some of the handsome Annesley features.

"Ma'am!" The door opened abruptly to reveal the tall, broad-shouldered form of her stepfather. Both women turned as one to face him.

Brodrick Fortey, the eyes in his gaunt face dulled from lack of sleep, cleared his throat as Lydia eyed him warily. Still a handsome figure in his dark blue velvet frock-coat, he regarded Aunt Elizabeth stiffly for a moment before stepping forward to take the lady's hand, bringing it to his lips and kissing the fingertips briefly.

"Mr Fortey." The warmth had suddenly gone from Elizabeth Annesley's voice. "So at last we meet."

"Indeed we do, Miss Annesley." He stood, eyes narrowed with suspicion. "I'm sorry I wasn't here for your arrival yesterday. Business, you know. I trust your journey to London was comfortable?"

And, when Lydia's aunt inclined her head in acknowledgement, he cast his glance around: "Ah, I see Liddy has made breakfast!"

Lydia winced at the sobriquet - a diminutive she had allowed only her mother - and her lips tightened with distaste.

He was acting with impeccably good manners as usual but she knew just how he could turn that devastating charm to his own ends when it suited him. Hadn't he beguiled Mama in that way?

Instinctively, Lydia moved away. She couldn't bear to be near him. Handsome he might be, his tall figure still able to move with athletic grace, but Lydia, although inexperienced in the ways of the world, was sensitive enough to realise that outwardly charming people can, inwardly, often be ugly and cruel. Her eyes registered a cold indifference as she regarded him now. Two wings of thick dark hair sprung from his forehead to reveal an intelligent but sardonic brow. Yes, he was still a fine-looking man but already his cheeks were beginning to display a few broken red veins, come from too much port and too much time at the gaming table, and his beringed hands were mottled and showing signs of podginess.

Lydia dutifully poured some tea as she tried to stifle her disgust. Living alone with him these last six months had been intolerable. Not that she could accuse him of anything. His behaviour had been quite proper towards her whenever anyone was present. But she knew to her cost of his darker side.

He had never quite disgraced himself, explaining his fumbling attentions to her person as nothing more than solicitude for her grief. But she had heard his drunken footsteps outside her door on many a night, calling her name and begging her to let him in. And she'd lain, her young body shaking in the thin muslin of her night-gown, waiting for the worst.

But, thankfully, perhaps because of her stricken silence, he had eventually lurched away. He had never broken down the door as he had often threatened and lately he'd left her alone.

He'd started to console himself with other women again - just as he had when her mother had lain sick and dying - and there'd been many a night when she'd heard the coarse, shrill sound of female laughter come from his bedroom. That was surely the worst betrayal of all. Lydia would never forgive him that.

Her sombre reflections came back to the present as she heard her aunt's persistent voice in response to her stepfather's question.

"I did indeed," she was saying. "You received my correspondence, I trust?"

"I did, ma'am."

"Then you already know the reason for my brief visit here - and you are quite satisfied with the purpose of it?"

"Satisfaction is hardly the word I would choose," Brodrick answered sharply. "Especially as you are about to take Liddy away from me."

The old lady took a step forward. She was clearly not a woman to be intimidated, and her slight flush of indignation was only thinly veiled.

"You're blunt, sir," she retorted spiritedly, "and so I shall be also. It has been agreed. And it will be better for all of us if Lydia comes with me to Upwych."

"Away from her father? Come, Miss Annesley, is that how you see your duty?"

"Her *stepfather*, Mr. Fortey."

Lydia moved out of earshot, crossing to the open window and looking out as her aunt and Brodrick engaged in confrontation.

Her green eyes clouded as she watched a flock of rooks rise, wheel and caw above the poplars. She pondered momentarily on her destiny and wished she could be left in peace instead of being argued over like this, as if she were nothing more than a piece of fine china to be bargained for. After a moment, she turned back to them.

"Aunt," she began, her high clear tone breaking into their discourse, "my stepfather and I have already discussed my leaving and, in spite of his objections, he knows quite well my intention to go with you."

Lydia spoke as she felt; it was her fashion and, as she caught the look in Brodrick Fortey's eyes, her chin tilted defiantly.

"Good girl!" smiled her aunt. "Well, Fortey. . ?"

He spread his hands in a gesture of resignation, then stuck his thumbs into his waistcoat pocket. He shook his head wearily before taking out of his pocket a gold-chained watch, looked at the time and shrugged.

"What can I do? It would seem that I have no further say in the matter. If you must take Liddy, then you must, ma'am." As he replaced his watch, his dark eyes regarded his step-daughter coldly. Then, to Lydia's discomfort, he moved towards her, took her hands in his and pulled her towards him. "A delicate little flower like my Liddy needs a strong man to guide her until she finds a husband," he murmured thickly. "You know I don't want you to go. This is your home and you will always be welcome here, for your mother's sake."

"I am not your Liddy, sir," Lydia answered coldly as his words oozed over her like dripping marchpane, making her want to shrink away. "And I am well able to take care of myself."

A little nagging voice in her brain was telling her that maybe she was being too hard on him. After all, he had been mourning her mother, too, and she had perhaps not given him a chance. But, then, she remembered his womanising; the times he had caught her unawares, revulsing her with his wet kisses and fumbling acts of false condolence. Her eyes closed tightly against his face as he brought it down to kiss her on both cheeks. And a louder voice, crying over the ruin of her mother's wasted love, soon silenced the other.

He betrayed Mama, she thought grimly. *Now I must leave here and make my own life. No man is going to hurt me as Fortey hurt my mother.*

Some of the distaste she felt for Brodrick must have communicated itself to her aunt.

"Come, Lydia," the old lady was saying softly, her protective arm around her niece's waist, "it's time to leave. Hurry and put on your travelling gown and cloak. I will wait for you in the hall."

They moved away from Brodrick towards the door. Once there, Elizabeth Annesley turned again to Lydia's stepfather and said in a satisfied manner, "I'm sure Lydia will be most grateful to know that she would be welcome here, sir, but she's almost eighteen and must take her rightful place as the future heiress of Upwych."

Then, turning back to Lydia, and in a different tone of voice, she instructed, "Now, go to your room, child, and change quickly. We must not be late for the train."

Lydia left the room silently, going upstairs into her bedroom on the second floor. Suddenly, she sat down in the comfortable wicker chair by the open window and, for a brief moment, felt her courage desert her.

She tried to reason. At least she would be free of Brodrick Fortey. But he was the only man she had known, her father dying when she was less than twelve months old.

Too many things were happening too fast, and it all seemed so unreal. She got up, and going over to her dressing table, brushed her long chestnut hair before putting on her new bonnet.

Then a feeling of excitement began to nip away at her stomach as she thought of the new life beginning. What did the future have in store for her now? What did she know of Upwych? What would she find there? Hadn't her mother once told her that it was *gracious in parts*? That it had an Assembly Room? Wasn't that where her parents had met each other, dancing together into the night? It had sounded so romantic to Lydia's young ears. Would she find romance, too?

And herself as an heiress was something she had to try hard to imagine. She racked her brain, attempting to dredge up the sketchy details Mama had confided. Annesley House was a grand place with a clutch of servants and stables and horses. How would she fit in? But, then, she was remembering her mother's tales of her childhood home.

"Upwych is a cheerful place and you will love it there, dear," Mama had promised. "And, one day, you will have to take your place as the owner of the finest salt factory in the world."

"The owner?"

"Yes, dear. Aunt Elizabeth is no longer young, and soon, perhaps, it will be passed down to you. It is a great privilege, but a responsibility also. The whole of Upwych life revolves around the salt works. You will soon have to learn of it."

"Learn of what, Mama?" Lydia had asked naively. "What can one possibly learn about salt?"

"You will see, dear. In Upwych, one cannot avoid the salt."

Lydia's eyes misted with tears as she remembered those loving moments with her mother but she knew, too, that she was wasting precious time dreaming like this. Moving quickly she changed into her blue woollen gown and packed a few of her most treasured mementoes into her travelling basket; a miniature of her father, a childhood sea-shell and a small pearl brooch that had belonged to her mother. Soon, she was ready. Lydia took one last look round at the only room she had ever known and then, picking up her bonnet and closing the door softly behind her, she went downstairs.

Her aunt and stepfather were still at their debate.

"Liddy, a business woman?" Brodrick was sneering as she reached the bottom stair. "My late wife's family, like my own, have little knowledge of trade."

"Trade, Mr. Fortey," her aunt responded sharply, "has assured my family of prosperity, and it is a situation that is decent and to be respected. You will note that I have no repugnance in mentioning money. In Upwych, salt men are gentlemen," adding caustically, "which is more than I have found during this thankfully brief sojourn in London."

Lydia saw Brodrick swallow hard. He was naturally a bully and resented anyone getting the better of him - especially a woman. But Aunt Elizabeth was not to be browbeaten and she rose from the ladder-back chair haughtily, straightening her rustling, purple skirts around her ample shape.

She gave Brodrick a sharp nod. "Our conversation is ended, Mr Fortey. You have been recompensed handsomely for the deprivation of your stepdaughter's company, and there's no more to be said. The hired carriage is waiting to take us to the railway station. We'll waste no more time."

Lydia's heart warmed towards her aunt as she moved with her to the door. It was clear she had the same opinion of Brodrick as she had herself and that alone made her her friend as well as her aunt.

"The sooner we are on that steam locomotive, the sooner we'll be back in Upwych," added her aunt.

Lydia smiled as she took her relative's arm and led her out of the house. With a cold goodbye to her stepfather - and wondering quite how much Fortey had accepted to relinquish his responsibility of her - she helped her aunt into the hard leather upholstery of the brougham and covered her legs with a rug. As Lydia climbed in herself, the driver secured her baggage onto the rack before they set off towards the station. It was only when they were safely on their way that she allowed herself a satisfied little smile. For once, Brodrick Fortey had met his equal.

* * *

The young stoker sweated away on the footplate of the train as he shovelled the coal. In the First Class accommodation, Lydia felt the furnace's warmth as she stared at a picture of an Evesham apple orchard and listened to the train's whistle and the rattle-rattle of its iron wheels.

21

They were the only occupants of the carriage now on that brisk autumn morning, quite different from the hustle and bustle when they had first boarded the train at the busy station. Many of its business passengers had alighted at Worcester, only a few remaining on the platform to continue their journey by the local train. And, Lydia observed, most of these were either old or invalid and, so Aunt Elizabeth informed her, on their way to Upwych to soothe their ills in the increasing popularity of the brine baths.

Now, three miles north of Worcester, and with the confused heap of that city's buildings left far behind, Lydia could hardly contain her excitement. She leaned forward in her seat, her green eyes glowing as Upwych drew nearer.

"Aunt, I think we're slowing down. Wake up! Do, please, wake up! We must be nearly there."

Elizabeth Annesley roused herself, rubbing her neck to ease the ache brought on by her uncomfortable slumber.

"Nearly there? Already?" She stirred, rubbing her still-drowsy eyes, and looked out of the red-curtained window of the train. The smoke from the engine was curling over them, blending like a cloak over the mist of the landscape. "No, Lydia, we're not quite there yet, but the train is slowing down."

"Why, aunt?" Lydia stepped quickly across to look out of the window. "Why is the train stopping here?"

"I don't know, dear, but people tell me it often happens."

Lydia's green eyes sparkled as she looked out at the gentle countryside around them, so different from the London scene she knew.

"Oh, aunt, what a pretty place. Is Upwych just like this?"

Her aunt smiled indulgently, settling back to finish her doze. "This looks like Fern Hill Heath. We've not much farther to go now and, yes, most of Upwych is as pretty as this - once one is out of the valley and away from the chimney-stacks."

"Then I must get ready." Lydia moved back to her seat to pick up her bonnet, setting it firmly on her head and fussily arranging the chestnut curls around it.

Its gossamy veil and sprigs of spring flowers along the brim suited her and, as she regarded herself in the tiny oval mirror above her seat, placing her head first to one side then the other, she felt her confidence grow. Lydia wasn't vain but she was pleased with her reflection. Somehow she felt much older, experienced even, almost a lady.

But the feeling lasted only a moment because, just then, the train juddered to a full sighing halt and, holding on to her hat, she almost lost her balance.

"Goodness me," her aunt said crossly, "I do wish these locomotives were more considerate to a lady's forbearance. Horse carriages are far more dignified."

But Lydia hardly heard her. She had hurriedly left the seat and had already pulled on the leather strap to open the window still further. Hanging precariously out of the upper half of the compartment, her eager eyes drank in the beauty of the high banks of ferns and grasses and trees. Surely, this was fairyland. And now that the sound of the engine had ceased, the air seemed unnaturally still with only the breeze sighing through the branches.

But the peace and quiet lasted only a moment. Soon she was aware of wild, raucous sounds all around her. Her head spun towards the spinney of elm trees where the sounds were loudest. There were voices - men's

23

voices - guttural, shouting. Dogs were barking and howling and then more shouting, until suddenly, the earth seemed to explode with the stampede of horses' hooves. It was pandemonium. Dogs, horses and riders were everywhere. Breaking over the hedgerows from the spinney, through the bracken, crashing across the fern. A horn bellowed stridently as a huntsman, cracking his whip, came flying past close to the train, almost close enough for Lydia to touch as he beat his frantic hounds away from the line.

"Why, it's a hunt," cried Lydia, craning her neck as the confusion of unruly dogs leaped around the wheels of the carriages. "Do come and look, aunt. This is marvellous. I've never seen anything so marvellous in my whole life."

The old lady smiled but remained quietly in her seat. She had seen many a hunt and it moved her but a little. Still, she mused, doubtless it must be exciting for Lydia, having come from London and not used to country ways.

Lydia's green eyes danced, letting the robust, colourful scene wash around her. Of hunting she knew very little, but how thrilling it all seemed. Her curls, beneath the pretty hat, glowed almost golden in the pale sunlight, and the vibrant hues of her sky-blue woollen gown gave her the look of a Gainsborough lady. She stood, rapt, framed like a picture in the train's window.

A rider crashed through the fern. A wild young huntsman in black jacket and stock, reining hard on his bay to prevent it plunging onto the tracks. He waved his whip boldly, overtaking and reaching out to drag at the reins of a second, scarlet-coated rider whose flailing whip had scythed through the air, causing his horse to stumble.

"Damn you, Caleb!" yelled the rider in red. "You rob us of our sport." He kicked at the mare's flanks as it careered into the side of the stationary train. "Out of my way!"

"You fool!" the huntsman in black shouted back, his words hoarse and urgent. "This isn't sport. Get away from the line. Hell's teeth, you'll have us all killed."

His angry, forceful instructions carried clearly into Lydia's hearing as, at that moment, he saw her. But he did not acknowledge her presence, gave no sign of regret that his tone might offend a lady, and Lydia gaped wide-eyed, first at him and then at the second rider.

The second one galloped nearer, doffing his hat to reveal a shock of straight fair hair and, smiling at her with the bluest, devil-may-care eyes she'd ever seen, he called quite shamelessly,

"My compliments, ma'am."

But, as Lydia nodded in confusion to the handsome face, the rider in black had already caught him up, turning his horse, forcing him up the bank and away from the train. She watched fascinated as they reached the brow of the embankment together and drew rein, both riders turning their heads briefly back as the fair one, grinning, waved his crop.

But the dark one stood his horse on the trampled earth, unsmiling, arrogant and impatient. The riding-jacket was open at the neck, cut perfectly across the broad shoulders and, even at such a distance, Lydia held herself still, stirred by his vibrant masculinity.

He held her gaze briefly. She imagined perhaps a flicker of interest in the dark, narrowed eyes. But if it had been there at all, it was quickly suppressed.

He turned his horse, his face determined and angry in the pale light. He snatched again at the rein of his companion's mare and then, as he snapped out a brusque command, they were gone - lost to the shelter of the trees. The dogs followed, more meekly now, as if they, too, were powerless against their master's imperious voice.

Then it was all over. The strains of the horn died away and all that was left was the broken undergrowth and the trampled brushwood.

Lydia was breathless. As she sank into her seat, the train hissed back to life, gathering its mechanical strength more slowly than the natural force of the horses and riders. Sitting quietly beside her sleeping aunt, Lydia closed her eyes and thought of what was waiting for her soon in Upwych. Would it be all she hoped?

She sighed. It didn't seem to matter now. Somehow, try as she might, Lydia found herself unable to drag herself completely away from the spectacle and back to reality; felt an odd reluctance to leave this place in the hope the dark rider might come back.

The Great Western locomotive chugged on around the loop of line skirting the River Salwarpe, entering at last the unlovely surroundings of the industrial belly of Upwych, with its low chimneys and ugly sidings.

On reaching the small station, the view was disconcerting, the most prominent objects being a conglomeration of tall chimney-stacks and a confused huddle of ugly old houses that seemed to teeter on the edge of a broad canal.

And, as she stepped off the train, Lydia's nostrils were assailed by the pungent vapours of sodium chloride, a tang ten times stronger than the therapeutic healthiness of the salty air she remembered on a day's visit to Brighton.

But Lydia wasn't really seeing any of it. Her attention

was still with the hunt and the two handsome young horsemen but, particularly with the rider in black. She could not bring his features quite into focus, yet his presence had crowded and jostled her thoughts. She wished his manner had been more friendly, and she remembered the faint trace of red in the dark hair, under-pinning the temper that had already been in evidence. And Lydia remembered, too, the way the brown eyes had faintly mocked her.

"How absurd," she murmured, aware of the beating of her heart. Then hurriedly stifling her spasm of exhilaration, followed her aunt on to the main street of Upwych. Yes, it was ugly here, but there was no question of turning back now.

Lydia's green eyes glistened. Strangely, she felt quite optimistic. She might never get used to the ugliness, but the lovelier picture of the hunt would always remain with her and sustain her. Yet she was puzzled, too. Puzzled at the feeling of joy it had brought, and of the knowledge that she would never forget the thrilling power the black-coated huntsman had exuded over the scene about him.

* * *

Chapter 2

Caleb Vyne bathed and threw on a dressing robe, dismissing his manservant and expressing a wish to be alone.

The servant bowed and withdrew as Caleb poured some brandy into a crystal goblet and, moving to the window, looked out to the mist-shrouded ridge above the river, glad that this hellish day was almost over.

His mood was sombre as he swallowed the liquid fire. He did not want to think any more about the morning's incident and cursed aloud that he had agreed to go hunting with Charlie in the first place. He should have known better.

His half-brother was a liability; too impetuous, too rash, and would not listen to reason. The knowledge annoyed him. Caleb didn't suffer fools gladly and Charlie was a fool, seeming to thrive on controversy.

He moved stiffly into his dressing-room, glancing cursorily at the attire so carefully laid out. Caleb placed his goblet on the small table by his bed and pulled on the fine serge trousers.

He was tired, but not too tired to seek out some warm companionship tonight - the companionship of a friend he could trust. And, as he wound his cravat and shrugged his broad shoulders into his grey frock-coat, he thought again of the morning's hunt.

His displeasure deepened. A fierce anger still burned in his belly. Caleb Vyne did not easily damn a man, but he had seen too much of the world not to deplore the weakness of his feckless younger brother.

More disappointment settled coldly on him as he thought of the man whose blood sprang from the mother they shared. Of his lying; his cheating at cards; and, most of all, at his abuse of the privilege that the salt works accorded him by right.

And knowing he could prove nothing, Caleb fought off an overwhelming desire to wring his brother's neck.

For long Caleb had hoped it was Charlie's youthfulness that made him so imprudent, and that one day he would learn to act like a man. But that day was long coming. Instead of a brain, Charlie seemed to have a head filled with sawdust - and especially when it concerned a pretty woman. *My God,* he thought grimly, *just look what happened this morning. He could have been killed - and the others, too - careering into the train merely to bring a blush to a young girl's cheek.*

A curious rage caught at his loins as he remembered the girl. There was no denying that her beauty had left him breathless too. Caleb couldn't remember seeing anyone look so fragile before, so unreachable, and he had felt something akin to pain when those startling green eyes had smiled so shyly into those of his half-brother.

Caleb's frown deepened. The image of the girl's face lay imprinted on his mind. Why, in God's name should he think of her now? Hell's damnation! She was only a girl, and he'd glimpsed her for only the briefest of moments. He grimaced. He would have to mend his ways. He knew plenty of eager ladies who, even without

29

the offer of a small sum, would be more than willing to share his bed.

It occurred to him that, lately, perhaps his energy had been directed too much towards his work. He'd been spending too much time at the works. He had almost forgotten that there were still pretty women in the world - and he'd been too long without one. But this one was so young - and virgins had never been his fancy.

He turned abruptly from the dressing mirror, experiencing a strange feeling that, at first, defied analysis. But, moments later, when he realised what the feeling was, Caleb Vyne allowed himself to smile. He desired the girl - it was as simple as that. From the moment he'd seen her framed in the window of the compartment, he had been attracted to her. A profound sexual hunger settled itself deep inside his gut and he would have to be a liar if he were to deny it.

Swiftly, he turned back to the mirror, forcing his attention away from his fanciful lust and back to his cravat, tying it expertly before pulling on his boots. Women could come later. He had enough to think about with Raven's Mill.

Caleb reached for his cloak and strode to the door. Whether he knew it or cared, he was a handsome figure standing tall and straight on the stone steps outside his house.

In his mid-twenties, Caleb's wide mouth smiled too rarely, giving his features a sternness, an uncompromising gravity that was misleading; a steadfast severity that was intensified by the darkness of his brown eyes.

Tonight, he needed air. He would walk to the inn. The rain that had threatened earlier was now reduced to a fine drizzle and, for a moment, his features, lean and stern, were illuminated by the yellow glow of the lantern above the gates. And, so, deciding to leave his bay to its bed of warm straw, he set off, frowning against the world.

He wished he had someone he could turn to, but there was no one. And there was no point at all of him discussing the matter of Charlie with his grandfather, because the old man doted on him. And it was even more impossible to approach Charlie's father - his stepfather. He was no more than a drunken fool, a man not to be trusted. Thus, with his mother, Lavinia, too sick and weary to carry the extra burden of his own futile despondency, Caleb turned to Sam Shrike.

* * *

Caleb pushed open the door of 'The Talbot' and looked around for Sam. The barman, seeing Master Vyne in the doorway, touched his forehead and, for a moment, as though aware of the presence of a gentleman of note, the noisy laughter of the inn customers diminished.

"Master Caleb, sir?" Sam beckoned from a table in the far corner of the room, his face flushed, a tankard already in his hand. "Over here, sir." Sam's fair hair, darkened with its generous coating of Macassar oil, gleamed in the smoky light, and his thin shoulders hunched forward as he sat down again. He leaned his elbows on the trestle table, his hands securely gripping his pint of ale.

Caleb dropped easily into the vacant wheel-back chair opposite. "The young rogue drew the hounds right on to the line this morning, Sam," he said, signalling for more ale to the barman. "There was no way of heading them off. He had no thought, riding like a madman even

31

though the noon train was due. We've already lost six good hounds through my brother's recklessness."

Privately, Sam wished young Charlie Sheridan to hell, but aloud he said: "Take your ale, Mr. Vyne, and don't fret. It wasn't your fault."

"He distracted the dogs, threw them off the scent at the cutting and then rode like a demon after them. Near broke his neck - his horse's, too, and all because of . . ." Caleb Vyne broke off as he thought again of the girl on the train.

"All because of what, Mr Vyne?" asked the salter, glancing at Caleb inquisitively. The ale was warming him and a bit of gossip would be a comfort after a hard day in the brine pit.

"The train, standing there. . ." Caleb paused, somehow reluctant to mention, even to Sam, the advent of the girl. He gazed into his ale for some seconds then shrugged, saying, "Lucky the driver had his wits about him."

"Aye," smiled Sam, a little disappointed that it was not something more. "Mr. Charles has a grudge agin' trains." He took another swig at his ale.

The two men lapsed into a comfortable silence. Caleb was only three years younger than Sam but, looking at the two men, it seemed hard to believe. Sam's youth had been taken by the salt. He'd worked hard and long since he'd been ten years old, his father dying before his time and leaving young Sam to care for his mother and the ones who were left. But, in spite of the wide separation of their backgrounds, Caleb was in closer communication with Sam than anyone, and both men remembered fondly the times of their boyhood when the older youth had carried the rods for young Master Vyne to the Salwarpe, and of the fish they'd shared later with Sam's mother, Maria and his sister, Sal, in their tiny cottage.

Caleb asked quietly, "How is Sally, Sam?"

Sam frowned and shrugged. "Mam's not too happy with her, Master Caleb. She seems too peaky by half."

"I'm sorry." Caleb didn't want to betray to Sam just how worried he was about Sally; that her health was of some concern to him. "Perhaps it was wrong of me to put you both to work at Annesleys. Perhaps Miss Annesley's foreman is putting Sal to work too hard and too soon after her last sickness?"

"May be so, Master Caleb," muttered Sam, "but it's no use talkin' to her; she's stubborn is my sister. None of us can get anything out of her, try as we do."

Caleb nodded sombrely. "Sally's a close one, I grant you," adding with feigned nonchalance, "I didn't think she looked too well in church last Sunday."

For a while Sam didn't answer, sitting there taking long draughts of his ale. Then, with a fleetin smile, he went on quietly, "No, she wasn't, and right worried we all were." He paused again, scratching at the long fair hairs on his arm; fair hair that was also revealed by the open two top buttons of his flannelette shirt. Then he smiled a little self-consciously. "All we salters would be better off in Upwych, I shouldn't wonder, if you had charge of things. But getting us away from Mr Charles was no mistake. Take my word for it."

Caleb stirred uneasily on the hard chair, his dark eyes sharp and knowing he'd just been paid a high compliment.

"You know I have no say in the employment nor conditions of our salters, Sam. That's still left to my grandfather, even though he is turned eighty and only seems to listen to Charlie these days."

"Aye, and pity it is, sir. One of the old school he is. Just like Mr. Herbert Annesley was before Mr. Bertram and Miss Elizabeth."

Sam drained his tankard, setting it down again noisily. "But times change they say, and now there's another takin' charge. Funny, ain't it, Master Caleb, how women seem to be runnin' the whole of Upwych these days?" He shook his head. Sam was glad his mother, Maria, took notice of him. He wanted to be the only master in his house.

Caleb looked up from his glass. "Another taking charge, Sam?"

"Aye, sir, wi' Miss Elizabeth. A new heiress from all accounts, come up from London."

"From London? How do you know of this?"

Sam shrugged. "It ain't much that passes the salters."

"Have you seen her?"

"No, I haven't had the pleasure yet. But I hear tell she came today on the noon train. At least, so rumour has it."

"Is that so?" Caleb stared thoughtfully at the dark sockets of the window above Sam's head. The watery moonlight glimmered momentarily and then retreated, but Caleb's thoughts had turned again to the girl he'd seen that morning. A lovely girl with green wide-set eyes and stubborn chin.

"My ma went to see to Mrs. Blacket this morning and thinks it must have been her she saw getting into a carriage wi' Miss Elizabeth."

"Is that so?" Caleb repeated thoughtfully. Perhaps he *had* seen the latest Annesley heiress, after all. Then shrugging off his vague conjectures, he asked, "Why did your mother go to see to Mrs. Blacket? Is she ill again?"

Sam drew his shirt sleeve across his mouth and grinned. "No, not ill exactly, she had a run-in wi' the bear."

Caleb's dark eyebrows rose in surprise. "The bear? Pemberton's bear?" and when Sam nodded, Caleb asked, "Why? What happened?"

Sam chuckled, only too pleased to relate the story again of the most entertaining couple of hours Upwych had witnessed in a long time. "That old dancing bear o' Pemberton's always guarantees some good crack, Master Caleb. He had the poor, wretched creature doing his tricks on the High Street this morn and the constabulary were right nonplussed about it - said 'e was barring the Queen's highway and 'e'd have to move on. Well . . ." Sam chuckled again before going on with his tale, "they tell me that old Pemberton led Bruin to this very tavern, and the locals were paying for their entertainment with ale. Yon bear likes a good brew, truth to tell, but I fear he ain't got the head for it. Next thing, the old bear passes out stone cold and nobody could move him. The whole street came to a stand-still. A fair old dither it was."

Caleb shrugged. Pemberton's brown Russian bear doing his antics for biscuits or sugar - and especially for the tavern's good strong ale - was nothing new in Upwych. "But what had all that to do with Mrs. Blacket?"

Sam's pale eyes gleamed mischievously, clearly enjoying his recollections of the morning's spectacle. "She was coming back from the market in her cart and ran headlong into them. It caused a right upset. She screamed like a mad woman, scaring the daylights out of everybody.

"Next thing, all the horses were bolting and the dogs

35

were fighting and Mrs. Blacket fainted in fright at the sight of the old bear fast asleep on her doorstep."

Sam lapsed into a loud guffaw and, over more ale, the conversation drifted from bears to cock-fighting, and from cock-fighting to the price of salt.

Then Caleb remembered more important things he needed to discuss with Sam, and turned back to the matter of his brother and this morning's hunt.

He tried, as well, to discover more about the present frailty of Sam's sister. He was worried about Sally Shrike. She seemed so pale and withdrawn, so alienated. It disturbed Caleb a great deal and he felt he owed an obligation to her. He feared the worst and desperately wanted in some way to help.

There were other things, too - like Charlie's behaviour in general. He was determined to do something about that and he needed Sam's reasoning influence to guide him. But, in spite of a sympathetic ear, even Sam was unable to provide Caleb with an answer to any of his problems. So, when Caleb left 'The Talbot' over an hour later, he was still in a dark mood. He pulled the high collar of his coat more closely about his neck and set off back home. He pondered on the changes that were needed in Upwych - changes that would improve the lot of everyone - and prayed for the strength to one day, with God's will, bring them about.

And would the new owner of the salt works make any difference? He doubted it. Not that slip of a girl. For, if his instincts were proved right, this new young heiress was surely the girl on the train.

As the wind whipped around his boots, his mouth was clamped tight. Changes had to be made in this town. And, to Caleb, these things were much more important than a dancing bear or a pretty young girl who wore a hat more suited for a London park than for an Upwych winter.

* * *

The first and greatest difference that Lydia Annesley discovered, once her trunks had been unpacked and she had found her way around her aunt's great house, was that she hardly ever seemed to be alone. In London, she had always been so. She had been here almost a week now and, although immensely happy with her new lot, Lydia was growing restless.

Annesley House was perfect in every way, from its rolling grass and high elms, its croquet lawn and its ornamental ponds. And her aunt had been kindness itself. Every day since Lydia's arrival in Upwych they had walked, arm-in-arm around the gardens, well wrapped against the sharp frosts of winter.

On these excursions, her aunt told her of the history of her father's family, and instructed her in the responsibilities that would soon be hers at the works. She learned about the salt and the pits, of the shafts and the springs, and of the inexhaustible store-house of brine that eventually found its way around the globe as the very existence of other important industries.

And, almost reluctantly, Elizabeth Annesley told her briefly of their rivals, the Strettons. And how that family's fortunes seemed to increase year by year while theirs, the Annesleys, diminished.

When Lydia had asked what could be done to stem her family's financial descent, she was told affectionately that that was something she wasn't to worry her pretty head about just yet. Lydia Annesley had learned all of this but, so far, had not witnessed any of it at first hand

and she was already impatient to do so. Her green eyes followed the maid's movements as she entered the bedroom, bringing in honey-tea and sweetmeats on a silver tray.

"Miss Elizabeth says to tell you she will be in to see you directly, miss," the maid said, giving a little bob.

"Thank you, Sarah."

The maid withdrew and Lydia sipped at her tea until, a few moments later, her aunt came into the room and settled herself comfortably in a chair. The astute Elizabeth Annesley sombrely studied the expression on her niece's face. She bitterly regretted that she had not brought the girl to Upwych sooner, knowing now what an awful time Lydia must have had with that monster, Brodrick Fortey. Damn the man to hell.

Still, she was here now and, even though she had known her for so short a time, Elizabeth Annesley was well pleased with her niece.

"We need to talk more about our trade, my dear," she began, "and trade is a word that you must learn to say without offence or embarrassment."

"I'm not offended nor embarrassed, aunt."

The old lady gave a satisfied smile. What a girl her niece was. How forthright. And how right she'd been in her judgement of her.

Elizabeth Annesley went on, "You will soon learn that time is money and, even though I loved my dear brother - your father, he never really learned the true sense of urgency. That is why," the shrewd eyes drifted to the portrait above the grand marble fireplace, "your grandfather became exasperated with him on more than one occasion."

Lydia's eyes followed her aunt's and she stared at the stern face of the old man hanging there. She had

38

inherited the Annesley green eyes. That was confirmed in the picture's focal point and there was a familiar stubbornness about the mouth and chin.

"I wish I'd known Herbert Annesley," she murmured, "I think I would have liked him." But Lydia was also discreet. And although she admired the strength of the old man's face, she saw in it also definite signs of irritability. A family trait she hoped had perhaps followed him to the grave.

"He would have enjoyed your presence in this house very much," her aunt returned softly. "I feel you have inherited a portion of his ways."

"Thank you, aunt."

"It's getting near the time for you to visit the works. Soon now, I will arrange a suitable time and chaperone."

Lydia bit her lip. She was impatient to see the factory, but even more so to see Upwych. Oh, how she longed to see the whole of the town. But her joy of exploration would be ruined if her aunt insisted on a chaperone, and she replied demurely, "That's very kind of you, aunt, and, of course, I will need someone to accompany me to the works, not least to explain things to me. . ." Lydia hesitated, putting a nervous hand to the loop of tiny pearls around her neck. "But is it not permissible that I see a little of Upwych by myself?"

Her aunt gave another small smile, settling back in the chair and sighing audibly. "My dear, whatever would the good people of Upwych think of me if I let you wander unaccompanied around the town?" And as Lydia shook her head silently, Elizabeth Annesley gave a girlish chuckle. "But, of course, you will go anyway, won't you, whether I approve or not?"

"I wouldn't want to trouble you in any way, aunt?"

Her aunt smiled as she rose from her chair, moving across to plant an affectionate kiss on Lydia's cheek. "You are no trouble to me, child," she said, looking up again at the portrait. "When I was young I used to prefer going off on my own too. It's far more fun." She chuckled a little more. "I was just thinking what my dear brother Bertram would have said. Somehow, I do not think he would have approved of his daughter walking abroad alone in certain parts of our town."

"I would not go anywhere of which you wouldn't approve, aunt."

"Perhaps not, Liddy." Lydia did not resent the pet name from Aunt Elizabeth. "But how will you know of which parts I disapprove?" The old lady sighed gently, adding, "Nevertheless, I understand how a young girl needs a little freedom and you may have your time to explore."

"Oh, thank you, aunt."

Elizabeth Annesley put up a small, restraining hand. "But only on one condition."

"What condition, aunt?" Lydia enquired softly.

"That you will allow Blanchard to follow behind with the brougham. That way my mind will be at ease, and if you venture too far you will no doubt need it."

"But I don't need a carriage, Aunt Elizabeth." Lydia's eyes were glowing now at the prospect of a few hours on her own. "Please? May I go out this afternoon?"

Elizabeth Annesley's eyes flitted from Lydia's radiant face to the portrait, and back again. "You may, dear. But I must insist on Blanchard following behind, if only for the sake of our family's honour."

Lydia gave in gracefully. She knew when she was beaten. "Very well, aunt."

* * *

When Lydia set out a little later, snugly wrapped in a deep-burgundy wool cloak and a velvet hat tied under her pert chin in a cloud of pink gauze, the small carriage rolled round from the stables and proceeded behind Lydia down the long straight drive.

Erect and immaculate in his livery, Blanchard was also discreet, keeping the horse and carriage several yards behind the straight slender shape of his young charge. He was a loyal retainer who knew Miss Elizabeth well. Experience of her sharp tongue had taught him long ago to follow her stern instructions to the letter. He would not let Miss Lydia Annesley out of his sight for one second.

And, although Lydia knew he was there, she pretended he was not. For a little time at least, she was determined to enjoy herself in her own way, not only to get to know the little town of Upwych but, mainly, to bask in the luxurious feeling of simply being alone.

Annesley House had been built, like most of the town's important houses, at the top of a hill. And when Lydia reached its brow, she paused, looking out over the magnificent views spread before her like a patchwork.

The day was clear and cold but the overnight rain had left the narrow rutted track puddled and, starting off again, Lydia hitched up her skirt to avoid them. She set off down into the town, towards the church, remembering her aunt's warning to avoid the huddle of salters' houses known as the Vynes. She wasn't exactly sure where they would be but, no doubt, Blanchard would put her right should she stray too near. Lydia shrugged inwardly as she glanced at the pretty houses around her. It all looked peaceful enough now.

Walking the narrow High Street gave Lydia a dizzy feeling. The shops and houses leaned crazily where the salt subsidence had weakened their foundations, making them quite out of line with each other. She gave little nods of acknowledgement to people who passed her by, all of them probably curious as to who she could be, and Lydia smiled to herself a little. If she was any judge, the gossips would have signalled her arrival long before now, so perhaps the friendly smiles were tinged with kindly inquisitiveness rather than impertinent snooping.

Lydia had to cross the road by the Royal Hotel to reach the park. Almost as though Fate had shown her a way to throw off Blanchard, she suddenly felt quite daring.

Without a backward glance at the coachman, she turned quickly and disappeared through its gates, leaving him no option but to rein in the pony and wait for her to emerge again. The brief feeling of guilt that momentarily gripped her was soon shrugged off; she was free and alone at last.

The cinder path crunched under her boots and she snuggled her hands more deeply into her muff. Lydia was revelling in the glow that the cold, clear air was bringing to her cheeks and, as she walked beneath the great canopy of oak and elm trees, she wondered if her mother and father had walked together along this path, too, when they were young and first in love.

Footsteps sounded behind her, heavy and hurried, and Lydia felt a small stab of alarm. Without looking back she paused, stepping under one of the trees to let

42

the man pass, but instead of walking by as she'd expected, the sound ceased, and she looked up quickly to see the laughing blue eyes of a man she vaguely recognised.

She was alone. It was a most awkward situation. But as she gathered herself, the man bowed, raised his hat and acknowledged her most correctly.

"Good afternoon."

His tone carried an accent which Lydia found hard to place. Now she knew who it was. It was the red-jacketed huntsman who had so boldly approached the train on the day she came to Upwych.

Lydia inclined her head slowly, silently praying that Blanchard would appear through the trees with the comfort of the blessed brougham.

The man was certainly handsome with his fair hair tied back into a narrow silk ribbon and his wide, slightly insolent mouth smiling quite brazenly. And he was tall, very tall. He stood with his back to the sun and Lydia had to squint from its dazzle as she looked up into his intense eyes.

"Tell me, ma'am, have I the pleasure of speaking to Miss Annesley? Miss Lydia Annesley?"

"You have, sir, but I am not accustomed to speaking to gentlemen without first being introduced."

"Then permit me to amend the oversight right away." To Lydia's discomfort, he placed a gloved hand on her muff. "As we are alone in the park I have no alternative but to introduce myself. My name is Charles Sheridan." He gave another small bow before adding, "However, this is not the first time we have met."

Lydia flushed. He was pleasant enough and clearly used to the formalities that were expected of a gentleman.

"I . . . I don't remember, sir," she fibbed, somewhat hesitantly.

"Come, Miss Annesley, you make an even prettier picture now than you did then."

Lydia flushed even more at his boldness, and drew herself up to her full height of five feet two in an effort to regain her composure. "You are forward, Mr. Sheridan," she returned sharply. "If you will excuse me, I would like to continue with my walk."

"Allow me to accompany you. The park is too hazardous a place for a young lady like yourself to be walking alone."

Lydia drew a sharp breath, her cheeks aflame. "That is not necessary, sir. My escort and my brougham are already waiting for me outside the gate."

"Then allow me to walk with you to see you safely there."

Lydia frowned and turned back towards the direction of the gate as he placed his hand lightly at her elbow. This was a terrible situation. How bold the young man was. And whatever would her aunt say if she should hear of this?

Lydia took a another deep breath and glanced quickly up at him as they walked. "Please, Mr Sheridan, don't interrupt your business on my account."

He waved a hand dismissively. "My business was over the moment I saw you, Miss Annesley," he replied gallantly. "When I saw that you were alone, my sole intention was to escort you."

It was such a pointed remark that Lydia began to realise, too late perhaps, how foolish she had been to venture alone in the park like this.

And, as they walked together, her attempts at conversation were very stilted indeed. She asked him of his horse, his leisure pursuits, his background. And it was during this discourse that she quickly discovered that he preferred to do most of the talking - which was perhaps as well. She learned, too, from where he had acquired his slight brogue.

He told her of his father's home in County Clare, Ireland and of his land there. And how fond his maternal grandfather, Lucas Stretton, was of them both.

Yet, even as he spoke, Lydia found herself growing more tense than ever. It soon became very clear to her that Aunt Elizabeth wouldn't approve of this casual meeting at all. Not only for its impropriety, but for the fact that this bold young man was none other than the grandson of Lucas Stretton, Elizabeth Annesley's greatest rival.

As he continued his story, Lydia found herself sinking into an even more intolerable situation.

Relief flooded through her as they reached the gates and her eyes darted first this way and that, searching for Blanchard but, to her dismay, he was nowhere in sight. Where the pony and carriage should have stood was a man. A man, tall and erect, holding the reins of a magnificent bay; and a man Lydia recognised at once.

With her heart thudding against her ribs she stood frozen as the man took a few steps towards them. Instinctively, she found herself backing away, looking round for a means of escape but there was none.

He approached slowly, staring at them both in a baffled rage as he raised his hat and bowed slightly to her. Before she could respond, however, she heard Charles Sheridan's angry snarl.

"You!"

"Yes, Charlie, me!"

"Why are you following me?"

"I am not." He turned his dark eyes back to Lydia. "Forgive me, Miss Annesley. It is not my custom to intrude upon a seemingly pleasant conversation."

Lydia felt her anger rise sharply. There was no doubt of his veiled insinuation. "You are not intruding, sir," she remarked pointedly. "Mr. Sheridan was kindly escorting me to my carriage."

The tall, dark man gazed around insolently before turning back to her. He was smiling but there was no warmth in the smile. And when he spoke again, his tone was edged with a heavy sarcasm. "Your carriage, ma'am? But I can see no carriage. Perhaps you will allow me to call a cab?"

Lydia looked around wildly. Wherever was Blanchard?

"That's enough, Caleb." Charles Sheridan remonstrated savagely, an uncomfortable flush deepening his good-looking face.

Caleb Vyne turned to his half-brother with deceptive calmness. "With you, Charlie, it's never enough. Now, why don't you fetch your horse from the thicket where you left him and ride off home, like a good boy."

Lydia froze, expecting an outburst from Charlie Sheridan at the high-handed order from the dark-haired man, but none came. Instead, and to her utter amazement, Charles Sheridan paused angrily for a few brief moments, as if in two minds what to do, then he shrugged carelessly. He attended Lydia with a curt bow and swung away without a word. She turned two unbelieving green eyes to the man still standing beside her, wondering what power he held to make others obey him so meekly, and without question. He was still smiling that cold smile and, as he moved further towards her, Lydia found herself backing away.

He laughed softly. "Don't worry, Miss Annesley, I will not harm you. But I would like to know how you came to lose your carriage."

She countered his question with another, turning on him imperiously. "How do you know my name?"

She spoke with such apparent fury that he laughed again and cast an insolent eye over her. And, in spite of herself - and her dilemma - Lydia felt drawn towards him. He was the most attractive man she had seen in her entire life.

"Oh, come, Miss Annesley," he chuckled, shaking his dark head, "surely, you can't believe that we in Upwych are so blind that we would not notice such an enchanting girl amongst us?"

His sarcasm was now bordering on insolence and Lydia threw back her head. "If you wish to behave in so impertinent a manner, sir, then I suggest you reserve it for more suitable company."

Caleb Vyne bit his lip in mock apology and Lydia sidestepped away. She began to walk in the direction of the hotel, thoroughly out of sorts, her precious hours of freedom soured by these two annoying young men. She heard him behind her. The clip of his bay's hoofs and the firm sound of his boots giving him away.

"I believe you are walking in the wrong direction, ma'am," came his amused observation. "If you will permit me. . ."

Lydia almost stamped her foot, then swung round. She didn't know what to do. She was, indeed, most hopelessly lost. She tried to retrieve her pride by fixing him with a cold, green stare, focusing her gaze on the fine bone structure and the dark crop of strong curly hair. He seemed to tower above her in a most unnerving way but, now, to her surprise, Lydia thought she saw a hint of earnestness in his dark eyes.

"Sir, your behaviour is intolerable," she snapped. "If this is an example of Upwych manners, then I fear I should not have left London."

He moved closer, his body shielding her from the piercing wind. "I am sorry that you feel that way, ma'am," he said quietly, yet in a manner that commanded instant silence. "But I can assure you that the *manners of Upwych* are usually beyond reproach."

"Then why do you follow me?"

"For your protection. And for the fact that I think I know where your coachman may be. If you promise not to move from this spot," he said affably, "then I will fetch him for you."

Lydia nodded and, as he disappeared through a narrow passage close by, she stood impatiently chafing her fingers and stamping her small boots in an effort to keep warm.

Within moments he returned. "Just as I thought, Miss Annesley. He is on his way."

And, with a tremble of relief, even as the man spoke, Blanchard and the brougham trotted round the bend of the road.

As Caleb Vyne helped her to her seat, his hands felt warm and strong. Once she was settled he turned sternly to the hapless coachman. "If I was in charge at Upwych, I'd dock your wages for disappearing like that. Now, take your mistress home and make sure you don't make a mess of that."

"Yes, Mr. Vyne. Begging your pardon, miss," uttered Blanchard miserably and Lydia found she could not let the coachman take the wrath of this man without her defence. After all, it had been her fault in the first place, giving him the slip the way she had.

"There's no need to scold Blanchard, sir," she called

out in a clear steady voice. "I dismissed him when I decided to walk in the park."

The dark young man bowed, throwing her a surprised look. "Just so." Then, turning back to Blanchard, he commented stiffly, "You're lucky to have such a generous mistress, Blanchard. Let us hope she remains so."

"Drive on, Blanchard," Lydia instructed, keeping her voice low but, before the coachman moved the carriage away, the man caught hold of the rein.

"I hope we meet again, Miss Annesley," he murmured, adding, "but perhaps in less awkward circumstances."

Lydia didn't reply. She sat very still in the brougham as it carried her along the High Street and in the direction of Annesley House. Once she knew she was out of his sight, Lydia allowed herself to relax. So his name was Vyne. Caleb Vyne.

She tapped her fingertips together within the confines of her muff. There was something about him that disturbed her very much. And it wasn't only the fact that he was clearly close - albeit, hostilely so - to a family member of her aunt's most implacable enemy.

* * *

Caleb Vyne, on the other hand, had not moved. He remained very still until the small carriage had taken Lydia completely out of his sight. Then he mounted his horse, turned it and galloped off, thinking what a damned attractive girl Lydia Annesley was. She reminded him of a bright burst of colour; an exquisite flower that had unexpectedly bloomed, filling his lonely day with joy and hope.

49

But then his handsome face darkened. This was something else he would have to sort out with Charlie.

* * *

Chapter 3

On the day of her eighteenth birthday, Elizabeth Annesley presented Lydia with Sophie, a roan mare and, as the greyness of winter advanced into a February of alternating frost and rain, Lydia found riding pure joy. She discovered mile upon mile of open countryside and, once she'd mastered the intricacies of controlling the high-spirited young mare, she began to revel in her unaccustomed freedom.

In Upwych, Lydia enjoyed the opportunities that she had never had in London, her sole regret being that Aunt Elizabeth still insisted that the reluctant Blanchard accompany her.

And, on these cold winter days, Lydia would ride hard and swift, making sure that the hapless coachman was at least a mile behind.

On these rides, Lydia thought of many things. Of how lucky she was to be in such a wonderful place; of her kindly aunt and all that she had given her; and of the responsibilities that would soon be placed upon her at the Upwych works.

But, most of all, Lydia thought of Caleb Vyne.

He edged into her thoughts now as her green eyes gazed out across the winter landscape and she braced herself, firmly closing her mind's eye to his disturbing face.

Last night's storm had blown itself out and a pale, watery sun was lighting the brown, slumbering earth, softening its cold armour of ice for the few, brief hours of a winter's day. It was enchanting. And, drinking in its wild, naked beauty, Lydia wondered, momentarily, why she should feel so edgy and strung-up.

Reining in the roan she turned, looking back at poor old Blanchard as he struggled to make up ground and Lydia, regretting her impulsive gallop, felt more than a little sorry for him. Without realising how hard she'd ridden, she had strayed far from the pathway, and the small copse she found herself in was dense, but well-sheltered from the bitter December wind.

Lydia dismounted, picked up a small stone and twirled it around in her gloved hand for a few moments before tossing it over the stark hedgerows. She looked around approvingly.

In spring, this place would be filled with snowdrops and primroses, perhaps even colourful patches of celandine. It was a peaceful spot; beautiful and secret, and she must come back here at some future date. Perhaps a day when she could be entirely alone?

Lost in her imagination, she thought again of Caleb Vyne and how, as a small dark-haired boy, he might have come here to play. As his handsome face drifted around in her thoughts, Lydia frowned glumly.

He puzzled her. Why were he and Charles Sheridan so much at odds? And what on earth was it that should cause Charles to show such a submissive attitude towards him? What hold did Vyne have upon him? And what had happened to cause such bitterness between the two men? Lydia gave a small, wry smile. Such enmity seemed a pity when they were both so handsome.

She stepped back, shading her eyes to watch Blanchard's

plodding approach, yet still the questions intrigued her and, inwardly, she vowed to find out why. Vyne's tall, taut frame was as strong as a bull but Charles Sheridan, big as he was, would surely be no match against such strength. And whatever their antipathy, Lydia was convinced that Charles was the more likely victim.

Of the two, he seemed far more approachable, far more amusing. His candid blue eyes held such an open look - a noticeable receptiveness that one found hard to dislike. But the other, Vyne, carried upon himself a brooding sourness, and it was a sourness that was already twisting the man's handsome features.

Still pondering as she remounted, Lydia scolded herself. Unless it affected the Upwych works it was really none of her business. And, anyway, it was probably something she would never know. So thrusting it out of her mind, she turned Sophie's head back towards Blanchard. It was time to return to Annesley House for lunch.

But, whether it was her business or not, the question remained. Relentlessly, the two men came back into her mind as she made her way home. And it occurred to Lydia that the more she thought of the quarrel, the less it made sense. But then she smiled another secret smile. It seemed no matter how hard she tried, Caleb Vyne just wouldn't leave her thoughts. It was funny how a woman could be attracted to the worst of men.

Hadn't the same thing happened to her mother when she'd met Fortey? Hadn't her stepfather enamoured her mama with his dark good looks and false words of love? Was the dark and brooding Mr. Vyne another such man? Secretly, in her heart of hearts, Lydia Annesley hoped not.

* * *

"You're looking very thoughtful, Liddy," observed her aunt, glancing up from her letters as her niece came into the morning room.

"Am I, aunt?" asked Lydia, stooping to kiss the top of the lady's silver head, adding somewhat apologetically, "It's nothing. . . Perhaps I was thinking that I ran Blanchard more than I should have today."

"Did you enjoy your ride?" Elizabeth surveyed the girl approvingly. What a lovely picture Lydia made with her animated heart-shaped face and her cheeks, once so pale, glowing from the clear air of the Upwych hills. Her new green habit and feathered hat suited her, and her chestnut curls were prettily restrained in the nape of her slender neck by a fine black net, giving her an aura of sophistication far beyond her eighteen years.

"Oh, yes, aunt," Lydia exclaimed. "And, with your permission, I would love to go out again this afternoon while the sun is in such a good humour."

"You have my permission, child - I have much to do here to keep me occupied."

"You always have much to do, aunt," Lydia remonstrated gently. "Very little seems to take you away from your endless papers." She smiled fondly as her aunt nodded her agreement, but Lydia's gentle expression changed swiftly to alarm as she noticed for the first time how pale Elizabeth looked today. "In fact," she added softly, "I'd say you do far too much."

Elizabeth Annesley leaned back in her chair, smoothing a pale hand across her brow and gave way to a deep sigh. "I'm tired, child," she murmured wearily. "I fear I may not yet have recovered from the journey to London."

"It is surely more than that, dear aunt, and I truly feel you should rest more," Lydia advised anxiously.

"Leave those letters for now. If you tell me what it is you wish to say, I will finish them for you later."

"No, indeed," her aunt returned with a dry little laugh. "These are works matters and they need my personal attention."

"Then let me help."

"They need not concern you yet."

"Perhaps, aunt, it *is* time for my concern. If I'm to know what I have to do."

But her aunt raised an admonishing hand. "Time enough, Lydia. There's all the time in the world for you to learn. I will show you when I think the day is come. Until then, enjoy your riding and your girlish dreams. Youth is gone from us soon enough."

"But, aunt, I can't indulge in such foolish pleasures while you are taking everything on yourself," Lydia protested stubbornly, growing more anxious at her aunt's pallor. "I'll stay by your side today and make sure you get some rest."

"Indeed, you will not," replied Elizabeth, just as stubbornly. "I don't want a fuss. I am quite, quite well."

"I'm not fussing. . ."

"That will do, Lydia. Now, let's take luncheon and then you must continue with your ride." Elizabeth Annesley would hear no more. And, after lunch, with the promise that she would take a nap, the old lady insisted that Lydia leave her alone and instructed her to take the mare out again.

Reluctantly, Lydia gave in and, after more futile protests, she made her way into the hall. Picking up her gloves from the hall table, she turned them over in her hand. *Oh dear*, she thought, *I can't possibly wear these again today*. They were ruined. Caked with the dried mud of her impetuous playfulness with the stone.

55

Irritated with herself, Lydia turned for the stairs to change them for another pair but hesitated at the bottom as the sound of furtive giggling caught her attention.

She heard the girlish voices again a moment later and Lydia stood stock still beside the tall potted palm. One of the two was undeniably Sarah, her maid.

Lydia stepped forward, about to scold the girl for wasting time, but then suddenly froze, instinctively drawing back into the shadow of the palm, all poise gone. A man's name had caught her attention. A name that immediately turned a refined young lady like Lydia Annesley into nothing more than a furtive eavesdropper - the name of Caleb Vyne.

"Oh, yes, Bessie - and Mr. Vyne . . ."

It was Sarah's whispered sigh that Lydia could hear and she held herself very still. She strained her ears but the whispering voices became muffled and Lydia could pick out only the odd, broken, sentence as the two girls gossiped on.

"Amy Blacket tells me he's a devil for the women," came the excited undertone of Bessie, the kitchen maid.

"Well, Amy saw . . ." more whispers then, ". . . up by Raven's and she says the two of them together . . ."

The voices rose and fell querulously until they became no more than confused giggles, dropping even lower until Lydia could hardly hear a thing. She held her breath, waiting, until the sounds became audible once again.

"Tell me what happened, Sarah?" It was Bessie again.

More sounds. ". . . Sally Shrike needed money. Oh, how could she let young master . . ?"

Again the words lowered tantalisingly out of Lydia's earshot. Then, suddenly angry at herself for sinking so low as to eavesdrop like this - or perhaps from the little she had heard - Lydia drew herself up. A deep rage fired inside at her unbecoming furtiveness and, taking a deep, uneven breath, she stepped briskly from behind the palm and into the hall.

"Sarah!" she called with a rare imperiousness. "Sarah! I know you're there. Come out from behind the stairs."

Sarah's surprised pink face emerged from behind the banister's twisted rails. "Yes, miss?"

"Sarah! Stop what you are doing at once and bring my black leather gloves from my dressing-table."

"Yes, miss." The maid scrambled to her feet and, with a little bob, she flew upstairs.

"And you, Bessie. Back to the kitchen with you."

"Yes, miss." The flustered kitchen maid flew past her across the hall and, with her cheeks flaming and her head erect, Lydia Annesley hurried quickly out of the house.

* * *

Blanchard had been Miss Lydia's most staunch and faithful companion since she had saved him from Caleb Vyne's biting tongue that day in the park. And although he was exhausted by his young mistress's unabated love of riding, he didn't openly complain.

He led the mare, and his own equally weary and over-weight gelding, from the stables for the second time that day, his expression showing nothing of his desire to put his feet up and sleep away the afternoon.

"Blanchard, I think we'll go another way this time."

Blanchard sighed inwardly, helping Lydia on to her side saddle. "Yes, miss."

"Can you suggest somewhere?"

"Wherever you like, miss - it'll be dark inside two hours, so it mustn't be far."

They trotted out of the gates. For the first time, Lydia didn't feel like riding and she tried to quell her apprehension. Aunt Elizabeth looked so frail. But Lydia's pleas to take over more responsibility while her aunt took more rest had, as always, fallen on deaf ears.

Her troubled mind was also reeling from the disjointed gossip she had heard from the two maidservants. It made her cross to think she had deliberately set out to overhear what was, after all, nothing more than downstairs gossip. But she had not liked what she'd heard. She had held her own doubts about Caleb Vyne, but was he really such a monster as they had made him out to be?

Recalling the girls' conversation, Lydia decided that perhaps she shouldn't be surprised to hear such things. After all, he was too good-looking for his own good - arrogant, and probably a bully. Doubtless, he had all the girls in Upwych after him. That kind of man usually did.

She would dearly have loved to ask Blanchard more about him, but of course, she couldn't do that. Inwardly, Lydia sighed. It was not easy being a woman. If she asked the questions she wanted to, it would put her in a very difficult position indeed. As the young lady of Annesley House it was most unseemly to be so curious of others, and so, for the sake of propriety, she was compelled to remain silent about the one subject that intrigued her most.

They approached the hill's brow. "I rather fancy following the river, Blanchard," Lydia said as they reached the bridge at last. "We've never gone that way, have we?"

"No, miss, but we mustn't go too far."

"No, Blanchard, I agree, we mustn't go far. I have no wish to leave my aunt any longer than necessary."

Taking the river's path was a good choice - a prettier ride could not be found. The path followed the Salwarpe which, in its winter fullness, was not the sleepy water of summer days. It tumbled and rushed over its spine of boulders before eddying and whirling into dark pools, silent beneath its ranks of spider web hawthorn and willow.

The two unlikely companions rode in silence for over half an hour until they reached a high bank. Here, they stopped and Lydia gazed around to see the river winding on towards Worcester and the mighty Severn. And, further on, turning from the foaming Salwarpe and looking beyond the trees, she suddenly caught sight of the house.

It stood in shadow, black and white, its twisted chimneys half hidden by the trees. And it held such a forsaken look that Lydia's heart suddenly chilled.

She asked: "What place is that, Blanchard?"

"That's Raven's Mill, miss," the coachman told her gruffly.

Lydia turned her head back to the house, strangely drawn by an invisible cord of foreboding. Raven's Mill seemed to hold a cloak of great unhappiness around it, as though sighing a lament for happier days, and as her eyes followed the mishmash of buildings that straggled around it, she caught sight of the huge wooden water-wheel that threshed and flailed at the spuming river. A timbered bridge spanned the narrow stretch of Salwarpe, and as her gaze came back to the house, it rested reflectively on the rows of brine huts.

A cold premonition gripped her. "Who could live in a place like that?"

"Why, miss, don't you know?" And when Lydia shook her head, green eyes wide with curiosity, Blanchard told her, "It belongs to Mr. Caleb and the rest of the Strettons."

Her gaze spun back to the house, this new disclosure causing her even more unease. So this was where he lived. This was where the Stretton salt came from. Was it possible she would find out more about him after all?

"Mr. Caleb?" Blanchard thought she sounded astonished by the news. "Tell me, Blanchard, why is there such bad feeling between my family and his?"

The coachman shook his head, looking away. He'd rather not be here at all. Miss Elizabeth did not approve of Annesley people being so close to Stretton land - especially to Raven's Mill. And Miss Lydia was being far too inquisitive for his liking.

Lydia waited, her green eyes half-trepidation, half-defiance. "Well, Blanchard?"

"It goes back a long time, miss," the coachman mumbled. "The old folk don't talk about it so much now."

"Why? What happened?"

Blanchard shrugged, pulling the brim of his hat further over his eyes, conceding reluctantly, "Some say 'twas when the Strettons went over to Cromwell, and they betrayed the Annesleys to the Parliamentarians. The Strettons took Annesley land and used it to dig brine."

"You mean they stole our salt?"

The man nodded slowly. "That's how folks saw it, though it were legal enough, so to speak. The Strettons have been banished by the Annesleys ever since, and many of their tenants, too. King Charles had strong support round these parts and the battles split many a family."

White-faced and astonished, Lydia countered, "But

60

those times were so long ago - two hundred years."

"Aye, miss."

"Surely, it must be more than that."

Blanchard nodded his agreement. "Mebbe so, miss, but folks have long memories and don't forgive."

Lydia let out a long, despairing breath, colour ebbing from her cheeks. "Then it's time they did."

"Aye, perhaps it is."

She glared back at the house called Raven's Mill. "And what about Caleb Vyne? Does he make a good master?"

"He ain't master at all, miss," Blanchard answered.

"Not master?"

"No, miss. But there's many says he should be."

"Then why isn't he?"

"It's known that old Mr Stretton fancies his brother."

Lydia glanced again at the cold facade of the house. She could well understand that, but she was still burning with curiosity. "Why, Blanchard? Is Mr. Vyne such a hard taskmaster?"

Blanchard shrugged, liking this less and less. He was hoping that his young mistress would soon tire of her questioning and start on their ride again. Besides, it would be very wrong of him to tell this young girl of the tangles around the Stretton family. "Dunno, miss," was his unhelpful reply at last.

But Lydia persisted. "The Strettons have as many workers as us, haven't they?"

"Indeed they have, miss. And a very powerful family they be." Blanchard threw Lydia an uneasy glance, watching her face. Would she never take her gaze off Raven's Mill?

A strange light was heightening the green eyes. Raven's Mill. . . Silent, mysterious, forbidding. How well the house suited him.

61

She stared at it a few moments longer, knowing the coachman was growing impatient. "I'm ready to leave now, Blanchard," she said finally, turning the mare's head and moving away.

There were so many more things she longed to ask. Chief among them was the simple question, *What kind of man is Caleb Vyne?* But it would be wrong - foolish and unfair - to ask such things of Blanchard at this time.

To the coachman's relief she questioned no more, and with a slight kick to the mare's ribs, Lydia started off again, following the river's bend. The ride on the sluggish ground was slow. It was a bitter cold day and, although she wore her gloves, the slight wind seemed to blow right through them. They must turn back soon. She mustn't jeopardise Blanchard or her mare, and after half an hour she suggested they head for home.

Lydia, half-listening to the crunching steps of the horses' hooves and gazing thoughtfully ahead, gave Sophie the barest more rein, letting her mare move just a little more quickly. Her thoughts were with her aunt, and how glad she would be to be back in the warmth of Annesley House. But her absent-mindedness was soon distracted as her attention was caught by a movement below to her left. She glanced in the same direction and her sharp eyes saw the shape of figures, walking closely together along the lower path. There were two: a girl, whose long black hair flowed to her waist and crowning a thin, white face, and a lad, an inch or two taller, and with what seemed a thatch of white feathers for hair.

Lydia turned her head quickly to Blanchard but he had already anticipated her question. "Salters, miss."

"From Raven's Mill?"

"No, miss. They're two of yours."

Lydia's astonished eyes darted back to the two figures below. Their clothes were in rags, and their faces blue from the cold. How could they possibly be Annesley salters? Why, even from here, they looked little more than wraiths, and especially the girl. Her threadbare shawl was useless against the biting wind, tied around her thin shoulders into an untidy knot. And even from the distance between them, Lydia could see beneath it the sharp outline of her angular bones.

"What are they doing here?" she asked quickly.

Again, Blanchard shrugged. "They may be sick. Doctor May ain't far from here."

Lydia stared again at the couple as they walked along the path. They were nearer now and Lydia's fears were confirmed. They were salters all right. Not only had the salt encrusted their inadequate clothes, but their skin as well. And they looked so poor. Lydia vowed she would ask Aunt Elizabeth when she got home, just how much the salters were paid.

"If they're sick and they're our workers," she murmured unhappily, "then perhaps I'd better speak to them myself. Call them, Blanchard."

"Better not, miss."

"Call them."

Blanchard sighed, cupping his hands around his mouth and calling loudly, "Hold on, you two!"

The pair paused. Then, looking up and recognising Lydia, the man touched his forehead while the girl, head hanging, dropped a quick curtsy.

"Come here, both of you," ordered Blanchard, wishing he was back in his snug little hideaway above the stable, and not a part of this undesirable meeting.

The pair scrambled up the bank, standing silently together and waiting. Close to, Lydia saw that the man's face was ashen. His thin shoulders were stooped and his face was lined and drawn. He seemed old, yet she felt he could not have been more than twenty five.

Her eyes rested on the girl. Her dark beauty was fragile and her eyes were fierce in her tear-stained face, tears not from the salt, but from weeping. Lydia's hands shook a little and she sucked in her breath. Instinctively, she knew they were in some sort of trouble and lamented.

Blanchard said: "Miss Annesley, this is Sam Shrike and his sister Sally, two of your salters at the Upwych works."

Shrike. Sally Shrike. Where had she heard that name before? Then she remembered, and she regarded the girl more closely. So this was she. So this was the Sally Shrike who attracted Caleb Vyne's attention.

"Good afternoon, Mr. Shrike." Lydia composed herself, holding her slender body erect in the side saddle and making an attempt at a tight little smile. "And to you, Sally."

"Ma'am." Their response was little more than a murmur.

"You are on your way home?"

"No ma'am," Sam answered. "We're on our way to the works."

"Aren't you a little late for that?"

"Oh, no, ma'am." The agonised despair in Sam's response tugged at Lydia's heart. "We always make our time up, you need have no fear of that."

"I have no fear of that, Sam," Lydia responded quietly. "My aunt has told me of your loyalty."

"Thank you, ma'am."

"You're one of our pit men, I believe."

"I work in the brine, ma'am."

Lydia glanced again at Sally, "And you, Sally, do you

64

also work in the brine?" She had hoped the girl would speak; would lift her head so that Lydia could see more clearly into the distressed face. But Sally Shrike remained silent, nodding her head in acquiescence and keeping it bowed, leaving her brother to answer for them both.

With a deep sigh, Lydia smiled again. "What are you doing so far away from Upwych? Is one of you ill? Have you been to see the doctor? I hear he's nearby."

She was aware of Sally Shrike's long, shuddering sigh as she gripped her brother's hand even tighter, but the only response came from Sam, urgent and frightened. "It's . . . nothing, ma'am, we'd best be back at the brine."

"You would fare better if you let me help."

But Sam Shrike smiled wanly, the smile not reflecting in his pale eyes. "No, ma'am. There's no need."

A silence fell and Lydia looked thoughtfully down at Sally Shrike. That the girl was suffering was as clear as day, but it was also just as clear that she would get no more from either of them, no matter how hard she tried.

Presently she shook her head. "Then I'd better not keep you. Go on your way."

The two respectfully bowed their heads once more before running off down the bank. Once on the path their pace quickened and Lydia watched them as they disappeared around the bend. Soon they were gone, two grey shadows in the receding light, but not before she had seen the girl clutching at her side, clearly in agonising pain.

Lydia withdrew from her riding skirt a small leather pouch. "Blanchard, I want you to do something for me."

"Yes, miss?"

She held out some coins. "Here, take these. Catch up with the Shrikes and give them this money."

"But . . . miss. . ." His eyes widened disbelievingly as he took the coins, ". . . that's too much."

"Do as I say."

Suddenly out of his depth and knowing now that it was useless to argue with Miss Lydia when her mind was set, the coachman touched his cap and turned his horse.

"Oh, and Blanchard . . ."

"Yes, miss?"

"When you have done that, don't bother to come back for me. I'd like to ride alone for a while."

Blanchard was horrified. "No, miss, I can't let you do that."

Lydia smiled at him. "Why ever not? Are you afraid that perhaps I'll catch sight of our rivals, the Strettons?"

"That, you could easily do around here, miss."

Lydia shrugged, her smile broadening. "Then I may get the measure of them."

Blanchard was clearly agitated. "But Miss Elizabeth would not like that one bit."

"Miss Elizabeth must not know, Blanchard, and she will not if you don't tell her, and I certainly won't. My aunt is not strong these days, and we don't want her troubled by something that may not happen, do we?" Blanchard shook his head. "Now, be off. I guarantee that by the time you have caught up with the pair, I'll be behind you."

"But . . . but I fear there's another rider about, miss, I can't leave you alone here."

Lydia smiled again. Moments ago she had heard a horse's whinny, too, and was curious as to whom it could belong, and who the rider could be. "Nonsense, Blanchard," she responded sharply. "I can take care of myself. Now, get after the Shrikes before it's too late."

66

Blanchard bit back his reply, moving off slowly and turning again to Lydia in dismay. Impatiently, she waved him on and, after another moment's hesitation, he went off on his way. He grumbled silently as he rode. He could do no more than obey his mistress. So, the faster he could reach the Shrikes, the faster he could get back to her. Because what Lydia didn't know was that Blanchard had already seen the rider, and he would have rather left her with the devil than with that rapscallion of an Irish rogue.

When Blanchard had gone, Lydia moved forward until she could see the rider hacking along below her and, recognising him, her heart lifted mischievously. Perhaps she would have a little fun after all now that she had come across Charles Sheridan. If he had ridden along the upper path he would have seen her too, but he was far below and seemed in no hurry.

He had clearly given his horse a hard ride because, as Lydia followed his track, she could see that the animal was stained with mud. In fact, Lydia concluded, Charles himself looked much the same, as though he'd been rolling in the mire. Keeping out of sight, she walked on above him.

But that was where she made her mistake. Lydia rode silently leading her mare down a narrow incline, keeping her presence hidden by the trees. But soon, instead of coming upon Charles Sheridan as she'd intended, she found herself in a small clearing; a hollow where fallen trees had trapped the river's flow, making a natural harbour. Of Sheridan, there was no sign.

She reined in, irritated, wondering whether to turn back or carry on the way she was going. But then, Lydia gave a small gasp as something else caught her eye. As she turned to look, her eyes narrowing at the touching little scene before her, her heart froze. Two figures were standing close together. A man, holding the reins of an impatient bay, and a girl. A dark-haired girl with her head bowed, a threadbare shawl masking her thin shoulders. It was the salter, Sally Shrike. And the man was Caleb Vyne.

Of Sam there was not a sign, and Lydia wondered how this could be. She wondered, too, what Blanchard would be making of it all, finding only the girl's brother at the works. She shuddered, the events of the last hour flitting across her mind and its ugliness sickening her. And the mare, learning patience, took her mood from her rider and stood, silent.

For many long moments Lydia gazed transfixed as she watched them talk so earnestly together. After a while, the man let go of the rein and reached into his jacket to take out a pocket book. He drew out some banknotes, handing them to the salter and his arm came protectively around her, drawing her more closely to him. Then, as the girl leaned forward, tucking the notes into the neck of her thin dress, her dark head lolled gently against the cloth of his jacket. It was the posture of lovers.

Lydia's cheeks burned. Not only had she seen the man offer money to one of her workers, but he was embracing her now so affectionately that she felt physically sickened. She turned away quickly, averting her eyes. So, the things she had heard were all true. The overheard innocent chatter of the servant girls had been based on reality after all, and Caleb Vyne was a man who paid for his favours.

Lydia shivered as the sun hid behind the gathering evening clouds, feeling she would never be warm again. She turned quickly, thudding her heels into the mare's flanks and galloping away towards the river. The mare's startled whinny carried to the hollow and both Caleb Vyne and Sally Shrike looked upwards in surprise.

Someone else had heard the commotion, too. Charles Sheridan broke cover, increased his speed, and was fast catching up with Lydia. "Miss Annesley! Slow down! You'll break the creature's neck at that pace."

He caught the reins.

Lydia turned quickly to face him, angry tears stinging her eyes. "Let me go. I need no one's help, Mr. Sheridan."

"What are you doing so near to Raven's Mill?"

He smiled tightly, palms clamped around the reins and holding on fast. He looked terrible. His eye was blackened and there was the unmistakable evidence of blood congealing on his swollen lips. And, in spite of her own tears and temper, Lydia could see that there was nothing pleasant now about the scowling face before her.

"Answer me," he gritted impatiently. "What are you doing here? And alone at that."

"I . . . I lost my way," Lydia lied, gasping from the effort of the scramble to the path. "But what's happened to you? You look awful."

"Don't fret about me," Charles Sheridan snarled. "I've been in more trouble than this."

Lydia looked around. They were in a deep spinney in the centre of a lonely field and, suddenly, she felt afraid. She backed the mare up, stumbling a little. "I . . . I must go," she stammered. "Blanchard will be waiting."

"Do you make a habit of losing Blanchard, Miss Annesley?" he asked, his grin no longer the friendly one he'd shown her that day in the park.

"No, of course not. . . I . . . ." She looked around wildly, hearing the jangle of harness as another horse approached at speed. "Look! Here he is now."

But it wasn't Blanchard, who broke through the trees. The black horse and the flying cloak could belong only to one other man - Caleb Vyne - and Lydia felt she was surely living a nightmare.

"So it *was* you I heard, Miss Annesley," he remarked crisply. "It is indeed fortunate that I am on hand to protect you once again."

Lydia gaped at him. "*Fortunate,* Mr. Vyne?"

"Precisely so." Then, turning immediately to the other man, he accused coldly, "I should have known you would not be very far away, Charles. Haven't you done enough damage for one day?"

The two men faced each other. One, mud-splashed, his face showing an ugly grin and the other, pale, his face set as a mask. Between the two, sat Lydia, shaking, afraid, and cursing her foolish impetuosity.

Charles sighed mockingly. "You condemn me yet again, Caleb?"

"I do."

The fair haired man shrugged nonchalantly. "The devil if I care."

Caleb Vyne's disgust was measured in his voice. "You know the devil well - you were spawned by one."

"Oh, come now, Caleb, let us not air our family differences in front of a beautiful girl like Miss Lydia," Charles responded, turning to catch another hold of the mare's reins. "Come, I will see you safely back, Miss Annesley."

"Take your hands off her, Charlie." Vyne's tone was cold.

Sophie was skittering with Lydia trying to control her.

"Tut, tut, Caleb," came Sheridan's mocking reply. "Can't you see the lady wishes to leave?"

Lydia drew a deep breath. That was true enough. She

had no wish to be between the two of them again, fighting as they did like prize cocks.

"I must return home," she ventured. "My aunt will be waiting."

Caleb Vyne's fingers closed tightly on the reins. "Then I will escort you."

Lydia stifled the inner twinges of doubt. "No, Mr. Vyne," she said in a quiet firm voice, moving the mare forward. "You need not trouble. I believe you already have someone waiting in the hollow."

She saw his expression harden. "If you refer to your salter, Sally Shrike, she's on her way back to your works."

"Sally Shrike!" Charles Sheridan leaned forward savagely. "What's she doing here? What have you been saying?"

Caleb turned to Sheridan, his eyes black with rage. "It is what I'll be saying to you that need concern you."

Both men stared at each other in silence; one cruel and violent; the other, angry and grim.

Sheridan shook his head slowly, his blue eyes cold, yet showing the tiniest wariness. "I'll pay you out, Caleb," he murmured. "My father will see to it, that much I can promise."

But Caleb Vyne threw back his head, laughing bitterly, before turning his gaze back to Lydia. "Do not judge me by what you hear from others, Miss Annesley."

Lydia felt bewildered, her own glances trapped and held by both men. To cover her confusion she said as coldly as she could, "I do not know you enough, sir, to judge you in anything."

But Caleb Vyne ignored her remark and went on quietly, "It would be wiser if you stayed away from Raven's Mill - for your own good."

71

Lydia's face flushed angrily as she answered, "I ride where I please, sir."

Caleb Vyne inclined his dark head. "Then beware, Miss Annesley."

"Of what, sir?"

His voice lowered threateningly. "Raven's Mill is not the place for innocent, tender hearts - I say these things for your protection."

Lydia swallowed nervously, her lips dry. "You speak in riddles," she scoffed, moving the mare further forward. "I have no fear of Raven's Mill - nor you, sir."

"Ha! Hear that? Now, out of our way!"

Charles, pulling on his horse's head moved jerkily to follow Lydia, but he was too late. Caleb Vyne's strong grip had reached across and was restraining his horse, fuelling his rage.

"Get out of my way!" Charlie shouted. "Miss Annesley and I have things to do."

Sheridan struggled again to follow Lydia but, as she rode away, Vyne had forced Charles's mount in the other direction.

As she glanced back, she saw the fair-haired Sheridan was behaving like a fury. She watched him raise his whip, bringing it down on the other in a hail of lashes. Lydia's green eyes glittered wildly as she urged the mare on, thankful that, although she held no like for him, Vyne had evaded the onslaught by ducking his head away from the blows.

"Miss Annesley! Stop! I beg you, stop!" It was Vyne's voice, urgent and pleading.

But Lydia didn't want to heed him now. She didn't want to hear him. All she wanted was to get as far away from the two men as possible, as fast as her mare could take her.

This then was the result of her wayward behaviour. She should have listened to Blanchard. Because, whatever it was that lay so malevolently between the two men, she wanted no part of it.

Imagining she heard the sound of hooves on the hardening earth behind her, Lydia urged the mare ever on. She didn't let up until she caught sight of Blanchard hacking towards her.

The servant didn't question her pale face, but inwardly worried what had happened to the young mistress. When they reached the gates of Annesley House, Lydia was quite breathless and weakened from her efforts.

But, even as she rode into the warmth of the stables and left her sweating mare to the groom, she resolved that this evening, after supper, she would ask her aunt more of the Vynes, the Strettons and the Shrikes. And she was grimly determined to ask her aunt even more of those madmen from Raven's Mill.

* * *

Chapter 4

"How Upwych suits you, Liddy." Aunt Elizabeth's quiet voice drifted across the long, elegant dining-table as the two women waited for the redoubtable housekeeper to serve dinner. "Those roses in your cheeks bloom prettier every day. It does my heart good to see you looking so well." Her soft white hand hovered above her plate. "Thank you, Wilson, that's quite sufficient."

Lydia smiled, glancing across into the discerning eyes of Elizabeth Annesley and wishing she could say the same for Sally Shrike and the other salters of Upwych. "Sophie and I have had a good day by the river. But what about you, aunt, did you put aside your papers and rest as I asked?"

"I did."

Lydia smiled wryly at her aunt's pursed, disapproving lips but she was, however, glad to see a little more colour in the old lady's cheeks. It pleased her that she had kept her word and had taken a long nap this afternoon, and because of it, seemed more rested.

They began their meal in silence. Lydia's troubled thoughts were still lingering on the two fierce rivals from Raven's Mill. She was wondering how much she could persuade her aunt to tell her of them without causing her too much upset; or arousing too much suspicion.

Caleb Vyne's words were more than an echo in Lydia's mind. At first she had believed he had not seen her watching him and the girl, but his subsequent words revealed the opposite.

He had asked her not to think ill of him. But how else could she? And those terrible marks on Sheridan's face! Had the two men fought each other earlier? Had Vyne inflicted those dreadful cuts and bruises? And, later, hadn't she herself witnessed Sheridan's attack on Vyne with the whip? Was that no more than Sheridan's revenge against him for an earlier beating?

Lydia found she had no appetite for food as she ladled the thick, brown sauce over her meat. She took a mouthful and then pushed the food around the plate with her fork, her thoughts focussed firmly on the events of the afternoon's ride.

"Blanchard tells me that you saw Raven's Mill today - and two of our salters."

Lydia caught her breath, glancing up quickly as the old lady's words cut sharply across her thoughts. So, in spite of her instructions, the coachman had told Aunt Elizabeth their secret after all. Lydia wondered why she should she be so surprised. After all, it must be hard for any of the servants to keep things hidden from their perceptive employer; perhaps it had even been forced from him.

Poor old Blanchard. She had made his task very difficult by her actions this afternoon and she must make amends. But at least his momentary lapse of loyalty towards her had given her the opening to ask the questions she'd intended and she answered contritely, "Yes, aunt."

"The Shrikes," Elizabeth continued. "The lad's an excellent worker."

"And the girl - Sally? What of her?" Lydia waited but her aunt made no response, seeming intent on her food once more. After a while, Lydia prompted, "Is she ill, aunt? Does she get enough to eat? She looked so terribly thin and Blanchard spoke of a doctor in those parts."

Her aunt looked up, the expression in her eyes hardening a little. "If she doesn't eat enough, then the fault is her own. Our salters are paid as well as any around here - and better than some.

"And if they need a doctor, they use the one in Upwych. I can't imagine what the girl was doing out by Raven's Mill at that time of day."

Elizabeth paused thoughtfully, "Unless her mother had called her home - their cottage is hard by, less than a mile."

Then the old lady added somewhat impatiently, "Sally Shrike has always been delicate. Her mother had much worry with her when she was first born and sometimes it's difficult to know whether she is really ill or whether it is her play upon her mother, which keeps her from her work. The mother has tended our salt pans since her husband died and is a hard-working woman."

"I see." Lydia's thoughts had turned once more to Sally's thin shoulders and her head pressed against Caleb Vyne's black riding cloak. "From what I saw of her, aunt, she looked ill indeed."

Elizabeth Annesley sighed deeply. "Get on with your supper, Liddy. If Sally Shrike is ill I'll hear of it soon enough. Now, tell me," she asked more lightly, "what did you think of Raven's Mill?"

It was instantly clear to Lydia then that the subject of Sally Shrike was closed as far as her aunt was concerned.

So she shook her head, replying softly, "I thought it seemed . . . an unhappy place. But I must confess, I

76

didn't see much of it. It looked neglected, run down, but . . ." she hesitated slightly, "I saw the brine huts and the water-wheel - and I believe I saw some new machinery in the yards."

Her aunt's head jerked up, the grey eyes fixing Lydia with an unbroken stare. "What did you say?"

Lydia was suddenly flustered. Her aunt's face had drained of what little colour it had held and was now a sickly white. "There was . . . there was a machine, I think," she answered quickly, "well . . . something covered by water-proofed sheets by the gates.

"But perhaps it wasn't machinery at all. I'm new to these things and maybe I made a mistake in thinking it was so." She waited as her aunt took a hurried sip of water, then added with a small smile, "I wouldn't know a salt drill from a plough, aunt."

"Let us hope you are mistaken, child, and whatever you saw was indeed a plough. Raven's Mill is undercutting us enough as it is. New machinery would only add to our troubles." The formidable old lady paused, composing herself and attempting a smile. "Now, tell me more, what else did you see?"

A flush spread across Lydia's face. Now that the subject had arisen, she had no wish to deceive her aunt and she confessed falteringly, "I . . . I saw Mr. Sheridan." She looked quickly down at her plate, gazing fixedly at the untouched slice of meat and waiting anxiously for the reaction that was sure to come as she murmured, "Mr. Charles Sheridan." And, after a brief silence, she glanced up again, reddening more at her aunt's surprised stare.

"Charles Sheridan? How did you know it was he?"

"I met him before . . . when I went into Upwych. I went into the park and . . ."

"You went into the park?" Elizabeth gasped accusingly. "*Alone?* Without Blanchard?"

"I assure you, aunt, our encounter was quite by accident," Lydia hastily explained. "I'm sorry, it was very remiss of me. . . I should have told you of it."

"Yes, Liddy, you should." Two bright spots of colour were now burning in Elizabeth Annesley's cheeks. "I do not trust the man. He is too much like his father." Then, almost to herself, "Lavinia Vyne was a fool ever to have married him. Such a waste."

"Lavinia *Vyne*?" Lydia was suddenly confused. "Then who is the other man? The one they call Caleb?"

"So, you have met his brother also?"

"His brother?"

"Yes, child. Mr Vyne is Charles Sheridan's brother."

"But how can that be?" Lydia was stunned by her aunt's disclosure. How could Sheridan and Vyne be brothers? Not only were they so different - in every possible way - but they were sworn enemies, too.

"*His half-brother.*" The sharp eyes held Lydia in their shrewd gaze. "Caleb's father was Harry Vyne, Lavinia's first husband - and a finer man no one could meet. A fine man indeed."

"And . . . and what happened to Harry Vyne?"

Elizabeth Annesley gave a deep, sad sigh. "He died, child. He had an accident a long time ago. Before the boy had time to reach manhood." Her aunt's eyes reflected her troubled memories. "When he was thrown no one would believe it, no man could sit a horse like Harry Vyne." Elizabeth Annesley sighed again, remembering, and shrugged sadly, "But good horseman that he was, he was thrown at a fence by Fern Hill and never recovered."

The old lady lapsed into a long sad silence before she

spoke again and, when she did, the eyes that held Lydia's were sombre. "I believe all of us were a little in love with Harry Vyne," she ended softly.

"And Mr Sheridan?" Lydia asked curiously.

An unwilling smile touched her aunt's lips and her voice dropped slightly. "Poor, silly Lavinia. She was always so easily spoiled by a man. She met his father, Billy, in London, when he was over from his estates in Ireland. He had money then, of course, but it's been squandered away since. Mostly on strong drink and gaming."

Lydia looked down at her plate again. How like Brodrick Fortey this Billy Sheridan sounded. And how odd to think that Caleb Vyne's childhood so closely resembled her own. Perhaps that was why he held such a strange attraction for her?

Her aunt was still speaking, her voice sounding faint and far-away, "So, dear Liddy, you have met them both and I have been unaware of it."

Lydia glanced at her aunt in embarrassed anguish. "It would seem so."

"And you did not know they were brothers?"

"No."

A vexed frown shadowed the old lady's brow as she chided, "Blanchard had no right to allow you to walk in the park alone. Nor had he the right to take you so near to Raven's Mill today. I will speak to him about it in the morning."

"But, aunt, it was I who . . ."

"Silence, Liddy. I will hear no more of this. You are new to our ways yet. You have much to learn. But, for the present, suffice to say that I would rather you had nothing to do with anything that comes from Raven's Mill. They mean us nothing but harm."

79

"But, aunt, I have no intention of . . ."

"That's enough. Raven's Mill bodes ill for us and I do not want your good Annesley name dragged into any scandal of theirs."

"Scandal, aunt?"

But Lydia got no further. She broke off anxiously as her aunt gave a muffled groan and suddenly clutched her hands to her chest. Elizabeth Annesley's face was grey as she lurched forward in her chair, her hands grasping even tighter at the black brocade of her heavy dress.

Swiftly, Lydia leapt to her feet and ran to her aunt's side, not liking the look of the crumpled, ashen face, nor the small beads of sweat that were already standing out on the hot, fevered brow. "Aunt! Oh, dear goodness!"

"Leave me, Liddy, leave me. I'm . . . I need some air."

"No. No. I won't leave you, aunt, you are ill and you need a doctor. I will send Blanchard for one right away!"

"Don't fuss, child." The old lady's breath was coming now in great choking sobs. "Open a window."

"Hush, dear aunt. This time you will do as *I* say." And, refusing to accept Elizabeth's stubborn, gasping protestations that there was nothing wrong with her that couldn't be cured by a good night's sleep, Lydia Annesley rushed to the writing desk and scrawled a hurried note, called for Blanchard and sent him out into the night.

* * *

Lydia blamed herself. That was the worst. If she hadn't spoken of Raven's Mill. . . If she hadn't told her aunt of Sheridan. . .

She was desperately worried. She had hardly slept at all. And now, as the sun streamed onto her bed, its light making the gold silk-embroidered cover shimmer, Lydia rose and opened the shutters further.

Last night, the doctor's face had been grave. "For now, and for the foreseeable future, Miss Annesley," he had told her, "your aunt must have complete rest. No breath of the works at present; no anxieties at all."

"Of course, doctor, I understand."

When the doctor had examined his old friend and patient, Lydia had stroked her hand along the parchment-pale brow as Elizabeth lay so weakly in the high bed. And, filled with misgivings, she heard her mother's words once more as they jolted with alarming clarity into her disturbed thoughts, *The whole of Upwych life revolves around the salt works - you will soon have to learn of it.*

She had begged to remain with her aunt but the doctor had insisted that she rest too, leaving the capable Wilson in charge. Lydia had listened deferentially as he had given his instructions for her aunt's care and she had lifted her worried eyes to his when he had addressed her. "Miss Annesley, come, your aunt is sleeping now."

"Must I leave her? Can I not stay?" she had pleaded. "I will rest here, in this chair and . . ."

But the doctor had been adamant. "You are very young, child," he'd murmured softly as he'd led her out of her aunt's darkened bedchamber and onto the wide landing, "but you must rest too. Wilson knows her duty to your aunt well. Her family have been servants here at Annesley almost as long as your kinsmen have been its masters. Now, my orders are that you should rest tonight. You will have much to do from tomorrow. You will need your strength. You have to take up the reins now."

81

"Yes, doctor, but . . ."

"In the morning, call in the foreman and the bailiff; they will be of great help to you. Both of them good men and loyal to Miss Elizabeth."

"Yes, yes, of course," Lydia had replied abstractedly. "Of course I will do as you say but . . ."

He had smiled sympathetically. "No *buts*. Your aunt will sleep for many hours now. I have given her a sedative so you would be wasted here."

Then, noticing her bright cheeks telling of her anxiety, he had added quietly, "You will find the task not as difficult as you may think. Your shoulders are young and inexperienced but, I warrant, you will find them strong enough to carry the burden of Annesley works until your aunt recovers. I will call in again tomorrow."

* * *

Lydia Annesley looked out into the grey light of morning. Had all that happened just a few short hours ago? Was it only last evening that Elizabeth Annesley, frail and sick but still in command, had suddenly succumbed to her illness and left Lydia alone with such an enormous responsibility?

She put on a robe and went softly to her aunt's chamber. The worthy Wilson was still seated by her side at the foot of the three steps that led up to Elizabeth's great bed, the housekeeper's grey-streaked head lolling against her bosom as she slept; rough, work-worn hands folded loosely in her lap.

Lydia glanced anxiously at her aunt. Thankfully, she was still sleeping. But now her face was as white as any salter's, her thin grey hair spread out over the embroidered linen of her pillow and her breath shallow. Elizabeth Annesley was hardly finding the strength to breathe, let alone run a salt works and a vast house like Annesley.

Lydia felt numb. It was a daunting thought, but the doctor was right. She would have to take up the responsibility of the salt works now and, running her fingers along the wood of the bed's frame, she took a deep breath.

Where should she begin? But then her chin tilted.

She was an Annesley. She would find the way.

* * *

The bailiff was the first to arrive. Somewhere, a big clock was striking nine as Lydia brought her aunt's tray down the stairs and Blanchard let him in. He was a tall man, his rough shirt clean and his shoulders straight. And, even in so short a time, Lydia soon discovered that Elizabeth Annesley's illness was already the talk of the salt sheds. As she preceded him into the library, the doorbell rang a second time, this time to admit the foreman, Dobson.

Once seated, Lydia found she was not expected to say anything, but merely to listen and to learn. This she did, attentively, as the two men of Upwych talked to her of matters of which she had no knowledge. They talked of sinking and boring, boiling, and cutting blocks, and as they spoke, it soon began to dawn on Lydia how necessary the support of these faithful servants of the salt would be. For without them, how would she be able to face such a new and fearful responsibility?

When they had finished, she regarded them both with gratitude and keen interest. "All will be well," she confirmed. "We will continue as we always have until I see what needs to be done."

The two seemed satisfied and left within the hour,

but Lydia found that her next visitor was not so amenable. It was the bank manager. A dapper man with a balding head that seemed to hold nothing else but figures. And it was of no consolation to her when he admitted in his dry way that, although there were still many assets, the Annesley fortune was not quite so solid as their salt.

"Your aunt had many worries of late, Miss Annesley," he said plainly. "She carries a heavy burden and I feared something may happen of this sort. However," he consoled, "the bank shall support you in whatever way we can. Not only because of the circumstances of your aunt's illness, but for our long years of loyalty to your family. "But," the man's pale eyes narrowed shrewdly, "it may become more difficult as time passes. And I cannot stress enough the importance of gaining more profit."

Lydia thanked him as he made his leave, keeping to herself the fact that, so far at least, she had no idea what that support would entail, or in what way she could use it best.

And, apart from satisfying herself that everything possible was being done for her aunt, she spent a great deal of the day's precious time receiving the kindly good wishes of an assortment of visitors.

In between, Lydia Annesley hid herself away in her aunt's study, trying desperately to familiarise herself in the company's books and papers. It was difficult, but Lydia forced her concentration on the task that lay ahead; to shut away everything except the workings of the salt factory.

When the last caller of the day had departed, Lydia Annesley refused dinner, taking a tray into the study and working well into the evening. . . She looked up from her papers wearily as Blanchard told her of yet another visitor. A glance at the marble clock on the mantelshelf told her it was already half past nine, and she sighed audibly.

"I can't possibly see anyone else this night," she said, leaning back in the hard wooden chair and rubbing her fingertips along her aching forehead. "Please convey my apologies to whomsoever it may be and ask them to return another time."

Blanchard made an apologetic little cough. "I'm afraid the gentleman insists that he see you tonight, miss." He cleared his throat again. "He says he will not leave without doing so."

"Who is the gentleman?"

"Mr. Vyne, from Raven's Mill."

The total stillness of the room seemed an eternity as Lydia's hand tightened around the quill. She could not possibly see Caleb Vyne. How could she, when it was partly his fault that she found herself in this position? She was still sitting speechlessly when the door behind Blanchard opened wider. Unaccountably, as the man stepped in, the room became alive and vibrant.

"Miss Annesley." Caleb Vyne removed his hat, tossing it onto the seat of an adjacent chair. "Thank you for seeing me at this late hour." He straightened his broad shoulders and regarded her a little oddly, moving soundlessly towards her across the room.

"You can go, Blanchard."

Lydia rose from the desk, and waited until the coachman was safely out of the way before turning her gaze back to this unexpected caller; to this quiet, mysterious man who seemed so full of contradiction. "Mr Vyne. You are the last person I expected to visit me today."

85

A dark flush spread across the man's handsome face but he responded calmly enough, offering his hand to receive hers. "Yesterday, by the river, I felt the same, ma'am."

Lydia ignored his courtesy and moved across to the fireplace, hoping to hide her confusion by her action. She gathered her wide skirt to her side with an unsteady hand, its soft fullness enhancing her slender form.

"I'm afraid these are no happier circumstances, sir."

He moved towards her slowly, staring momentarily into the brightness of the coals, then sweeping across her and at the shimmering bronze of her gown as it reflected the fire's glow.

"Far from happy though our meeting be," he said quietly, "nevertheless, I come to offer my help."

Lydia glanced sharply at him. What help could he offer? How could she take him seriously? Wasn't this man her rival in business? Did he think her so naive? And what was it about him that communicated itself to her so blatantly, and made her so uneasy?

She demanded bluntly. "Your help, sir? In what manner?"

He smiled, his answer confident. "In any way you wish."

"Please, Mr. Vyne," she said cautiously, intending to put him in his place, "the hour is late and I am not in the best humour for such distasteful drollery."

A short silence fell and, when he next spoke, his low words were filled with accusation. "I would not make jokes with your aunt so gravely ill."

Lydia frowned. She suddenly felt nervous and irritable, perhaps the aftermath of her recent worries, or perhaps the disturbing effect this man seemed to have on her; disturbing and uncomfortable.

"Then what else could it be?"

Caleb Vyne bowed, smiling with elaborate politeness. "No more than what I say. I come to offer my help."

Lydia moved away slightly. "I need no help, sir. I have my foreman and my bailiff. All will do their part."

"Well guarded then, Miss Annesley," he replied shortly. "However, my offer stands. Should you need it, send Blanchard with your request and I will do my best for you."

She met his gaze levelly as he gave another curt bow.

"Convey my best wishes to your aunt, I wish her a speedy recovery."

Lydia inclined her head stiffly. "I will inform my aunt of your wishes."

He moved back into the centre of the room, pausing by the desk and looking around. "I had forgotten what a charming place Annesley House is," he murmured, turning back to catch Lydia's wide-eyed glance of surprise. "Of course, ma'am, you would not know of my familiarity with it."

He bowed again.

"No, I did not know."

He smiled slowly. "I've been well entertained here." Then he turned full on to face her, wrong-footing her again as he admitted, "The room smells of roses, and I have never seen it look so beautiful before."

It was the most direct and unmistakable compliment Lydia had ever been paid and, for a moment, she could not speak.

He smiled again, bowing slightly, "Goodnight, Miss Annesley."

Recovering a little, Lydia answered, "Goodnight, Mr.

Vyne. Blanchard will show you out."

"No, leave the man. I know my way." He moved to the door and picked up his hat from the chair then, turning, his face serious, he added, "Should you receive another visit from a member of my family, I should be wary."

"What do you mean, sir?"

"I'm referring to Sheridan." His voice was like ice again now as he turned away.

"Do you not mean your *brother*? Why, sir, he is a charming fellow."

He turned, regarding her whimsically. "Oh, yes, my *half-brother* is certainly charming. But that, of course, is a lady's opinion."

"And you, sir, know a great deal about a lady's opinion?" The old Lydia was rising, the one who had stood up to Brodrick Fortey and who had wrested her mare's head away from the sight of this man and Sally Shrike.

"I take my leave, ma'am, before I learn even more."

Long after he had gone, Lydia Annesley stood by the window looking out at the lonely night. Was she being foolish to reject Vyne's offer of help so dismissively? After all, her aunt had said no wrong of him, only of Raven's Mill. Was she wise to heed her head and not her heart?

But then she turned away, snuffing out the candles briskly. How could she allow him to help her? And, as she silently closed the door behind her, her Annesley head was already affirming that she was right in not trusting the most fascinating and dangerous member of the family at Raven's Mill.

* * *

"Are you still awake, aunt?"

"Liddy?" The voice from the bed came weakly. "Is that you, Liddy?"

"Do you need anything, dear?"

"I want for nothing but peace of mind. What have I brought on you, child?"

Lydia gently smoothed the wispy white hair away from her aunt's brow, answering her soothingly, "Hush, hush, everything is well. I'm surrounded by help, and tomorrow I'm going to the works. There is nothing to fear, aunt. All you have to do is get better."

Elizabeth Annesley closed her eyes, the lines of anguish smoothing away. She smiled faintly, "I was right when I said you were like your grandfather, Liddy - he could soften the blow, too."

She tried to lift her head, her hands tightening around the linen sheet. "But, beware of our rivals, dear. I know all about those at Raven's Mill. . ."

"Hush! Do not think of those things now, wait until you are stronger. I will take care of things."

Aunt Elizabeth's old hand patted gently against Lydia's. "Raven's Mill has always been a thorn in Annesley flesh, ever since poor Lavinia." The dimmed eyes held Lydia's for a moment then closed again wearily. "Such a foolish girl! She couldn't resist a handsome face."

"Hush, hush now, aunt."

Her aunt sighed. "Foolish . . . foolish girl . . . so long ago. . ."

Then, as Lydia bent to kiss the old cheek, her aunt fell silent, the sound of her breathing steady and deep. Lydia tiptoed softly out of the bedchamber. Elizabeth Annesley was already fast asleep.

* * *

Chapter 5

Hardly a blade of grass grew on this side of Upwych. There were no trees, no burgeoning blossoms, and nowhere could a bird's song be heard. Here, there was only the salt. It pervaded everything. The stench of it filled the air - the nostrils - and the soul. If Lydia Annesley had believed herself prepared for such a feeling of repugnancy, then she had grossly under-estimated. The ugliness of the salt works had ingrained itself on everything around. Even the church had not been spared.

And, as Blanchard helped Lydia from the carriage, her face grew more stern and unsmiling. She was wondering how God could allow His house to look down on such a repellent sight.

She turned brusquely back to her maid in the brougham. "Wait with Blanchard for me, Sarah," she directed quietly. "If you put the rug around you, you will not feel the cold too much. My visit here should not take very long."

"Yes, miss."

With her face puckered in determination, Lydia hitched up her skirt and trod carefully across the untidy yard towards the foreman.

Matthew Dobson had been waiting for Annesley's new young mistress for over an hour and now, as she drew nearer, his dark-ringed eyes stared uncertainly from his bulbous face.

He raised his cap. "All is prepared for your inspection, miss."

Lydia acknowledged the man with a curt nod. "Then let us get on, Dobson."

"I think we'd be best starting wi' the pump." The foreman pointed upwards, and Lydia lifted her eyes as his blunted finger drew her attention to a barn-like structure of brick, with a covered tower on top. "Yon's the shafting that connects the engine," he explained briefly. "Below us here is a river of salt - mightier even than the Severn - and the engine pumps it up to our sheds. But you'll see better inside how it works."

Lydia nodded again and followed him into the works. They crossed a narrow covered courtyard and passed through a door that stood ajar. But then, as she stepped inside, Lydia stopped suddenly. This was surely the brink of hell. As her eyes grew accustomed to the shuddering, smouldering cauldron, she wondered how anything - human or otherwise - could endure this pit of fire and brimstone.

The salt was choking her now. Even in so short a time, her velvet cloak was encrusted with a million particles of ubiquitous brown dust. Her green eyes smarted and the back of her throat had already become bone dry with the heat.

"Here, we pump up the brine," she heard the foreman explain. "Then we boil it to extract the salt but, if you'll follow me, miss, you'll see more of that further on." He paused uncertainly and Lydia felt his concerned glance. "Are you all right, miss?"

"Perfectly." Lydia straightened her shoulders and gave a little cough to clear her throat. "Carry on, Dobson, I wish to see everything. Don't concern yourself with me."

"Well, if you're sure, miss. . ."

"I am."

As they walked along the narrow passageways between the rows of salt pans, Lydia felt a sickness rise in her throat, stifling her breathing. Beneath her feet, the rough, flagged floor seemed to burn through the soles of her inadequate boots and the sweat from her brow trickled down her face. She pursed her lips grimly. She knew now why her aunt had waited so long to show her this. The old lady had been shrewd enough to know that it took more than an eager, determined heart to be certain the salt works prospered. It needed a strong stomach, too.

How could these workers bear this hell? All around were the blackened, sweat-streaked shapes of men as they hurled coal onto the fires beneath the salt pans. And the women, as black and as sweat-streaked as their men, stood by in pairs, ladling and raking the salt with heavy iron shovels.

As she passed by, the women instinctively pulled their thin chemises further up around their shoulders. It was a small sign of respect but Lydia did not blame them for their state of undress. It was too hot to be fully clothed, so they, like their menfolk, worked near naked at the top. Lydia noticed, too, the deep shadows across their haggard faces, thrown by the flames and illuminating their watchful eyes as the new mistress of Annesley passed them by.

Further along the narrow aisle Lydia paused, her eyes lighting on a girl ladling the salt; a girl whose thin shape had, thus far, been hidden by the deep red shadows cast by the flames. The girl glanced up as Lydia caught her eye. She bobbed a vague, deferent curtsy before wiping her mouth with the back of her hand and bending once more to her work. A damp muslin rag stretched tightly across the tips of her breasts as she pulled on the ladle, and the straggled black hair was tied back from her face.

There was a sudden glare of white heat from the fire and Lydia shielded her eyes. But, even as the smoke curled around the thin, wraith-like form, Lydia recognised her. It was the girl whose face had been buried against the broad chest of Caleb Vyne. It was Sally Shrike.

Lydia Annesley watched the girl with close attention. It seemed impossible that so frail a body could so skilfully wield a spade. Sally Shrike brought it round full on as she emptied it, then rested momentarily, her hand clutching at her side as she moved to let another woman take her turn.

"Why is that girl doing such work, Dobson? Surely she is too frail for the pans?"

"Sally Shrike's as strong as they come, miss. All the Shrikes are." Dobson laughed, but it was false laughter and Lydia knew it. "Over there's Maria and she's a good 'un. Strong as well." He continued to grin.

Lydia looked and realised by her features that the middle-aged woman was probably Sally's mother of whom Aunt Elizabeth had spoken.

She frowned. "I think you are mistaken, Dobson."

"I put the girl to work where I'm told, miss," growled the foreman sulkily, "but, if you think she must be moved, then that's a matter you must take up wi' Miss Elizabeth - begging your pardon, miss."

"It is for me to decide what must be done now, Dobson," Lydia informed him quietly. "And I would like her moved to lighter work."

Their eyes met and Dobson's betrayed a little alarm.

"She wouldn't like that, miss. Lighter work wouldn't pay enough for Sally Shrike."

"You will do as I say. I will make sure that she does not suffer any loss for it."

"Yes, miss. As you wish, miss."

They reached the other end of the building. It was cooler here by the open door and Lydia took long, grateful breaths of the reviving air before she made any further comment.

"It is truly back-breaking work to be a salter, foreman."

"Aye, miss, it is. We use only the strongest for this work. Four men on the fine and two on the broad."

A movement distracted her from another door. She turned quickly, aware of *something*; something fleet and furtive, and very, very fast - so fast that she wasn't sure it had been there at all. "What was that, Dobson? Surely, not a child?"

"Aye, miss, it was young Jemmy."

"Young Jemmy?"

"Young Jemmy Yarwood, miss. That's his pa yonder."

Once more Lydia's gaze followed Dobson's indication. The boy, no more than five or six, handed his father a red spotted bundle. The man's face was grey like the rest of the salters, his features pouched. He had the look of a man whose face had once been skinned by fire.

"Young 'uns bring in food for their fathers when the salt is running well."

"Why do they bring in food? Do we not give them time to eat?"

"Not always, miss. Sometimes, the men can't leave the pans. There's many a time a good salter'll tend his pan a full week - even sleep by it."

"Why should he do that?"

"The family's livelihood depends on it, miss, and he earns more money. The more salt pumped, the more his pay."

Lydia sighed deeply, leaning back against the door and grateful for the coolness. How she longed to be with Sophie, striking out across the white frosted fields with the sigh of the wind against her face. She closed her eyes, wondering how she could improve the lot of these salters of Upwych without jeopardising their living more than she had to.

A few moments later she opened them and looked around. The boy had gone, and her attention turned once more to Sally Shrike. The girl looked wretched. She was leaning now against the wall, her hands clutched across her stomach and almost in a faint.

Uneasy in her mind, Lydia started hastily towards her, avoiding the flames that leaped at her skirt. As she made her way through the pans, the other women looked on sullenly, none of them making a move to help Sally Shrike. Yet, even as Lydia reached her, a quick glance over her shoulder told her that the girl's brother, Sam, had laid aside his shovel and was standing back from his work.

The foreman came swiftly up behind Lydia. "Miss Annesley, you shouldn't be here . . ."

"Silence, Dobson," she ordered sharply. "Can't you see the girl is sick?" She gestured to the salter. "Come here, Mr. Shrike. Your sister is ill; you must take her home."

"Home?" repeated the foreman. "In the middle of the day?"

"Yes, Dobson. I will not have a woman treated so." She looked up into Sam Shrike's worried face as he came respectfully to her side and, as the man hesitated, she added softly, giving his arm a comforting pat, "And do not be afraid of losing your pay, I will make it up."

Sam Shrike raised his face, smiling faintly. "Bless you, Miss Annesley," he said, his intelligent eyes examining his young mistress against this background of hell.

How small she was, how delicate, and how prettily her hair hung in the ringlets around her shoulders. And she was an Annesley. It was a wonder Charlie Sheridan hadn't set his sights on this one.

Gratefully, he took hold of his sister's arm and led her away. At the doorway he paused, turning and looking back doubtfully. He waited until Lydia nodded, assuring him again of her permission, then he said again, his words barely audible above the shed's clamour, "Bless you, Miss Annesley, for your kindness."

When the Shrikes had gone, Lydia turned her attention back to her inspection of the rest of the works. She followed the foreman around, her nimble brain learning quickly of the salter's trade, yet her mind still troubled. Her attention was still dwelling on Sally Shrike.

She knew the girl must be ill. Surely, it was not only the salt that was making her face so pale? She must find out and do the best she could for her. And whatever she meant to Caleb Vyne was nothing now to Lydia. She must have people fit to do the work.

"Oblige me by escorting me to my carriage, Dobson," Lydia said when there was nothing else left to see. "I have many things to do, not the least of which is another visit to the Upwych bank. This I will do straight away."

"Yes, Miss Annesley." The foreman watched Miss Lydia step into her carriage aided by her coachman. He was feeling very doubtful indeed. She had far too soft a heart for a brinemaster. He didn't know what was going to come of it all.

Once inside, Lydia leaned back against the cushions. Blanchard held the horses still, waiting for orders.

Lydia looked into Sarah's nervous face. "You've brought your basket?" The girl nodded. "Good. Then you may go to the butcher's while I visit Mr Smith at the bank."

"Very good, Miss Annesley." The girl popped her head out of the window and called to Blanchard. "High Street for miss, Mr Blanchard!"

Tipping his hat, Blanchard geed up the greys and pulled away from the factory gates.

* * *

Lydia's suppositions, regarding Mr Smith, had sadly been correct. The bank manager's head indeed held nothing but figures.

He was perfectly polite as befitting a financial servant, whose bank had made some sizeable profits out of Annesley's better days, but he was quite unbending. He reiterated the fears he'd expressed earlier on, when he'd visited Annesley House to inquire about Aunt Elizabeth's health:

"Profit will only come from the sale of salt, Miss Annesley, and although it pains me to say so to you when you have many anxieties, Annesley Works has staunch competition, which is eating away at its profit."

"You mean Strettons?" Lydia's chin set determinedly. "But they have always been our rivals. I don't fear them."

"Ah, Miss Annesley," he said, unclasping his hands. His bald head was glinting in the sun, which streamed through the office window. "Strettons are investing - or so I believe - they set much store by constantly updating their machinery and making provision for further bore holes. In that way they can be sure that salt flows freely."

"Annesley brine is not drying up, Mr Smith," she re-proved, "and that is the purpose of this visit. With the bank's help, we, too, may think about investing."

The manager looked worried, nor made reply for a moment which Lydia took to be a grave sign. Then he was shifting papers before him. He cleared his throat. "Forgive me, Miss Annesley, but behind this lay the nature of my call on you earlier. Miss Elizabeth has been a wonderfully competent manager and mistress but without her holding the reins, how could Annesley fortunes thrive? She has a lifetime of experience."

Lydia flushed. "I may be young, Mr Smith, but I have Annesley Works at heart. I intend to learn all I can about the trade and make it a success. But I can only do this if the bank will extend me credit."

The manager leaned back in his chair, thinking what an enchanting picture she made, her green eyes eagerly holding his. But he knew his board would not agree. She was far too young and inexperienced to risk large funds. Faced with such heavy responsibilities, she might surely take fright and run back to London at a moment's whim. And, given her beauty, it was even more likely she might find a husband and lose interest in her salt empire.

"I'm afraid it's not that easy, Miss Annesley," he said. "We need a business plan and substantiation of your position. For instance, who will furnish you with knowledge? Whom can you consult on this?"

"I was thinking that might be a part the bank could play," said Lydia quietly. She could see she was getting nowhere. The possibility of the dapper and friendly Mr Smith helping her cause was becoming more distant with every sentence.

"Perhaps you should talk it over with Miss Elizabeth. When she's feeling better," said the manager.

"But she can have no worries the doctor says," cried Lydia.

Mr Smith was ignoring her pleas and shuffling papers about on his desk. Then he picked them up and placed them in a flat box.

Lydia knew that her interview was almost over.

"I can assure you the bank will be sympathetic in the near future. However, should your aunt's condition worsen, then my board will want to quickly take stock of our position."

"To put it plainly, Mr Smith," answered Lydia in her forthright way, "should my aunt die . . ." the manager looked shocked, "you will foreclose and force me to sell out."

She pushed back her chair, and next moment Mr Smith was hurrying round to her side.

"Not so, Miss Annesley. I hope such an unfortunate occurrence may be prevented on both counts. At present, this is all the advice I may offer. If you could find yourself a backer of substance, a guarantor, then my board would be of a different mind."

"A backer?" It was a new idea, a straw to clutch at. But whom? As Mr Smith hurried to open the door for Lydia, the serious face of Mr Vyne rose up in her mind. Was this what he meant when he offered his help?

Stepping out into the bright sunlight, she dismissed the thought, which was quite impossible as he was a Stretton and they were sworn enemies and competitors.

Once in her carriage, she ordered Blanchard to drive on down the High Street so that Sarah could visit the butchers and obtain a brace of pheasant to tempt her aunt's poor appetite.

* * *

Seated in her carriage, the crooked High Street held no beauty for Lydia that day. She watched Sarah enter the butcher's shop then leaned back against the cushions. Whatever would she do? A backer? But whom? She gazed out of the window again across to the milliner's. The sight of two extravagantly decorated hats did nothing to lift her spirits; suddenly, she was remembering the day she had come down from London with Aunt Elizabeth to take her place as the future owner of the salt works. Then, the only matters she had to think on were fashionable hats. She sighed.

Sarah was coming back now, looking frozen, the pheasants' tails protruding from the basket. She climbed in and Blanchard stirred the patient horses.

The carriage was almost at the top of the street when a great deal of rough shouting assailed the occupants' ears. Sarah looked at her mistress in horror, her hands up to her mouth, while Blanchard brought the horses to an abrupt halt. Then Lydia was leaning from the window.

The whole of the street was packed with a white host of factory workers, the marks of their trade on skin and clothes. They were jostling into an enormous haphazard circle.

Lydia gasped. At the centre was a young man with hair tied back in a ribbon, his full mouth twisted in an arrogant leer. He was facing a tall, gaunt young man, who stood aggressively, fists clenched. Lydia recognised both assailants. Mr Charles Sheridan and Lydia's own salter, Sam Shrike.

"Come away from the window, miss," squeaked Sarah in a frightened voice.

But the shocked Lydia could see what was about to happen. Her man was challenging Mr Sheridan - a most unseemly and dangerous thing to do. And then he struck Mr Sheridan a blow to the chin. The salters let out a wild cheer of triumph.

"Blanchard, let me down!" cried Lydia imperiously.

She must put a stop to such impertinence. The odds were quite unequal and she had the power to change the balance.

Charles Sheridan was hurling himself at the ring of men, looking for a means of escape, but they wouldn't let him through. Lydia's heart went out to him, although her hands were perspiring greatly. And she couldn't blame Mr Sheridan for his language. He had no idea she was present.

"Damn you, damn you all," he screamed. "Old Mr Stretton shall hear about this."

Sarah had her hands over her ears as Blanchard opened the carriage door a crack. "Miss, I beg you. Don't interfere. The men are in an ugly mood."

The groom's face was white under his hat. Suddenly, one of the men was turning. "Look!"

They were all staring as Lydia pushed Blanchard aside and stepped down from the carriage - but the circle didn't break.

"Miss Annesley!" The salter doffed his dirty cap.

Charlie Sheridan saw a chance to escape and made a desperate lurch again. However, next moment he was sprawling on the street, having been tripped up by another worker.

"Stop, men! I order you!" cried Lydia. The ring broke. "Mr Sheridan, are you hurt?" She bent over him. He was looking up at her. It was then she felt a hand on her sleeve, restraining her.

She turned. The salters fell back.

It was Caleb Vyne.

"On your legs, man," he said.

Charles tried to get up, but tottered. Lydia made as if to help him, but Caleb Vyne was still preventing her. She looked down in sheer amazement at his strong hand. That he dared touch her was intolerable.

"I beg you to leave me go," she said.

"When I have tamed this whelp," he retorted. And then she realised Caleb Vyne must have been watching it all. And doing nothing.

Sam Shrike was standing, head erect, jaw thrust out, fists still clenched. Suddenly, she felt the pressure on her arm cease. Lydia couldn't believe it. She was horrified. Caleb Vyne was clapping Sam on the shoulder as though he had done no wrong.

"Go home now, Sam. Nothing will be mended by such behaviour."

Suddenly Sam and the other salters were backing right off. As they turned away, they doffed their caps deferentially - to Caleb Vyne. Meanwhile, Charlie Sheridan had struggled to his feet, his chin blue under the bruising and a trickle of blood coming from his mouth. His blue eyes were staring out of his head.

"You see, Miss Annesley, how I'm persecuted by my own kin?"

Lydia's hostile eyes stared into Caleb Vyne's. "This is the most shameful encounter I have ever witnessed," she said, her breath coming fast.

Caleb's dark eyes stared back at her. Eyes, which had been so warm and probing when he had promised her his help.

"Get off home, Charlie," he said dismissively.

Charlie was feeling his chin gingerly. To Lydia's amazement he didn't remonstrate. He was stumbling a little as he acknowledged Lydia with the briefest of bows. Then he walked off.

His half-brother turned to her. "Did I warn you to be wary, Lydia - or not?"

How could Caleb Vyne use her name in such a familiar way? Was he a monster?

"The salters had good cause for anger. You should not have meddled," he added.

"How dare you, Mr Vyne!" Lydia drew herself up haughtily. "You encourage *my* salter to brawl with your own kin, and you call it *meddling*? You have a nerve. Good day to you!"

Lydia could stand no more, but her heart was thudding as if it would burst. With Blanchard close by her side, she was handed into her carriage, where Sarah was seated, crying into her shawl.

As Lydia tried to console her overwrought servant, she felt almost as dizzy as the street outside.

When Blanchard finally wheeled the carriage round the corner, she caught a glimpse of Caleb Vyne standing tall and erect, still on the spot where she'd left him, staring boldly in the direction of her retreat.

* * *

She questioned his behaviour over and over again. What kind of man was he to stand by and see his brother beaten? And he had said there was good cause.

Lydia quizzed Sarah as the carriage made its way smartly back to Annesley. "I know you were frightened, and not without reason, but you must not let yourself go like that." Lightly scolding her maid gave Lydia herself courage.

"Weren't you afraid, miss?"

"A little, but they wouldn't have hurt me."

"They would have Mr Sheridan."

"Do you know why it happened, Sarah?"

"No, miss." Scarlet cheeks had replaced the tears.

"Perhaps you do?"

"I can't honestly say, miss." Lydia knew she shouldn't question a servant.

"All right, Sarah, I believe you. However, as I'm new to all here, I'll ask you one more question. . ."

"Yes, miss?" Sarah looked quite afraid.

"Is Mr Sheridan not liked?"

"He is not, miss." The reply was vehement.

"And Mr Vyne?" Sarah's look was furtive.

"Dunno, miss. He's the master."

Lydia had to conclude the worse from that. There were so many things she had yet to find out about the Strettons. But from whom? Would she ever learn the secret of Raven's Mill or understand the brutal behaviour of its inhabitants?

* * *

Chapter 6

If Caleb Vyne had been in a better mood, he wouldn't have failed to notice the beauty of that frosty morning. But Sam Shrike's attack on that rascal Charlie was fresh in his mind. To think the fight had been played out in Miss Annesley's presence.

And it had been carried on when he had returned to Raven's Mill. There had been more harsh words, and more. Caleb swore with frustration.

To outsiders and workers alike, he appeared cold and insensitive, but no one understood how much the hard, young taskmaster of Stretton had a great reverence for the presence of beauty, especially that in the countryside around solitary Raven's Mill.

Caleb was no poet. Nor could he put into words what he felt. But he realised that, as a boy, he'd loved every shady den in the trees, every dark outhouse, smelling of hay and cowcake; he'd loved every quiet pool, stuffed with grayling and perch. Now, as a man, he was often able to find in those heedless boyish haunts, peace and release from the cares of running Stretton Salt Works under such violent family pressures.

But, that day, there were too many troublesome things on his mind. He couldn't have stayed in the house with those damned Sheridans a moment longer.

As Caleb strode over Stretton land towards the river,

bruising and trampling the delicate marsh plants underfoot, he was too out of sorts even to notice how wild and unkempt the land had become for lack of pruning.

What was uppermost in his thoughts was a determination never to show any softness that risked destroying the stern composure he retained, whatever ill luck followed him. He had no desire to become a drunken fool like his stepfather, nor a wastrel and womaniser like Charlie Sheridan. But he could not share with anyone the injustice to which he was subjected daily.

His boots strode on subduing the hummocks of grass, proud and stiff under their white-whiskered burden of early morning frost. The bare sticks of the hazel bushes, which grew so profusely about the wild gardens of the Mill, cracked as they brushed against his body, showering him with a bloom of frost to which Caleb was oblivious; as oblivious as he was to the shining, biting earliness of that fairylike winter morning.

He reached the Salwarpe, stared into the water, wishing it could wash away his resentment and anger. But it was as furious as he, throwing itself around fallen branches and soaking grasses, dragging them hurriedly on to the bursting Severn in floods of foam.

He closed his dark eyes, breathed in to shut out the world in an effort to calm himself then, opening them, looked down. Suddenly he could see the nodding specks of white emerging from a heap of rotting sticks close to the edge. Caleb crouched to look.

A cluster of snowdrops!

He stretched out and plucked a single flower, stared at the lovely delicate head hanging from the transparent stalk and found himself thinking of Lydia, who had stood before the great fireplace and denied him the chance to help her. He knew she thought ill of him for thrashing his brother, for his apparent sternness,

But how did he think of her? Something stirred inside. *The secret world of the Raven's Mill he alone knew, must never touch her.* Already, his anger was ebbing at the thought of Lydia Annesley. He bent once more and picked a bunch of those white heralds of spring, placing them in the clasp of his cloak. Then Caleb turned away from the river and made for the house.

* * *

Somehow, his mother had made her way downstairs without help. As Caleb hurried through the flagged hall, he could hear the pleading tone. Surely she was not crying already?

"Billy, I beg you!"

"Back to your bedroom, Livvy!" Billy Sheridan's command was, as usual, followed by a curse. Caleb clenched his fists as he walked through the door into the drawing-room.

What had once been a beautiful place was tawdry now. The carpets were brown with age, their brightness dimmed. The silver was tarnished; the furniture scratched and worn. The oil paintings he'd loved as a child still hung intact, but they were spotted and fly-blown. Billy Sheridan had soiled everything with his drunken and violent behaviour.

Lavinia was seated at the table. Caleb's heart quickened at her paleness. His mother's long red hair hung loose and flowing over her robe, which displayed remnants of its once brilliant green and was now, in places, just as sadly faded. She was afraid to let Caleb buy her new and had told him so often spoiling her would make it worse for her. How many times had he begged her to follow him from this hell-hole? But there was still something inside her which clung to Raven's Mill and the feckless Sheridans.

And there was something in Caleb too. He would stay and claim his birthright as a Stretton. He'd been here first, was part of the place, and it would belong to him finally.

"Don't fret, mother," he said, ignoring Billy Sheridan's hostile glance. "Are you feeling worse?" She shook her head. "Look, I've something for you." He unclasped the snowdrops and handed them to her. Then he poured himself a drink, his stepfather watching all the time.

This morning, Billy Sheridan could sense Caleb's mood and wouldn't curse him for bringing snowdrops and ill luck into a house, where all was bad luck and devious planning.

"You like them, mother? I found them by the Salwarpe."

"It means spring's on the way," she said softly.

"Yes, and I shall take you out as soon as the weather's better. Away for a while."

"No, no, I can't, Caleb. There's the workers to think of and all that new machinery."

Caleb shook his head at her words, put an arm about her. Lavinia hadn't been to the works for years. It was just her defence against what was happening to her own weak body. And all the time Billy Sheridan sat watching them with sneering hate in his eyes, while Caleb hated him back for how he had met, duped and ill treated his mother.

Billy had been handsome once; he still had some curls on his head but they were thinning. Where he'd been lean as a young man, he was now paunchy, come from a monstrous appetite for drink, which showed in the florid red of his face.

All that was left of the good-looking Irishman who Lavinia Vyne had met at the London exhibition, were his brilliant blue eyes, which he'd handed down to his son, Charlie. Their look had been the downfall of too many women.

Charlie was his father's son all right. Caleb looked at Billy with contempt and thought about the latest wrong Charlie had wreaked on an innocent female. At that moment, Caleb would have liked to have beaten both of them to a pulp, hang or not.

"Don't look like that, Caleb," pleaded Lavinia. She was frightened at his face. She could stand no more trouble that morning. She'd heard Caleb and Charlie cursing each other late in the night, and then Billy had come up, heavy with drink. She was feeling sick.

"I'll take you back upstairs, mother. You need to rest."

Lavinia was grateful. When Caleb had flung out of the house to control his temper, she'd feared it wouldn't work. But her son was as good a man as his father had been. *Why did you have to die, Harry?* she asked under her breath. *Why on earth did you have to die, and leave us like this?*

"And you need warmer clothes than this in the house," Caleb added, feeling her gown. "This old thing is made of nothing."

"No," she sighed, leaning on her son as they left the room, "I can't part with it. Your father brought it from Birmingham as a present when we were first married."

Caleb smiled. "All right, mother, you keep it. But put some warmth beneath it." He could show his mother that he had loving feelings, but only her and no one else.

* * *

When he came downstairs, his stepfather was waiting.

"Snowdrops for mother!" he sneered.

"Aye, flowers, man," said Caleb, jumping the last five steps and catching Billy by the arm.

"Leave go!" shrank the coward. "I would there were flowers on your grave."

"They'll be on yours before mine, Sheridan. And your cursed son's. But they won't be snowdrops."

"Watch your tongue, lad. Remember you're dealing with an Irishman."

Caleb knew he could have broken his stepfather's neck with ease, and the man was still full of pompous wind. "Then see you hold yours. I say what I mean. And where is your precious Charlie? Perhaps I should tell his grandfather that he is still in bed. Or about one of his indiscretions?"

Caleb was determined Billy would know of his son's reprehensible behaviour, and the best way to scare him was to intimate the Sheridans might fall from favour with old Mr. Stretton, who kept to his room, but still held the reins of control.

He added, "Grandfather Stretton may dote on Charlie, but would he condone rape?"

"What lies are these?" stuttered Billy. Yet, for a moment, Caleb had seen surprise and fear in his eyes.

"Aye, rape," repeated Caleb. "And I have proof."

"What? The word of some whore who's after a place with the master?"

"No whore," said Caleb evenly, "but a girl of respectable family. Charlie has overstepped severely this time - and he'll suffer for it." He was thinking of the way the salters had ganged up against his half-brother outside 'The Talbot'.

Caleb should have let them get on with it. He would

have done so if Miss Annesley hadn't been watching. Charlie was a real coward and could never take punishment. And a mere girl had managed to save him this time.

Later, as Caleb ate his breakfast, he was thinking how Charlie only took advantage of females, and why women always looked for and found the worst of men to be with.

* * *

The rest of the Shrikes had gone to work leaving Sally alone. She lay quiet on the hard bed-stock which she shared with her mother, wondering why things always went badly for her.

Mrs Shrike had often said her troubles had begun the day she'd had Sally. That hadn't been a kind remark but Sally had learned to live with it. She had to admit she enticed trouble easily.

Even as a little girl left alone for a second while her mother ladled salt, she had almost fallen in the pit. Perhaps it would have been better for all the Shrikes if she had done?

She turned her face into the prickly pillow. The only comfort she could feel on her cheek was her own hair, loose about her and thick as a blanket.

Sally ought to have gone into work but she felt far too ill. And hadn't the young mistress sent her home to gain strength? She thought about Miss Annesley, who had a fine figure and beautiful face.

Sally stared at a strand of her own hair. What if it curled and coiled like Miss Liddy's? But it would never be the colour of chestnuts, those bright playthings she, Sam and the boys had threaded on string and fought with; or made into the only kind of necklaces Sally could afford. And now this! She put a hand gingerly beneath her swelling breasts. When would it be her belly? When would they all start to notice and jeer her? She would be like the lepers in the Testament.

Sally began to cry. It was a wicked thing to have a child outside wedlock. A child without a father; a baby put inside her without her will. To hear *his* name spoken out loud was enough to make her sick. She wished Sam and the boys had killed Sheridan like they'd wanted to, but that would have been murder and they'd be hanged.

She could have murdered him herself. She'd never wanted him, never made him do what he did. And now part of him was growing inside her. Sally Shrike shivered, rolled off the bed and crossed the room which served the Shrikes for living, eating, sleeping, all in one.

The fire was almost out, but she was afraid to put on coal because of the expense. Living near the coal yard was more tantalising than advantageous. However, sometimes, at night, she and her young brothers and sister would go out and riddle through the discarded slack to find small lumps for the fire. Today she'd have to go outside and gather some sticks. . .

She found the bundle leaning against the privy and blessed her brother. He'd broken the pieces small enough for her to handle, She brought them back in and fed them to the fire. As she watched the flames licking their twiggy sides, Sally went over and over what had happened in her mind, wishing her seducer would burn like that in Hell. . .

* * *

It had been only a few days before Christmas and Upwych had been on fire with oil lamps and candles, with the shops stuffed full with sweetmeats and presents for those who could afford them. Sally had taken two of her younger brothers and one small sister to see the church dressed in its finery. There had been ivy leaves twisted about the pillars - and baubles. Sally had told the excited children to stop shrieking excitedly in the house of God and then they'd crept about instead with only John's boots making a noise on the stones.

It had been his turn to wear them, so the brother next in age to him, Tim, had stayed at home. Sally had promised to take him out tomorrow. Her sister had done well because the vicar had sent Mrs Shrike a parcel from the Aid Society, containing two pairs of girls' boots. The littlest boy, Tommy was wearing the other. He didn't care whether they were girls' or too big, as long as he could see the Christmas dressings.

Outside the church they were lucky to meet two of the wives from the Vynes, who'd been blessed with good money from their men, and took the young Shrikes off for a farthing each of sweets. Sally was glad because her arms ached from dragging the children along. She was free to walk up the crooked lane and look in the watchmaker's window. She heard the tinging bell on the shop door and stood aside to let the customer out. Then she was looking up into the blue eyes of Mr Sheridan, the young master from Raven's Mill. She hung her head.

"Sally Shrike," he said.

"Sir?"

"Shopping?"

"No, sir. Out with me brothers and sister."

He was laughing pleasantly. "And where are they?"

"Down town, sir, with some Vynes women. Buying a pennorth of sweets between them." He was feeling in his pocket. She watched, fascinated.

"Here!" He was holding out a florin.

She stepped back. "Oh, no, sir. I couldn't!"

"It's a Christmas box, Sally. For you and the children." He laughed out loud. "Take it. And don't hang your head. Look at me." He cupped her chin in his hand. "Be happy."

She coloured under his gaze. She'd never seen such bright, blue eyes. "I can't, sir."

"What nonsense. You can - and you must - or I shall be offended. And that will do you no good at all." He was pressing the coin into the palm of her hand. And she couldn't resist.

* * *

Looking back, Sally realised how she'd been trapped. Like a little beast in a snare. Being in Sheridan's employ at that time had made her so vulnerable. She couldn't have thrown the money into his face, but she shouldn't have taken it either. Both ways he was too powerful as master and there had been no way out.

That florin had bought all the Christmas boxes they'd ever had. The Shrikes lacked a father. He'd died after falling when shovelling coal under the salt pans. Sam, she and her mother were the only breadwinners. Sally knew her father would have wanted to die again anyway if he'd known what had happened to his daughter.

But her brother was braver.

At first, Sam had put down his head and sobbed. Whether from anger or sorrow she was too frightened

114

to ask but, after, he'd clenched his fists and set his jaw until the veins stood out.

"The brute'll pay," was all he said. But how? Soon her pregnancy would be the butt of every dirty mouth in Upwych.

But not all gentlemen were the same. She had to believe that. If it hadn't been for Mr Vyne she might have died. Sally forced herself to think of that too. . .

* * *

There was a stable not far from the yard where the coal horses were kept. The Shrikes' red brick cottage was about a quarter mile from it between the canal and the river. Sally loved the place. It seemed remote from the noise and dust of the coal yard and the shouts of the workmen as they loaded their barges.

When she and Sam were small, they'd creep into the stable, climb through the mangers and on into the loft space. In the summer dusk they used to sit up there and listen to the owls crying, watching the bats winging their way about the yard and down the thoroughfare of the water. There was a special smell about the stable and it was always deep with straw. Beneath the floor was a small room where winter feed was kept which could only be reached by a trapdoor. No child with the exception of Sally and Sam could ever find the entrance. It was their secret place.

When the horses were brought in steaming from work, Sally used to stand next to the beasts and take comfort from their warmth through her thin dress. She loved them and when she was grown, watered and fed the animals, which were used to pull both coal and salt carts to the station. Sally might have been short on book-learning but she was bright with imagination. The day after she'd met Mr Sheridan she was in the stable singing a carol very loudly. Blossom, her favourite shire, was lying down peacefully, and as Sally sang happily she was thinking about Christmas and another stable far away.

The times she'd wished she hadn't been there. Nor decided to climb into the loft. If only she hadn't been singing, she would have heard him creep up behind her through the manger. How he squeezed through she'd never know. Charlie Sheridan was a big young man who would have squashed the life out of himself just to get at her. If she'd known what he was going to do she would have jumped out of the window, even if it'd meant breaking her leg.

He'd come at her from the back. Taken her by surprise. She could smell the soap on him. That was the only way she recognised him as none of the village lads could afford finery. Then he'd thrown her backwards on to the dusty boards, strewed with wisps of hay and chaff. When she came to afterwards, she had chaff mixed with blood in her mouth. His buttons had scored her skin and he cut her pitiful cries of pain by pushing his scarf in her mouth and fastening it behind.

It was no good struggling as he sought her breasts - nor could she raise herself from under the heavy length of his body as he began to do unspeakable things to hers. He was too hard to shift. . .

"If you tell on me, Sally, I'll have the lot of you out of the cottage and on the streets. D'ye hear?"

He was fastening his buttons as he said it. Then, when he'd done, he tweaked the scarf from off her mouth, pulled her up from the floor and clapped her on the bottom.

"There, that's better. Don't look stricken. You'll be

all right. Wasn't that bad, was it? Get off home now. And don't tell. Remember?"

She nodded, mute with horror.

He was gone with a thud. Jumped right out of the loft. Seconds later, she heard him ride off, his horse's hooves scraping and skidding on the cobbles.

It seemed an age before she had the strength to slip through the manger. Then she lay along Blossom's warm side for comfort and wept. . .

And *he* found her there. Not the brutish Sheridan, but Mr Vyne, come looking for trouble, after seeing his half-brother riding away from the stable like a madman. When she'd heard the hooves, she'd frozen with fear, thinking Charlie had come back for more.

Mr Vyne had not said much, but his eyes were wild. He had taken her home first after he'd promised to speak to Sam. And he had arranged for the family to leave Stretton employ and work for Annesleys. How he'd managed it with Miss Elizabeth, she didn't know, but at least that was one burden lifted. She had to work for Charlie Sheridan no more, but she still lived in the cottage near to Raven's Mill. Mr Vyne could do nothing about that, but on account of her fearful horror for the place where she'd been raped, he'd forbidden the use of the old stable for the coal horses any more, promising to have it demolished. Sally was glad of that. It belonged to her childhood; a childhood which was no more.

Their own cottage was derelict and he'd promised to have them moved, but Sam had forbidden it. Shrikes had lived there for two hundred years, and in any case, until the doctor confirmed Sally's pregnancy, none of the family were any wiser. She was forced to tell her mother then.

Maria Shrike was inconsolable after the confirmation.

But she was a female salter and had no weight behind her words. She knew there were villages all over the county where working girls had encouraged their master and paid for it. And, in the heated exchange that followed, Maria accused Sally of bringing trouble on herself and the family.

But Mr Vyne and Sam knew her better. And the young master had been the first, had borne the knowledge of Sally's rape by Charlie, had paid for her to visit the doctor on the day they had met Miss Annesley - and Sally had blessed him for his goodness. If anyone maligned Mr Vyne in Sally's hearing, she defended him fiercely. But perhaps she had been too vehement in his defence? Now folks were guessing at her illness, and several of the salters' women, who were jealous of the favours to the Shrikes like the new-found job at Annesley's, had started to whisper about Mr Vyne.

The injustice nearly killed Sally, but she dared not breathe a word about Mr Sheridan. Mr Vyne had ordered her not to for his mother's sake. He'd promised Sally and the child would be provided for and, so far, he'd done all he promised.

As she went over her predicament again and again, huddling beside the fire, Sally Shrike began wishing she might have fallen into the brine pit when she was but a little wench. If she had, then she would not have brought trouble on the two men she loved and respected most in the world, her brother, Sam and the honourable Mr Caleb Vyne. Sally stared into the fire anxiously . . . and came to with a start.

There was a faraway shrieking noise in her ears as she was torn from sleep. At first, she thought that it was the Bull, the factory whistle summoning them to work; that she had overslept. Then she remembered where she was. Sally struggled to her feet, stiff from the uncomfortable position in which she'd fallen asleep, and she hurried outside. She shivered when she recognised where the sound was coming from. The alarm was sounding at Upwych. Not Stretton. It meant some disaster had struck the Annesley pit. The whistle was always sounded when something terrible happened. Like when her father fell into the coals tending the pans.

All Sally could think of now was her mother, Sam and the children. Shocked, she dashed back into the cottage and threw her shawl over head and shoulder. Then, still feeling sick and ill, she emerged and began to run along the path in the direction of town.

She must make it to Upwych and find out what had happened. As she was forced to slow down because of a stitch in her side, she was praying that no more misfortune would fall on the Shrikes because that would be more than Sally could bear.

* * *

Chapter 7

Upwych was in uproar. The streets were crowded with anxious men, women and children, making for the works, while a press of carriages jammed the surrounding roads. Practically everyone in the town worked for or was connected in some fashion with the mining of salt. It was their livelihood. One blast upon the whistle which was not the customary one beckoning to or leaving work, was enough to throw innkeepers, shopkeepers and salters into chaos.

It was all a question of the town's survival and on that winter morning as Lydia Annesley sat down to breakfast, her wealth was already dissipating beneath her like the insubstantial white frost under the sun. She put down her china cup suddenly as the mournful siren wailed. Sarah, who was waiting at table, clapped her hands to her mouth.

"What is it, Sarah? What's that noise?" cried Lydia.

"The Bull, Miss. The whistle." The girl could hardly speak.

"What whistle? What do you mean? Tell me." Then Wilson was coming in. "Wilson, tell me quickly." The housekeeper looked as frightened as Sarah.

"It's the factory whistle, miss, on the chimney . . ."

"Yes, go on."

"It's called 'The Bull'. They sound it when there's been an accident at the pit."

Lydia's heart lurched. She looked from one servant to the other. "Well, why are you standing there? Find out what's happened." She was rising from the table and Wilson was already hurrying from the room. "Sarah, pull yourself together."

The girl was shivering, her eyes staring out of her head. "But, Miss Lydia, what about Miss Elizabeth?"

"I'll go to her straightaway. And Sarah, fetch my coat and tell Blanchard I shall need the carriage directly. I intend to go down there myself but get him to send one of the boys to the works to see Dobson and find out what is happening."

Lydia was determined not to let her anxiety show to the servants but, inside, she was dreading what effect bad news might have on her sick aunt and full of concern as to what might have happened at the works.

As she hurried up the broad staircase, she was thinking about those pitiful people who tended the salt pans. What misfortune could have befallen them now?

* * *

Elizabeth had woken, white and shaken by the whistle's blast. She had heard it several times in her life and each time wished she would never hear it again. Lydia did her best to console her, but had never experienced a factory disaster, which was a terrible thing.

Elizabeth could see that Lydia's place was at the works, but she was determined to delay her for a while. Soon, Wilson would return with news, which was better faced at home. If it was dire, the experience of waiting at the factory gates would have a shocking effect - and Lydia had to be strong to face the consequences.

"May I not go now, aunt?" begged Lydia, but Elizabeth Annesley shook her head.

"Let Dobson send us the news. I shall bear it better with you by my side." Elizabeth could see that this was the only way to prevent her leaving.

So Lydia paced up and down the room, while her aunt lay, fighting for breath and trying to calm herself.

Dr May had been sent for, but Blanchard had returned with the message from his maid that he, too, was at the pit, but she would convey the request to attend Miss Annesley as soon as she possibly could.

All the two women could do was wait. And Lydia thought it was possibly the worst moment of her life when Wilson entered the bedroom. Her face was sombre and she was clasping her hands as she broke the news.

No one had been injured, but the brine had ceased to flow; that when Dobson had dispatched men to find out the matter they had discovered sabotage. *The Annesley brine pipes had been cut right through.*

"Thank God, no one has died," whispered Elizabeth to Lydia, hand to her heaving chest. "But, Liddy, we are ruined if we have no brine." She coughed and clutched her side.

"Yes, aunt, let us thank Him," replied Lydia gravely.

Her shock was mixed with relief. Ruin was something she could face if she had to, but not the death of her salters.

It was only later when the doctor came and examined Elizabeth that the full importance of what had happened was beginning to strike.

Once her aunt was settled, Lydia ordered the carriage so she could visit the works and find out the damage exactly. What Lydia had not understood before, concerning her own company, was soon to become apparent. It was true that the Annesley Works depended on its own pit, into which the brine gushed daily from below the earth's surface. The liquid gold ran freely beneath the town, only needing local men to pump it up through Annesley's cumbersome machinery.

However, much of the young heiress's troubles stemmed from the fact that the brine was diminishing in the area of the works pit although old Herbert Annesley, being the good business man he was, had decided to expand all over the estate and bore holes to find more brine so the family fortunes could keep increasing.

There had been so many quarrels in past centuries over the rights to such estate, but the Annesleys had staked their claim and held on to their land.

The new bore holes had resulted in the laying of pipes to the Upwych brine pit and, beneath the ground was a network of pipes leading to the very heart of town. Evidently a person or persons unknown had severed the pipes leading from the most important brine seam of all.

* * *

When Lydia finally reached the works, her carriage had to pass through a crowd of silent workers, who stood back, looking like white ghosts. There was an eerie silence now the machinery had ceased and, inside the foreman's office Lydia learned of the felony.

"Totally severed, Miss Annesley." Dobson was afraid to tell the young mistress just how serious it was. Their supply was leaking away into the surrounding earth and the Annesleys were becoming poorer by the minute.

"Severed?" she repeated to the foreman. "But who would do such a terrible thing to us?" Dobson and the bailiff exchanged glances. Lydia looked from one to the other. "If you have any suspicion, I beg you, tell me."

"We have suspicions, miss," said the bailiff, "but no proof."

"Strettons, miss," said Dobson. "They're the ones who'll profit by our fall. Our competitors."

"But would they stoop this far?" Lydia could see by the men's faces that they believed it. "And you cannot prove it?"

"No - except the cutting of the pipes occurred at a spot not far from Raven's Mill," added Dobson.

A slight shiver passed through Lydia's body thinking of the sinister house.

"Where your land borders theirs," reminded the bailiff. "They had the prime opportunity, miss, and the motive."

"But they have new machinery. I've seen it." Dobson was looking at his mistress keenly. He had heard she was very fond of riding out near the Mill and he didn't care for the idea.

"Why would they need to cut our pipes?" pressed Lydia.

"Who knows, miss?" answered the bailiff. "But there is always greed. And Strettons have never loved Annesley since the old days."

"Yes, I heard about that from Blanchard," said Lydia dismissively. "But that was in the time of King Charles."

The men were gauging the atmosphere. Both sensed Miss Lydia seemed unwilling to hear tales against the Strettons. Was Mr Sheridan or Mr Vyne to blame for that? They had to be careful what they said.

"I shall go and see the damage for myself," said Lydia spiritedly, "as soon as I have chance. But now, I need to

124

decide what is to be done." She sighed, biting her lip while the men waited respectfully.

"Miss Elizabeth has suggested I call the Works Board together to discuss the future. The sooner we can gather, the sooner the men will be back in work. I think that is the answer, don't you?"

The men nodded.

"Dobson, can you see to the preparation of engineering work, so that we may begin as soon as the Board makes its decision as to how to proceed?"

"Yes, Miss Annesley."

"And, bailiff, I'm relying on you to make the arrangements for the meeting."

"At your service, miss."

"And thank you both for your explanation."

Lydia rose and began to pull on her gloves. Then her workmen were bending over her hand, mightily glad their ordeal with the young mistress had come to an end. And it had been a very ticklish one.

* * *

Later, as Lydia made her way back to Annesley House in the carriage, she was going over and over their accusations. She was sure that Mr Sheridan, all honest eyes and manners would not stoop to such a foul practice as cutting her brine pipes.

As for Caleb Vyne - she couldn't imagine that either. Stern and silent, he might be, but not a criminal, surely. Her heart ached at the thought. Only a few months ago she'd been full of hopeful dreams and fond imaginings. Just playing at life - and the expectation of love.

She remembered her first sight of the two young men when the hunt streamed over the railway line at Fern

Hill Heath. Who would have imagined they could do her harm? Or that only a few months after she was ready to accuse either of them of such a heinous crime? Had her instincts of admiration been so misplaced?

And yet, throughout the time she had known the Strettons, it had always been Caleb Vyne who'd offended her. That first walk in the park when he had treated her so arrogantly. Soon afterwards she'd witnessed his solitary and suspicious liaison with Sally Shrike beside the river and, in the wake of that unsettling incident, had seen him slight his brother quite openly.

He had never shown a sign of remorse. After, her own servants' conversation had proclaimed him *devilish with women*.

Lydia realised the odds were stacking up against Mr Vyne. But what could be presented in his defence? A visit to Annesley House with offers of help? But, even that was finished with a warning against his younger brother.

The more Lydia thought of the evidence, the more it pointed to him. But there was something inside her which didn't want to believe it. Although the man was arrogant and domineering, she had seen something in his eyes which made her stop short; told her to take care not to accuse him lightly. . .

As the bailiff said, they had no proof, and she knew she would have given a great deal to find some person unknown guilty of the crime, rather than Mr Caleb Vyne. It was at that moment she decided as soon as she had seen to the task of raising salt production again, she would challenge Mr Vyne herself and have the matter out with him.

* * *

Feelings were running exceptionally high. There was talk of sabotage and even murder and one name only was on everyone's lips. Strettons.

There was hardly one Annesley salter who didn't believe that someone working for Strettons or even a Stretton himself had cut Miss Liddy's brine pipes. Their anger was particularly directed towards Billy Sheridan and his foul young son. The latter was the devil in disguise. And there was the business of Sally Shrike and Mr Caleb.

The landlord of 'The Talbot' was afraid he was going to have to refuse to serve both young masters soon. He had no qualms in banning Charlie, but Mr Vyne was no Sheridan. Like many of the locals, he shared the opinion that Upwych would be a better place if Caleb Vyne was master of Raven's Mill.

People had nothing against poor ailing Lavinia, who'd been duped by that Irish bastard. Her dead husband had been much loved and there had been general sorrow when he was lost in the riding accident. It had been rumoured too that even Miss Elizabeth had been sweet on him.

All over Upwych, heads were shaken hopelessly. The thought of no wages was dire. They kept asking each other whether the new heiress had enough brass to lay new pipes. She had said she would order the work to be done, but would a young lady, fresh from the delights of London, bother?

Sam Shrike took it badly. He had everything to lose. He was now the head of a fatherless family, and his sister, Sally, had that devil Sheridan's bastard growing inside her. It was not the child's fault, but how could he sustain it?

And he couldn't speak of the matter to anyone having promised Mr Vyne, who was goodness itself. And he was being blamed. Suddenly, Sam Shrike was making a vow. That he would get even with the Strettons whatever he did and Charlie Sheridan would pay dearly for the evil he'd done to Sally.

* * *

The morning after the Annesley pipes had been cut, the salt workers' thoroughfare was busier than usual. The workers were collecting outside the gates again, stamping their feet and blowing their fingers to warm them. The night had been particularly cold and not many of the salters were dressed adequately for the weather.

Most of the women wore a thin coat only over their calico and the woollen shawl covering their heads and shoulders was about the best protection they had against the frosty weather.

The few bare trees outside the factory walls only tended to make the industrial aspect starker and more miserable, if that was possible.

As Lydia's carriage rolled down to the works, she thought she'd never seen such a desolate sight. The six great Covercroft chimneys dominated the scene like ghostly monuments to an industry stricken with ill-luck. The low buildings were dwarfed completely by these gigantic reminders of her present and difficult situation. The workers, hearing the approaching carriage, were craning their necks to see the lucky visitor who was snug inside. Then they recognised the driver.

"Miss Annesley." The mutter ran around the waiting salters and men were pulling off their caps in a gesture of respect. Women all around were bobbing awkwardly.

As Lydia caught sight of all those livelihoods

dependent on her, she prayed she could find a solution. Blanchard was slowing while the gates were opened. Suddenly, a face appeared at the window of the carriage. Lydia heard Blanchard shout.

"Get away, man!"

But Lydia called out: "No!"

The carriage stopped and Lydia waited. She was hoping to hear what the salter wanted. Blanchard's face appeared, his nose red from riding outside and his eyes were watering.

"It's not advisable, Miss Annesley. The salters are in a rare mood, not knowing where their next wage packet's coming from."

"More reason why I should speak with them then," decided Lydia. "I intend to go to my meeting fully informed." The Annesley chin was thrust out once more.

Blanchard had lost again.

"Very well, miss," he said, opening the door. "You! Come here."

The man appeared. He was pale like the rest, shivering in his threadbare working coat, a muffler about his throat and a cap which he carefully removed in front of his mistress.

"Timmy Boone," introduced Blanchard.

"Well, Timmy?" asked Lydia kindly, conscious of her own warm clothes and not wanting him to be standing bareheaded before her.

As spokesman for the salters, Timmy was more used to Miss Elizabeth's scorching tongue. He would have preferred dealing with the old lady as he was not used to kind words. But as he was spokesman, he must continue.

"Beggin' your pardon, miss, but we wants to know what's happenin' over yon. Shall we be let in?" His strong

Upwych accent was hard to pick up. But the real problem was she could give him no answer.

She decided on a compromise.

"You will be told, Timmy, I promise you. I will send the foreman out after my meeting, and you and your fellow workers will be fully informed. I know you are gravely worried. However, I hope to resolve matters quickly."

"So you ain't shuttin' down, miss?"

Lydia sensed how much anxiety had fuelled the clumsy question.

"Don't be impertinent, Boone," said Blanchard. "Miss Annesley will not be questioned."

Timmy Boone backed away.

"Stop, Timmy," she said and Blanchard stared in astonishment. "You can tell this to all my salters. I have no intention of closing the pit. The brine will flow again soon and your jobs restored. I promise."

Blanchard's mouth remained open like a fish.

Timmy replaced his cap and touched its side with a respectful gesture. Then he and the other salters stood back as Lydia's carriage passed through the gates.

She could feel their eyes boring into her, as keenly as they cut her salt blocks. She had to keep her promise, whatever the cost. Now all she needed was to attend the meeting to try and salvage her business and discover what was best to be done.

She had taken the bank manager's advice and ignored the doctor's. Her aunt, though very weak, had delivered the names of those gentlemen best suited to help and they had answered the summons. But if they'd be prepared to help was quite another matter.

* * *

The spacious board room was smart but hardly fit for such a rare young lady as Miss Annesley. The heavy oak panelling appeared not to have seen a feather duster for weeks, for over the wood was the shimmer of salt, which blew in through the window crevices and beneath the heavy door.

The red-bloom of the mahogany table was dulled and there were lighter marks in the wood grain. The handsome piece of furniture had been brought back from the Tropics by some distant Annesley ancestor while the chairs matched its dull severity. If one looked closely, there might be a button missing from their leather backs or a shininess of seat from age.

Yet the pictures on the walls were fine; one, a heavy oil painting of a livid sea attempting to engulf a three-master. Once again, a testament to the family's fondness for foreign travel.

The men who waited for Lydia that morning had the company's success at heart; if it went down they were ruined - with one exception - Mr Smith, whose bank represented all the salt aristocracy of Upwych. However, he felt sympathy for the lovely girl, who'd been forced to take on such a troubled inheritance when she should have been enjoying youthful pleasures.

Mr Smith coughed into his handkerchief, then blew his nose. "Chilly," he said, and sniffed.

"'Tis that," replied the foreman, rubbing his hands.

He was extremely uncomfortable. He had no experience of the board room, but he'd been called in because he knew how the factory worked. The chief engineer was away and thus he was the only substitute. He had already seen something of the new young heiress. He hadn't agreed with her decision then and he was almost sure he wouldn't now. Her treatment of the Shrike girl had been in keeping with a young lady's charity, but there was no place for softness in the hard world of business.

He could feel his colour heightening at the thought of his brine pipes being cut. To cover his sudden anger, he concentrated on looking at Doctor May.

The doctor's eyes were shut. He'd been called out twice in the night. One to a difficult confinement in the notorious Vynes, where the child had lived. One to a fatal consumptive case. He would rather have been in his bed than waiting for Miss Annesley. He knew why he was present. To report on Miss Elizabeth's state of health.

Two others on the board had not yet met the heiress. One, the vicar of Dodderhill, who was a shareholder in his own right; and Lord George Tulham, whose land bordered on the Annesleys, and who had in the past allowed the family to bore holes in his fields.

Besides being a beneficiary when they found salt, he had grown up with Elizabeth and had some feeling for her since boyhood. He had felt it his bounden duty to attend the meeting and give the young lady any protection he could.

"Any sign of her, man?" asked Lord George, who had given up a morning's hunting.

"Yes, here she is," cried the foreman. "I can see the carriage now. It must have been held up by the salters."

"They say she is much like her grandfather," said the vicar, straightening his stock.

"Then she'll be no beauty," quipped Tulham, "and we'd best watch out."

There was a gust of laughter around the table, which raised the atmosphere.

Lord George was wrong only on the one count. He

caught his breath as he and the others rose to their feet as Blanchard ushered in the caretaker mistress of Annesley Works.

She's some looker, thought George, as they took their seats again. He and his fellows were to find out very soon that they needed to watch Miss Liddy most carefully for she had a number of radical ideas which were entirely her own.

* * *

"And that's it, miss." The foreman finished his explanation of the damage. "The only way we can recoup some of our losses is to lay more pipes. We're lucky to have another small outlet to the brine seam, but it isn't coming quickly."

"Can we bore another?" asked Lydia.

The bank manager sniffed, then cleared his throat delicately. "Miss Annesley, may I remind you boring is a very expensive business."

"Ah. We cannot afford it?" smiled Lydia.

There was a general clearing of throats.

Lord George smiled too. "Miss Annesley doesn't shrink from the truth. It's an expensive business, I agree, but it could be considered, Mr Smith."

The manager was wriggling in his seat. He nodded. "I don't wish to disagree, my lord, but, I, personally, couldn't take such a decision. I would have to refer it to Head Office."

"Head Office, Miss Annesley," repeated George.

Lydia liked his expression. He was elderly but had retained a sparkle of youth. Could Lord George help her? At that moment, and against her will, she was wishing for Caleb Vyne's opinion.

"So what do you suggest, my lord?" she asked.

"If it was my brine I would re-lay, not go to the expense of re-boring, nor recourse to Head Office approval."

"Really, my lord!" said Mr Smith.

"It's just the truth, man. There's no need to re-dig with such punishing interest."

"Thank you," said Lydia, sensing an awkward moment. "And I agree with Lord George. I want my pipes re-laid. But who is to say they'll not be severed again? Isn't it a possibility? Can I afford to take such a risk?"

The foreman stood up and leaned over the table, his calloused palms pressed against the smooth mahogany surface. "Begging your pardon, miss," he said slowly, "if you cannot, then Upwych is finished."

"Thank you," replied Lydia. "Now, gentlemen, I see it this way. Dr. May tells us my aunt needs time to recover. And no anxiety. I have thought about everything very carefully, and indeed, spoken to her of it.

"It would be easy for us to offer Annesley House and the works to the highest bidder. From what I deduce, that bidder would be a Stretton. And, if a Stretton is guilty of the crime against me, I can see no way to sell anything to him!"

"Bravo!" said Lord George.

"I will hold on to Annesley. I will set guards on my pipes on the land, and I hope Lord George will help me arrange that. While the workmen are re-laying I don't think we shall be attacked. But if an attack comes I shall take full recourse to law, and hunt the culprits down. In short, they will be made to suffer." Her green eyes were very bright.

"I do not like being bullied," she added. "And my salters will not starve." The foreman was open-mouthed.

"Dobson, I want you to tell my workers that their jobs are safe. From personal funds I will add an extra coin to their wages if the work of re-laying gets underway by tomorrow afternoon."

"Yes, miss," replied the foreman. "May I go and tell them now?"

As the man hurried from the room, Lord George was thinking how magnificent Annesley women were when roused - and was remembering Elizabeth.

Then Lydia was turning to the bank manager. "I will call at your office at ten tomorrow to go over my accounts."

"I'm afraid, Miss Annesley, that you may be extremely disappointed," said Mr Smith.

"Hush, man," said George. "You and I will have a talk as well. What's the use of neighbours if they cannot be neighbourly? In any case, some of the pipes are on my land. Miss Annesley, we shall make this a joint venture."

The bank manager's eyes were glinting. With Lord George Tulham's wealth at her disposal, the Annesley girl might name her terms.

"Thank you, my lord," cried Lydia.

"God bless you," added the vicar. Suddenly, the outlook for his shares was becoming so much brighter.

"There'll be happier talk in the Vynes tonight," remarked the doctor. What a way the young lady had with her. He'd be a lucky man who set his sights on Lydia Annesley but he'd have to be a strong one.

"And, Dr. May, I have some plans for my workers' welfare. I should like to discuss them with you."

"Only too glad, Miss Lydia, but if this meeting is nearly over, I beg to be excused. I've had a broken night."

"Of course. I've kept you far too long already," cried

Lydia. She took out the pretty watch which had belonged to her mother. "Goodness, nearly lunch time. Can I extend the hospitality of Annesley House to any of you?"

All but one declined. Lord George was very keen to see and hear more of this amazing young woman. He also intended to make her a handsome joint offer for the re-laying of her pipes. They left together in his brougham and, as they passed through the factory gates, a cheer went up from the shivering salters. They had decided to stay outside until the young mistress left the premises.

Timmy Boone stepped forward, removed his hat to doff it to Lydia and Lord George. "I speaks for all the salters, miss," he said in a hoarse voice. "Thank you."

The carriage moved off and Lord George noticed the brightness in Lydia's eyes. "You have accomplished what we have not, my dear."

"What's that?"

"The respect and approval of the workers."

"I hope so with all my heart," said Lydia. "They have miserable enough lives, and I'd like it to change."

"Well done, Miss Lydia, well done," said Lord George expansively, as his chestnut horses trotted on down the wide thoroughfare past the ugly chimneys of Upwych.

Later, Lydia was very glad she'd invited him, as he was able to give her some further insight into her family history. She was touched by his evident concern for her aunt. He had asked to be brought up to see her, but finding Elizabeth fast asleep, he and Lydia had tip-toed out. There was still a tender look on his face as they descended the staircase and entered the drawing-room.

"You've known my aunt a long time, my lord?"

"Since we were both children. Although I was at Eton, I was a frequent visitor to Annesley in the holidays."

"You were boarded out then?" asked Lydia.

"Indeed I was, but not happily. My father had more preference for the place than I certainly did. If I had married, I should not have sent my own son." Lydia could see the remembrance of schooldays long ago was painful, so she didn't pry.

"And my aunt? Did she have a governess?"

"A fine one, but exceedingly severe. And an excellent chaperone." He was evidently feeling better because his eyes were twinkling under the heavy white brows. "Ah, yes, quite excellent - and now - poor Elizabeth. To think she has come to this."

"I'm sure she'll be well again," Lydia interposed, hoping he wouldn't be sad again. She was wondering if Lord Tulham could have been her aunt's suitor, he spoke so tenderly of her.

"You have a kind heart, Miss Lydia, like your aunt." He got up and walked over to the window to look at the park. "She and I have been ever close. In fact, I would have asked her to marry me, but she had other plans. A strong-willed young woman." Lord Tulham cleared his throat. "Very much like you, my dear. I thought it when I listened to your speech today."

"Thank you." Lydia was annoyed to find herself blushing. "I hope you will not think it an impertinence, but I'd be happy to hear some more about my aunt."

"It's quite simple," said Lord George. "Although I was bewitched by her, she was not enchanted by me. But that is the way with love." He looked so crestfallen that Lydia just had to go up to him and place her hand on his arm.

"I'm sorry," she said.

"Elizabeth cared for another man, you know. It still hurts to think of it. . . . He wasn't free."

"I see. . ." It was clear now why her aunt had never married. She believed in love, not gain. "From a local family?"

"Unfortunately so."

"Why unfortunately?" asked Lydia.

"My dear," said Lord George, looking into her green eyes, "the man was Harry Vyne. Elizabeth fell head over heels in love with him, but he was married to Lavinia Stretton. Besides, she was a good deal older. In fact, there were, I believe, twelve years space between Elizabeth's birth and your father's.

"Your grandfather was incensed about Harry Vyne," he continued, "not only that he was a married man, but that he was tied up with the Strettons. She was forbidden even to speak with him. And, in those days, the Annesleys were glittering stars on the social scene. Mrs Stretton and Elizabeth's mother vied with each other in concert and coterie." Lord George looked sad once more as he added: "My father and hers attempted to press our marriage, but I refused as I knew her heart would never be mine."

"Harry Vyne died, didn't he?" Lydia asked, thinking about how sad it must have been for her aunt.

"He did. . . But he left a son. . . The image of him."

"Caleb."

"You've met the young man?"

"Several times," she replied, hoping her voice wasn't trembling.

"I'd say he was the best of the Strettons. The other lad's a . . ." Lord George suddenly remembered he was talking to a young lady. "I beg your pardon, Miss Lydia."

She smiled. "I'm sure you were only going to offer some innocent charge against Mr Sheridan," she said.

Lord George was sure then she hadn't met Charlie.

"He's a good rider, but a bit of a hothead," mumbled George to cover himself.

"Would he have had a hot enough head to sever my brine pipes?"

"I'm sure I don't know, Miss Annesley, but I am more inclined to believe him guilty than Caleb. However, a young lady like you should have other things on your mind than brine pipes. But, again, you are so like your aunt," he sighed, taking Lydia's hand and brushing it with his lips.

Throughout the afternoon Lydia was thinking about his words. Rather Charlie than Caleb. Just why did everyone slight the younger and favour the older, when to her, it seemed the other way round?

She concluded it must be on account of the popularity of Caleb's late father and the low regard in which Upwych held the Sheridans. Now, sure she had found the answer, she was even more resolved to seek out Caleb Vyne and level her charges. At least, then he would have to defend himself.

Later, when Lord George's carriage was about to pull away, Lydia thanked the old man for his magnificent offer of a joint financial venture in salvaging her brine pipes.

But as his horses trotted off, she was thanking him too in her heart for illuminating her hitherto secret family history, and how it tied up with that of the Strettons of Raven's Mill.

* * *

Chapter 8

The reassurances Miss Annesley had given to the salt workers on the day of the meeting seemed to be coming to nothing. 'The Talbot' was no longer a place for noisy laughter and relaxation as there was hardly any money in the town to buy ale. Those who had any, made their beer last.

Timmy Boone and Sam Shrike were sitting at opposite ends of a trestle table, their faces confirming their anxiety. Timmy had a half pot in his hand and he was staring into it miserably. He was thirty-five but, like the rest of the salters, seemed much older, his skin wrinkled and shiny from exposure to salt and his back bent from heaving heavy loads.

Timmy had some responsibility at the works, being the salters' representative but, more often than not, he slept beside his salt pan, his life consisting of hard labour and monotony.

Quite often he would set off on a Saturday evening and not return home until the following week. Like the rest of the salters, he had to stick at the job day and night even to get a living.

Maisie Boone used to send two of their smaller children to take their father his meat and drink, which he ate while he was working. Timmy had no option; he was paid on a piecework basis with a bonus for the salt he produced over and above the quote.

But not that Saturday.

He still had a wife and children to feed, but here he was in 'The Talbot' because some felon had severed Annesley brine pipes. He cursed the Strettons out loud.

Sam stretched out his hand and laid it on the other's sleeve. "Come, don't take it too hard, lad. You know Miss Annesley's promised to keep us fed. They say there's a soup kitchen being set up. And the new pipes will be coming here by canal in the next few days." He wanted to believe it himself.

Brave talk, though Sam was tired to death. The pipes they'd had in stock were nowhere near sufficient, and had been shifted by wagon to the site.

And tomorrow was Sunday.

There'd be no work then.

He yawned, flexing his weary muscles. He'd taken advantage of Miss Annesley's offer of the extra coin in their wages - had they any! Tim had done the same and they had lugged pipes until their backs were breaking and others, desperate for the chance of any wage at all, had taken over.

Now they'd run out and were waiting for new. Rumours were rife. Some said that the young heiress had been talking through her bonnet and that there was no cash to pay for new stock. Others had confidence in the Annesleys allied to Lord Tulham, and maintained stoutly they'd not be swayed by this news from Stretton. This latest caused Sam some real anxiety.

It was rumoured that their rivals were embarked upon a new bore hole as their engineer had found a rich salt seam. Boring would furnish fresh work, and that week, it was all the starving salters needed.

Sam feared that loyalty to the Annesleys was waning

given the fickle nature of the workers when they had empty bellies. As for himself, he couldn't stomach the idea of working for Sheridans any more, given what had happened to Sally. But he had young mouths to feed too.

He scratched his head in pure frustration, then jumped as, suddenly, Timmy was thumping his fist on the table making the pots rattle. The few other customers and the landlord were staring.

"Strettons should be made to pay," he shouted. Timmy's outburst was indiscreet in an alehouse which took any salter's money, be he Annesley or Stretton.

"Hush, Tim, 'twill do no good. We all have scores to settle with Strettons."

"Aye and we should do somethin' about it." Tim's expression was ugly in its desperation.

"Ye'll do nothin', Boone, I tell you, or your missis and the nippers will have no father to support them. For he'll be in gaol. Then where will they be?"

"I hear ye, Sam, but it doesn't stop me wishing Strettons and the whole Raven's Mill crew at the bottom of the Salwarpe." He thumped the table again.

Suddenly, a gasp arose from the bar. With a flurry of cloak and boots, Caleb Vyne was towering above the trestle. He had come in unawares and heard Tim's outburst. He looked down into the haggard face of the salters' representative. When Timmy Boone was near to losing his reason, it was a bad look out for them all.

"I hear you too, Tim," he said and the air was thick with breathless fear. "And, though you wish me at the bottom of the Salwarpe, I've come to say that it's true there'll be work at Strettons."

A murmur ran round the room.

"'Tis no rumour," Caleb added. "We are boring new

and we need men for the job. I have no wish to pick a quarrel with any of you here. But, I can tell you this," he looked round, "I am not given to make rash statements like some." Tim hung his head. "But I swear that I, for my part, had no complicity in the whole of this foul business. Sam!" He nodded to the salter. "Good day to you."

"Mr Caleb!" The salter was on his feet. Not only were his limbs aching, but his heart was full of pity for the injustices levelled at Mr Caleb.

"And good day to you all," said Caleb curtly, turning to the door. As he left, the customers' voices were rising in an excited hum. . .

Caleb sprung into the saddle. He had ridden into Upwych against his better judgement. The salters were in an ugly mood and who could blame them. Not only Annesley men, but his own as well.

The latter feared that the bringing in of Annesley workers on the new bore hole would cut their bonuses. But neither Billy Sheridan nor his grandfather cared for that. They had only profit in mind.

Caleb was still unsure who had wronged Miss Annesley over the matter of the pipes, but he was sure Charlie had something to do with it. His excesses were many, and he saw the ruin of Annesley as an opportunity for Strettons to advance their production.

There had been many lapses in morality in the salt business, and the astute Caleb knew there'd be many more. Tapping new brine springs, as old Herbert Annesley had been lucky enough to do, had served his family well for years, but now the Strettons were the lucky ones. But the Sheridans were greedy.

And there were always new salt men coming on, hungry for profit. At that moment, Caleb was sick of the whole business. He could see no way, given the favouritism shown to Charlie, of changing things for the better. Should he peach on him to their grandfather? But the old man was near senile.

The thought of Strettons passing to Charlie changed his misery to anger. Not only would Annesley be ruined but Stretton too. There had to be a way out of the predicament.

He was thinking of Lydia Annesley as he rode down Friar Street, past two more alehouses full of disgruntled salters. She had not known what she had been coming in to face when she'd stood innocently smiling, framed in the window of the train. She, like Caleb, had been pawns in the game of life.

As Caleb made his way along the course of the river back towards Salwarpe, skirting between it and the canal, he was wondering how long it would take for her pipes to arrive. Would it be time enough to save her fortune?

Caleb was surprised how much she remained in his mind. He was not used to dwelling long on young ladies. He left that to his scoundrel of a half-brother.

He wished that he could have explained to her in his own fashion that he held her in regard, and would not have harmed her. But he had not the words, nor the opportunity. Caleb was no ladies' man; the women he had known had offered only his body comfort. He had no knowledge of women's minds, save his poor mother's.

Besides, Miss Lydia thought ill of him. Each of their meetings had ended unfortunately. Again the fault was Charlie's. The young rogue was the bane of Caleb's life and, probably, always would be.

But, like Lavinia, Caleb was patient. For, at the back of his mind, he had some belief in the Almighty's power to wreak retribution. Raven's Mill was as much his as

Sheridan's and he would bide his time under injustice until that day when Charlie fell into some trap of his own making.

And Caleb knew that, given the opportunity, he would help that day come about as soon as possible.

* * *

Riding alone always gave Lydia the opportunity to think. Once again, she had told Blanchard he wasn't needed, and as usual, felt guilty deceiving her aunt whom she knew would not approve of her actions.

But Aunt Elizabeth had taken the sabotage of the pipes very badly and was under constant sedation by Dr May.

Lydia was mistress now, although she didn't feel like it, and Saturday afternoon was as good a time as ever to get away from the house. The new pipes would not arrive till Tuesday at least, and Sunday in Upwych was oppressive, especially given the present mood of the workers.

She had so many cares which plagued her day and night, and it was only with the white grass flying below her, and the steady thud of Sophie's hooves eating up the ground, she was able to forget her troubles for some hours at least. Although work had started on the laying of new pipes the delivery of extra stock by canal seemed to be held up. And the brine kept seeping away.

But Lydia, at least, was keeping her promise. Although she couldn't provide steady work, she was seeing the salters' families did not starve while they waited. With the help of Dobson, she was in the process of setting up a soup kitchen at the factory, but she realised its establishment was limited. She just had to start full production again soon.

She'd also been told the salters were meeting to decide on a course of action. Lydia had been furious when she knew why. Strettons were enticing them with offers of work on a new bore hole. Only two hours ago, Sarah had told her that Caleb Vyne had been to the inn on the High Street touting for workers.

Her soup kitchen was a poor substitute when one had a large family to support, and Lydia didn't doubt he'd succeed. *What else will you add to my sufferings, Mr Vyne?* she asked grimly. *But I shall have it out with you.*

With the wind biting at her veil, she concentrated on her riding, shutting out the memory of the still figure lying in the great bedroom at Annesley; the thin, white faces of her salters; the continuous noise of the distant Stretton machinery and the ugly mood which had overtaken Upwych, setting one family against another.

She was about to keep another promise too. *Seeking out Caleb Vyne.* If her aunt and Blanchard knew she intended to ride right up to Raven's Mill and demand to see him, both would have taken an apoplexy. Several times she'd almost turned back. But, soon, down below, she could already see the gables of Raven's Mill.

Caleb Vyne was down there somewhere. *Is this rashness, Liddy?* she asked herself, bringing Sophie to a halt. *How dare you come here? You refused his help. You turned him down. Now you're about to accuse him? You are courting humiliation if he's innocent.* Every nerve in her body shrieked at her foolishness, but her heart was telling her that what she wanted most at that moment was a glimpse of Caleb Vyne, however stern and unbending. Her breathing was coming so fast that she turned Sophie to walk the mare a little. *What would the inhabitants of Raven's Mill say when they saw her?*

She needed to compose herself before the confrontation.

Her curiosity increased as she guided Sophie down on to the wide path that bordered the river. There were bare hazel bushes stretching out their fingers to prevent her making for the Mill, but she dodged them skilfully.

She saw a pretty spinney to her left where the pink berry bushes were fruiting. The smell of salt was in her nose. Somewhere over those fields was where her brine pipes had been cut. Perhaps she should go and look. Her own salters would be working there. Perhaps it would be a better plan than seeking out Caleb Vyne.

Lydia knew instinctively her nerve was failing.

But, suddenly, Sophie was skittering as a black and white animal lumbered across in front of her.

"Whoah, Sophie, it's only a badger."

She watched as the sturdy animal disappeared behind the massive trunk of a fallen tree covered with ivy and made for the spinney. She didn't notice the horse tethered amongst the trees, nor the fair young man, hair fastened in a thin silk ribbon, piercing her back with keen blue eyes. But Sophie started again nervously when she heard a terrier's bark in the distance.

"Shush, Sophie," soothed Lydia, preparing herself to ride towards the bridge that led to Raven's Mill.

It was then they both heard a horse coming fast along the path. Lydia turned in the saddle and her heart leapt when she saw the black cloak flying and the strong, curly hair escaping under the hat. Her wish had been granted. She would have no need to ride on down to the Mill. For Mr Caleb Vyne was approaching her.

He looked sterner than ever, his strong lips set in a severe line. Suddenly, Lydia was wishing he would smile when he saw her as he had done the night he'd visited her at Annesley. But there was no chance of that.

As he drew alongside, he looked extremely grim, his dark eyes questioning her presence there.

"Good afternoon, Miss Annesley," he reined in, his horse sweating about the flanks. He'd evidently been riding the bay hard. "I assume that you would not like to be questioned as to why you're so far from home, and riding unchaperoned."

"Good afternoon to you, sir," Lydia flushed. "No, I would not. I ride where I please. And I assume the path by the river is common ground to all."

There was silence as their horses strayed together. She could see he was hoping for some explanation and she was trying to furnish one. She must be more courageous.

"I came," she said, "rather to question you."

He reined in to a halt. She had never seen such a fine eyebrow lifted quite as high - and there was the suspicion of a smile at the corners of his lips.

"Indeed. Ask away then."

The horses were walking, head to head, champing at their bits and in Lydia's ears was the sound of the rushing river and the throbbing of her heart.

"It has pained me to come this far," she said, "but I intended to speak with you."

"You were going to visit *me* at Raven's Mill?" She caught the hint of sarcasm. "Was your business that pressing?"

"It was, sir," she replied briefly.

Caleb noticed that her chin was as determined as her voice. She was challenging him with eyes, the colour of his mother's old worn robe and her chestnut hair blazed like fire.

"Then tell me of it and be done," he answered just as

briefly as he could to cloak his emotions. He could sense what was about to come; all he wanted was peace and being thought well of by her.

"I came, Mr Vyne, to find out if you were responsible for the dreadful act which has brought my company near to ruin." Once Lydia had dared speak the words, she felt as if a burden was lifted from her.

Below, in the protecting shadow of a willow, a small boy pulled in his fishing line and crept to peer at the sparring couple. However, when he saw it was Mr Vyne and the mistress of Annesley, he shrank back against the bank, terrified that, noticing, they might take their whips to him.

Caleb's response to her accusation was quite unexpected. He shook his head and laughed, but there was bitterness in the sound, rather than humour.

Finally, he took out his handkerchief to wipe the salt dust from his face. Then he bowed to her in the saddle.

"And is this court that I now stand accused? If I protest, Miss Annesley, will you believe me. Or am I judged guilty already?" He was staring into her eyes earnestly, his horse on a level with hers. "You think I am that much of a villain? And, if I was, would I confess it to you. Fie, ma'am, that you cannot tell a true man when you see one."

That had made her hot green eyes rake over his face more than ever.

"I have no need of absolution," he added. "My sins are numerous, but should I have wished to harm *you* I would have done more than cutting your brine pipes? You seem surprised, Miss Annesley? Perhaps more surprised than when I called to offer my help?"

The veiled reproof made Lydia flush once more.

"Your help," she repeated. "Although I felt in need of it then, sir, I have changed my mind. Your wit is biting, Mr Vyne."

"I have no wit, Miss Annesley. I'm a man who has little knowledge of London fashion and speech. I speak my mind and have done with it."

"That is most obvious," she flashed. "You have behaved boorishly since we first met." She could see Caleb's eyes brightening with anger, but she stood her ground. "I fear, Mr Vyne, I do not like your plain talk when its cruelty is directed towards me."

"Cruelty?" he replied, amazed. "And, pray, how have I wronged you?"

"From that first day in the park - when I was lost," she cried. "And you made sport of it. And, after, when I saw you in the High Street. When you stood by and let your brother take punishment from a common salter."

Lydia sat haughtily, her head erect, ignoring his black expression. Caleb Vyne and she were like tinder box and flint, ready to explode.

"Aye, I stood by all right. And saved the rascal from his neck being broken, and you from being harmed by interference. A brawl outside 'The Talbot' is no place for a lady."

"How dare you, Mr Vyne." Lydia lifted her riding crop involuntarily, her Annesley temper bursting forth. "You cannot insult me like you do your brother."

"I have no wish to insult you, ma'am," he said, eye on the crop, ready to catch at it should she strike out. "But I shall continue to curb his vices."

"Who are you to speak of vices, sir?" cried Lydia, "when you scold me so severely. What are your vices, Mr Vyne?" Her voice was clear and high. She was thinking of Sally Shrike and her own maids giggling at his expense. "I think you are the most arrogant and insufferable man I have ever had the misfortune to meet."

He bowed stiffly, but his lips were set hard once more. "Oh, enchanting words, Miss Annesley. And I have no defence except to say that I prefer to remain silent, rather than be a lapdog whose hanging on every word makes him attractive to a woman."

Lydia could hardly believe his insolence. She had never been spoken to in such a fashion. She tried to bring Sophie's head about, but Caleb had the rein. He leaned over, so near that she could have touched his curling lips.

"I will not say, Miss Annesley, that I have enjoyed hearing your opinion. Nor will I ever resort to uttering what you would like to hear. Your accusations are entirely false. All I have done to you is keep you safe from harm. Believe me."

Caleb had had enough of injustice. His patience had stretched to the limit. He plunged in head first, as he'd done so many times as a boy at play in the Salwarpe. The unreachable fragility which had attracted him first to her, was forcing him to warn her. He had to warn her. He knew she had the rashness of Annesley spirit in her nature. *He could not bear to see her harmed by Charlie.* Anger against his half-brother's wilful fecklessness with women spurred him on.

"Remember I told you to be wary of my brother? It is from *him* that you need saving. He is a womaniser and a wastrel."

Lydia gasped.

"I repeat that if I had wished you harm I would have done more than sever your brine pipes. But - I would never do you harm." There was a sudden sincerity in his eyes, which shocked her. The man was pure quick-silver in mood, like herself.

"If you think ill of me, think twenty thousand times worse of him. For he deserves it."

Lydia was on the point of saying that she was ready to change her mind, but he added quickly: "You have misjudged me, Miss Annesley, and I would have wished to be your champion." He was staring at her as if he'd never seen her before. "I beg you, misjudge him, for he will be your downfall. And, please, Miss Lydia, stay away from Raven's Mill."

She swallowed at his words, heard the pleading in his voice. Was it because he didn't want to see her again or because he feared for her safety?

"What do you mean about Mr Sheridan?" cried Lydia, almost afraid.

"He has no goodness in him." He could put it no other way.

"How do I know you are speaking the truth?" she said, confused, backing off as he let go Sophie's rein.

But Caleb came forward again, and reaching out, closed his hand over hers. She felt a stab of fire run through her at his touch. She looked down at their hands and then up into his face. There was a sweetness about his stern lips she'd never noticed before. Another thrill ran through her. Why had she thought this man her enemy?

And all the time he sat quietly, superbly controlling the restive horse, a sombre figure in black, raking her face with his eyes. Then he withdrew his hand and she felt the cold wind blowing about her.

"You do not. But, if you cannot take my word, then I urge you to seek out someone even more unfortunate."

"Who, Mr Vyne?" urged Lydia.

"Your salter, Sally Shrike."

Lydia drew in her breath. Was she about to discover the mysterious relationship that existed between the girl and Caleb Vyne? And did she want to?

She must.

"Then I will take you at your word, sir, and speak with the girl."

"Tell her I bid you to," commanded Caleb. "And take much notice of what she says."

Lydia's cheeks flamed at his imperious behaviour.

Then, again, like the sun comes from behind a cloud, his attitude softened. "I don't wish to command you, Miss Annesley. Indeed, I am your obedient servant, and have your well-being at heart."

"Have you, Mr Vyne?"

Suddenly, Lydia had no desire to curtail the conversation. There was so much she wanted to hear, to know of Caleb Vyne and his life at Raven's Mill. She had seen another glimpse of the man who had come to Annesley and offered his help. But would the opportunity present itself again after she had said such hurtful things?

Caleb hesitated. He didn't possess Charlie's skill with words. Nor was idle flattery what he wanted the young mistress of Annesley to hear.

"You know that I admire your courage, and . . . and your coming here."

They were the softest words she'd ever heard him speak.

Then he sat back in the saddle, adding, "I wish you good fortune with your questions. If they are answered well enough, perhaps then you might find sound reasoning behind my warnings.

"Although we have spoken harsh words to each other, it may be to both our benefit if we remain as *friends*."

153

And, suddenly, with a tiny inclination of his head, he turned the bay and dashed off along the path.

Lydia watched, her mind in turmoil. He negotiated the timber bridge across the Salwarpe, and rode on until his powerful figure was swallowed up amongst the buildings surrounding Raven's Mill. Finally, he was lost to her sight.

The conversation with Caleb Vyne had left her both dazed and elated. She was at a loss to understand the emotions which rioted within her. She had accused him, and he'd denied all her charges, countering them with ones of his own. That he hated his brother, Charles Sheridan, was apparent, but he said he held her in high regard, wanted to *champion* her and yearned to protect her from him.

These were not the words of a blackguard. But then he had laughed at her too. In fact, Caleb Vyne was impudent, making feelings rise in Lydia which she had never experienced before. The man was an enigma.

And he had given *her* licence to speak to Sally Shrike. That in itself was insolence. The girl was one of her own salters.

But, suddenly, thinking of his hand on hers and his admiring words, Lydia was realising that knowledge of Sally and Caleb Vyne's strange and seemingly ill-matched relationship was what she wanted to discover most of all.

Caleb Vyne's own words regarding Sally had laid him open to suspicion. He had a hold over the girl, for sure. Lydia's cheeks were red, as for the hundredth time at least, she recalled seeing Sally lean against him for support and Caleb furnishing her with bank notes. She didn't understand any of it.

Well, Mr Vyne, Lydia said to herself, *you shall not stand condemned until I have proof. I will do as you bid me in this, at least. I shall call on Sally Shrike and convey your message to her. Then I might learn the truth.*

As Lydia trotted Sophie away from Raven's Mill down the path beside the river, across towards the tow path of the canal in the direction of the coal yard, she was thinking over and over of the words which had passed between them. Caleb Vyne had said their being *friends* would be of mutual *benefit* to them both. What did he mean? She would have not been female if she had not known what was the implication.

But was he talking only business? Her womanly instincts told her not. Lydia realised that Caleb Vyne stirred feelings in her that she wanted to relish again and again. But only if she could trust and respect him.

She felt so frustrated and confused. And what serious charges he had levelled against his brother. What vices did the latter have? He had seemed an honest young man, although somewhat uncouth in his behaviour. Would Sally Shrike be able to enlighten her on those?

She shivered a little as she rode on.

Lydia was so deep in thought and the noise from the coal yard so loud, that she failed to see or hear the rider who was following at a distance.

The only one who did was young Jemmy Yarwood, who'd given up fishing and had found a more interesting pursuit of spying on Mistress Annesley and his master. He had not understood most of the conversation which had passed between her and Caleb Vyne, except that it was heated - and when Mr Vyne rode off in a temper, Jemmy returned to his rod until he was disturbed by that young devil of a Sheridan riding past, following the path taken by Miss Annesley.

* * *

Lydia, who was used to unlovely sights at Upwych, was somewhat nervous in the proximity of the coal yards. She had to pass by the wooden palings that led into the massive open space where mountains of coal were piled, to be shovelled into carts and carried to the barges and the railway sidings.

The air seemed black with dust. Whilst it was Saturday, she could see in the distance men, hard at work, bending, sweeping, shovelling, cursing and wiping their hands down their leather aprons. They were lugging rough sacks on their backs, and dumping their contents into carts, where the horses waited, heads bent under their load.

Lydia spurred Sophie on, confident she hadn't been noticed passing, and extremely conscious of the gritty taste of coal dust in her mouth. Inside, she was longing for open meadows again, away from the ugliness of Upwych and its chimneys, over which hung a pall of smoke so thick that passengers on the trains had complained they could hardly see the town at all.

She had no one to ask where the cottage lay, but she was remembering Blanchard's words. She found it quite easily after all, and was shocked at the degradation.

The Shrikes had once lived on the end of a small terrace, built for coal and salt workers. But the rest of the houses had been deserted long ago, and fallen into ruin as their occupants moved away or died. Dr May had long ago pronounced them unfit for human habitation, but old Mr Stretton had been a parsimonious landlord and made no improvement. Joseph Shrike's fatal accident had prevented any chance the family had of moving and so they'd remained, isolated, making the best of a bad job.

Lydia gasped when she saw the place, but she was determined to see Sally. At first, she thought that no one was in but, dismounting, she led Sophie round the back, picking her way through nettles, bricks and rubble.

She was in luck. Sally Shrike was standing, stretching to take clothes off the line, then placing the garments, stiff and board-like from frost into a washing basket.

"Sally Shrike?"

The girl started with amazement and stood, prop in her hand, staring. She bobbed an awkward curtsy, her eyes dark with fear. Her body, thin and fragile, seemed clumsy and awkward.

"Miss Annesley, what brings you here? Have you . . ?" the girl seemed to frightened to speak. "Is it . . . bad news, Miss? Is it Sam? Mother? They'm all right, ain't they?"

"Oh, Sally, of course they are." Lydia was angry with herself. Naturally, the girl would be afraid. What master or mistress would visit otherwise? "'Tis you I've come to see."

The girl was flushing through to her hair roots. She hung her head. Lydia didn't know why, but something inside was telling her. Sally Shrike looked fit to drop where she stood.

"Shall we go in?" asked Lydia, tethering Sophie to the clothes line.

"In there?" cried the girl.

Lydia nodded, preparing herself. She followed Sally Shrike into the poorest cottage she had ever seen.

"Are you all alone here?"

"The Saturday wash, ma'am," said Sally. There were heaps of clothes everywhere and a great dolly tub standing on the bare floor. "Mam has gone into 'wych with the nippers. I wasn't . . . well enough."

"And you're not well enough to be doing this." Lydia looked with horror at the paddle and the heaviness of the baskets, the scrubbing brush and the tub.

"I has to, miss. There's no one else."

"Yes, but I gave you time off to rest."

"Rest? What's that?" asked Sally. She was still staring. "Would you like a cuppa, miss? Come, sit by the fire. 'Tis a poor one but, at least, it is going."

"I would take some water." Lydia watched Sally go into the tiny scullery and heard the clank of the pump. When Sally handed her the cup, it was a fine one with a handle, and the water was sweet and pure.

Lydia drank thankfully. "Good water, Sally."

"From the well, miss. The only clean thing round here."

"And the cup. How pretty it is?"

"Part of a service, ma'am. Mr Vyne gave it." She clapped a hand to her mouth.

"A service, Sally?"

"Yes, ma'am, but 'tis not what you're thinking. Mr Vyne is a good man. He's provided for us many a time."

"I'm sure he has, Sally," replied Lydia, her cheeks as red as the girl's. "And that is why I'm here."

"I don't understand, miss."

"I'm here at Mr Vyne's instigation. I was just speaking with him."

"Is he here too, miss?" The girl's eyes were wide with longing.

Oh, Caleb, thought Lydia to herself, *her looks alone are betraying you.* And, disappointed, Lydia regarded the girl, trying to see what Caleb Vyne saw in the waif.

"No, he is not. But he sent me here."

"Oh, miss, he's the kindest gentleman in the world."

"Is he, Sally?"

"Yes, miss, he's done a deal for us. Sam has taken a great fancy to him. He'll have no word spoken against him. And they are saying Mr Vyne cut your pipes. 'Tis a foul lie, miss, he would do nothing like that."

She took the cup from Lydia and placed it on the table.

"Come, bring your chair nearer the fire," ordered Lydia.

The girl obeyed. As she was dragging it, Lydia noticed her thin dress and shawl, comparing it with her own comfortable riding habit. Sally Shrike was about the same age as she and yet how different were their lives. When Sally sat down opposite, her hands clasped in front of her, Lydia felt too young and inexperienced to behave as this girl's mentor. What experiences had she been through?

"I have come to inquire about your health, Sally. Your illness."

"Am I to have the sack then? Please, miss, no. I need the place. I'll be back at the pans soon," she pleaded.

"I've not come for that. I want to help you, Sally, if you'll help me."

"Help you?"

"By answering some questions - that may be painful."

The girl looked frightened to death. However, she nodded.

"Just now, you mentioned the accusations levelled at Mr Vyne."

Sally nodded again.

"I had heard them too, and that is why I wished to set my mind at rest. Our discourse was, in the least, very puzzling. I'm speaking to you in confidence, you understand? Mr Vyne has denied all the charges that I set against him. Indeed, he has laid them at his brother's door."

Lydia was suddenly afraid that Sally was going to faint; the girl looked so pale and was gripping the sides of her chair with whitened knuckles. But she had to go on, find out for herself what Caleb Vyne had intimated.

"He seems to think that *you* will be able to throw some light on those accusations. Indeed, his very words were that he *bids you tell me* the truth of the matter. I can only guess to what he is referring but, Sally, if you care for Mr Vyne, then you must exonerate him from my blame." Lydia was quite sure that this would not come about, given the expression on the salter's face.

"The truth, Miss Annesley?"

"Yes. What exists between you and Mr Caleb." Lydia didn't know how she was going to bear it but she was waiting.

"Mr Vyne has asked me to tell you the truth?" Sally repeated, rocking to and fro on the hard, old chair, her eyes cast down and fixed upon the bars of the dull red fire. "Then I suppose I must. I would not have him hurt for anything." She looked up, her mouth working as if she was wringing out the words:

"I'm . . . with child, miss."

Lydia swallowed, the blood rushing to her face. Then it was worse than she imagined.

"But . . . . I couldn't 'elp it. I told Mr Caleb I couldn't."

Lydia blazed inside, not only from the shock of it, but because of his brazenness in putting the girl through telling her. *And because of the feelings she knew she had for him.* Yet, she had to say something to comfort the girl.

"I believe you, Sally. Mr Vyne is a powerful master," she answered slowly. Sally was staring at her. "You couldn't resist him." Of that, Lydia was sure.

"Not Mr Vyne, ma'am. He ain't the father. 'Twas that devil, Charlie, who did it to me." She bent, hugging herself with her thin arms. She looked at Lydia through anguished eyes.

"Mr Sheridan?" Lydia's head was reeling.

"Aye, miss. *Him.* He's a bad 'un, miss. A right bad 'un. He took me, miss, in the stable and . . ."

"Oh, Sally, I'm sorry, I'm sorry."

Suddenly, Lydia was kneeling on the bare floor, holding the shivering salter in her arms. While she listened to the terrible explanation punctuated by the drip of the girl's tears she was hating herself for the joy she was feeling deep inside that it was not Caleb Vyne's baby the girl was carrying.

When Sally explained what Mr Vyne had done for all of them, Lydia listened mutely. How had she misjudged him. What wrong she had placed at his door. How could she ever face him again? And Sally. She must help Sally.

"So he got you the job at Annesley Works?"

The girl nodded.

Lydia was thinking he must have been to see Elizabeth and probably pleaded with her. What had he said when he visited? *That the room had never looked lovelier.* Perhaps her aunt had entertained him on account of those feelings for his father, which Lord Tulham had intimated. And my lord had a good opinion of Caleb too.

"I'm glad, Sally," cried Lydia. "Glad you have told me the truth. And I'll protect you too. No more slaving over the salt pans."

"Then you won't be giving me nor Sam the sack?"

161

"Never. You'll work for Annesley as long as it thrives." Those very words put her in mind of her own predicament. Would there be an Annesley to support the Shrikes? *There had to be. Suddenly, it seemed a certainty. And now she could seek Caleb's help with a happy heart.*

Lydia breathed in deeply, letting some of the burden she'd been carrying these last long weeks slip from her shoulders. Patting Sally on the shoulder, she rose from her knees and, taking out her fine handkerchief, blew the coal dust from out of her nose.

"I will keep all you have told me secret," she said, "but I'll allow no man nor woman to be cruel to you. None of this has been your fault. Remember."

Her heart was full of anger towards Charles Sheridan. So many things were clearer now. She remembered his bold attentions in the park and was wondering what might have happened to her had Caleb Vyne not interposed. She understood now that SamShrike had been defending his sister's honour outside 'The Talbot' and was sure she would have done the same as Caleb Vyne about the blackguard's behaviour!

"Thank you, miss," said Sally Shrike, "and you'll not think bad of Mr Caleb no more?"

"No more," repeated Lydia, "I promise. And, together, we may work something out when the baby comes."

"God bless you, miss," cried Sally. She was dreading the day his bastard would come into the world, but at least she wouldn't lose her job for it.

* * *

Lydia felt a different girl from the one she had been when she'd woken that morning. Not because her business problems had been eased, but on account of her heart.

Looking at her watch gave her a shock. It was getting very late and, probably, her aunt would have been asking for her. She stood up.

"I must go now, Sally. My aunt will be asking for me."

"God bless you, miss, for comin' here. Safe journey." The two girls shook hands outside the cottage, then Sally went round and fetched Sophie.

Lydia, her head full of what she'd heard, trotted away quickly from the Shrikes' cottage with the forlorn figure of Sally watching her from the doorway.

* * *

Chapter 9

Charlie couldn't believe his luck. An afternoon's badgering had brought about not only the sight of his quarry but a fairer one as well. He had had to lose one, so he'd decided on the badger. The two small terriers beside him had whimpered as he'd sent them home after the grunting beast disappeared down into his set. And afterwards he had caught sight of Miss Annesley in close conversation with Caleb.

He'd made sure to keep the couple full in sight. It had been a long conversation, and from Charlie's vantage point in the spinney he'd sensed their meeting had not gone well.

Therefore, he'd followed the heiress with a growing sense of foreboding. First, his damned brother, and then waiting an endless time to see her emerge with that trollop, Sally Shrike.

How much did the lovely Miss Annesley know? Was it conceivable Caleb and Sally had told her of his misdemeanours? Charlie had to find out.

* * *

Passing the coal yard was even more eerie; all the workers had gone and the gates were barred. Lydia spurred Sophie on but, as she rode, she was sure she could hear another horse behind her, its hooves drumming along the canal towpath.

She was right. Soon the rider was drawing level. She caught her breath sharply as she recognised him. It was the man she wanted to meet least in the world. Charlie Sheridan. He was wearing no hat and his curly fair hair was streaming brightly in the half-dusk, unconstrained by any ribbon. She looked at him coldly, hoping that her manner would not betray the unladylike thoughts her mind was entertaining. And the rogue was smiling in a most enchanting manner.

Lydia reined in as his knee, covered in elegant riding breeches, was almost pressing hers. If she had not been the wiser she would hardly have believed Mr Sheridan could hurt anyone. He had such an easy look and wonderful manner; was so young and utterly charming. Yet, *those looks hid the darkest of secrets.* And he had hurt too many. Little wonder his brother had ignored the slight against him and stood idly by.

Suddenly, she felt quite sick over the matter of Mr Sheridan and Sally Shrike. She'd hoped never to meet him again. Caleb Vyne's sombre face and warnings arose in her mind. She had to be careful. His half-brother's riding boot was still brushing her habit. She was suddenly afraid.

"Miss Annesley, how marvellous." His blue eyes glinted. "But what are you doing in *this* place?"

"I could ask you the same," she said. The words slipped out and Lydia was angry with herself. He was regarding her very strangely. She added quickly, "I'm on my way home. I had occasion to ride out of Upwych on business, and, as I had not taken this route before, I was interested in seeing more of its environs."

"Business, Miss Annesley? On the Stretton side?"

"Indeed not, Mr Sheridan. I was checking how the work was faring on my brine pipes."

Their conversation was stilted owing to the fact Lydia had no desire to give away her real reason for riding on the western side of the town. For a moment, his sardonic expression gave rise to the thought he might not believe her.

Suddenly, it was of the utmost importance that he did. She attempted to change the subject, but all the time she was full of loathing that his honest looks could hide such foul deception.

She glanced at him briefly but did not hold his gaze. "I believe your bruises are healing, Mr Sheridan."

"Indeed they are, ma'am. And I have no wish to obtain more."

She felt forced to smile at the feeble joke, yet she was desperate to twitch Sophie's reins and gallop off. But she had to keep up the pretence of civility at least. They continued to make polite conversation but Lydia sensed that something was not right in his manner.

"You have no need to accompany me on my ride, Mr Sheridan. I am quite content to be alone."

His blue eyes narrowed. "On the contrary, I feel bound to do so. Who knows what rough man you may meet on the two miles to Upwych?" There was no smile on his face, only a cool callousness and Lydia was thinking that under the fashionable jacket and breeches he was one of the roughest of all. "You study me, Miss Annesley?" His eyes were even keener.

"No, I'm sorry. I was thinking of my Aunt Elizabeth. She will be worried about me. And you, sir? Should you not be at home taking your dinner?"

He laughed. "They will not miss me, ma'am."

"Perhaps Mr Vyne will come seeking you?" Lydia said.

It was then she realised what a *faux pas* she had made. She hoped he would not take it amiss and, if he did, at least it would shorten their conversation and rid her of him.

"Mr Vyne and I have little in common. I think you understand that by now, Miss Annesley. He does not care if I eat in the house or not. My mother has some preference for him, while I have the ear of my father and grandfather. On the whole, this is to be expected as Caleb has a hasty temper and some reputation for violence."

This was not what Lydia was prepared to hear. "Please, Mr Sheridan, I beg some delicacy in this matter. I don't think it's proper for *you* to favour me with a list of Mr Vyne's vices." She was about to turn Sophie's head, but Charles Sheridan had a restraining hand on her bridle.

"You're forthright for a young lady, Miss Annesley, and I don't blame you for not wanting to know the truth about Caleb."

"I'm all for truth, sir, but no lies." Suddenly, Lydia wondered what foul charges he would lay on Caleb. He was quite monstrous.

Charles now looked more honest than ever. The blue eyes were almost sombre in their frankness. He would have been a master of the play had this been the theatre.

What followed then was ludicrous. He laid his hand on her sleeve. "I must advise you to have nothing to do with Mr Vyne. He can be exceedingly dangerous."

"Surely you go too far, Mr Sheridan? How *dangerous*?" She knew she didn't want to hear anything else. "I've no inclination to become involved with your quarrels with Mr Vyne. Please be kind enough to mention it no more. . . And I must go." She attempted to move her mare but he was still holding Sophie's rein.

"Have I offended you with my plain speaking? It's only for your good, Miss Lydia. I wouldn't wish you to think Caleb Vyne is more of a man than he is."

"Please let me go, Mr Sheridan."

"Caleb likes to coerce. He has a notion I should always do as he bids me. He is arrogant and domineering. Because I'm the younger, he attempts to guide me in everything. But that isn't to my taste.

"Caleb has set himself against me," Charlie Sheridan added, and his voice was ugly. "He will not rest until I agree to every whim. He has crossed me in a matter of which I could never speak to a lady."

Lydia was becoming extremely anxious at his mood and tone. The *matter* was very much on her mind. "No more, please, Mr Sheridan. Your enmity is obvious. I am glad I have no brother to cross me so. Let me go, please." She was pulling at Sophie and he was still holding on. "My groom will be wondering where I am."

"Although you have no brother, Miss Lydia," he said, smiling, "you will not lack protection from the master of Raven's Mill."

"The master? Of whom do you speak?"

"Why, myself, of course. I shall be master soon. And then . . ?"

Lydia was thinking of Caleb's warnings. This wild young man was behaving both rashly and indiscreetly. And she was at his mercy.

He pointed his whip in the direction of Raven's Mill. "Yes, I *will* be master," he added, "for Mr Vyne is out of favour. I have to bear all his slights. He has caused me much pain, and, Miss Lydia, I have often feared for my safety. He has set himself up against me. Against all of us." She was feeling quite shaky as she saw his strong gloved hand reaching out. He continued, in a voice like silk, "How could you know? You are new to this game. But, however painful this is, I urge you to listen. We Strettons are powerful. We have salt by the bushel and Annesley is weakening. . ."

"Let me go, Mr Sheridan. I warn you I won't listen to this." Her loyalty to Annesley and her aunt was in her mind, but now she was truly afraid of him.

"*United*, we would be unassailable. Bound inextricably." Lydia gasped. Charlie was piercing her with those cruel blue eyes and his other hand was on her knee. "If you favour me instead of him, we can outwit him together," he breathed.

"Let me go!" cried Lydia, bringing up her whip. "This is monstrous. How dare you speak to me so?" Her violence so surprised him that he dropped his hand, and seeing her chance, she wheeled the surprised Sophie's head away from the towpath and back towards the safety of the road.

But he was following fast. She could hear the thud of his horse's hooves as he drew level.

"You should hear me out, Miss Annesley. For your own sake."

She slashed out with her whip.

He shouted, "You have seen Caleb, haven't you? What lies has he told you about me?"

Both were galloping now, neck and neck as the shadows lengthened. The wind cut into Lydia's face and tore off her hat. Her hair was streaming behind her as she battled to reach the road. Lydia's whole self was centred on escape. Never, never again would she ride alone. How stupid she had been.

It was then she prayed that Caleb would appear as he'd always done before.

But this time Mr Vyne was not to be her saviour.

Lydia's breath was tearing out of her chest in painful gasps as the ground flew past her like a glassy sheet. Charles Sheridan was pressing so close to her that all she could do was dodge and bend in agonised fear. She could see the way off the path to the road and knew if she could make it she might be safe from him.

But there several trees overhanging and she was afraid she would hit one of their branches. If she did, she would most surely break her neck. And her pursuer must be aware of that too.

Perhaps that was his purpose?

She tried to keep her head, prayed that sense and luck would prevail, but stout little Sophie was foaming at the mouth as the bit began slipping.

"Help, help, help!" Lydia sobbed to herself, glancing aside at the determined face of Charlie Sheridan.

She paid for that tiny lack of concentration. Nearly upon the trees, Sheridan's horse swerved causing Sophie to lurch madly sideways throwing her rider wide and clear.

Lydia felt herself falling, remembered only the dark sky streaked with the glint of evening, the cold air and the hard thud as she hit the ground. Then nothing but black.

* * *

She didn't know where she was nor where she'd been. Her head and ears felt like a dark drum, all sounds muffled and strange. But, as she opened her eyes painfully, she thought it was a nightmare; she was looking into the flushed and sweating features of Charlie Sheridan.

Where was she? What was he doing to her? She struggled to get up, then fell back with a cry of pain.

"Be still, Miss Annesley," he breathed hoarsely. "You fell from the mare. Remember?"

She could hear the words but could hardly make sense of them. Fell?

Then suddenly, the whole terrible incident came rushing back through her half-numb mind. She began to shake uncontrollably, her body racked with sobs. She tried to move again, knowing the man, who was leaning over her was the person she most despised, from whom she'd been escaping. *It was a nightmare*. Was there no one to help her?

To her horror, he began stroking the hair off her brow, feeling all over her body.

"No bones broken," he was muttering as his despicable hands probed at her habit.

"Let me go, Mr Sheridan," she pleaded. "If you have any pity, leave me be."

"I'm seeing if you're hurt," he said as she lay mute beneath his attentions.

She tried to push him off but didn't have the strength. He was looking about him as if someone was coming, but no one came.

"No bones broken," he repeated. She put up her hand to ward him off and, to her horror, he took it prisoner in his and kissed her fingers.

"Leave me alone." She shuddered and her head was reeling.

"Be careful," he said, "I am the only one who can help you."

She was pushing him away but he put down his

head and nuzzled her neck. The bile was rising in her throat. Was this what he did to Sally Shrike?

"Stop, stop," she shouted with all the strength she could muster. "Leave me alone. I must get up."

"That's right," he said, lifting his head and looking her straight in the eyes. "You can't lie here." He was pulling her habit straight where he had disarranged it.

Could he be reasoned with? "You would not, Mr Sheridan, harm me while I am so much at a disadvantage?"

He didn't answer. Instead, he got up off his knees and pulled her half-fainting body towards him. Next moment, she felt him supporting her weight.

The effort of walking made her light-headed. Then her knees buckling beneath her, Lydia pitched forward into a fainting darkness, which quickly gave way to brief flashes of reality accompanied by the hot taste of some spirit forced into her mouth. . .

* * *

The sudden disappearance of Miss Lydia Annesley was the subject of so much speculation and gossip that the town of Upwych could hardly contain it. Local aristocracy and salters alike scanned the pages of *The Journal* in the hope of gleaning the tiniest amount of information. The editor's personal column proclaimed the missing heiress as already given up for dead, which the servants carefully hid from Miss Elizabeth on the advice of her doctor. Everyone in Upwych, from her neighbours to her workers, were afraid of what would happen to the ailing mistress of Annesley when she learned of Miss Liddy's fate.

Everyone realised that this shocking happening

coming hard on top of her other illness was likely to be fatal, but on the other hand, Upwych knew Elizabeth had the Annesley spirit, and had been heard to declare in exhausted and anguished tones that if Liddy had been harmed, Miss Elizabeth would see her attacker punished richly for his crime, even if it was the death of her.

What was uttered in 'The Talbot' was spoken very carefully indeed. No one wanted a thrashing from Mr Vyne, nor a beating from Charlie Sheridan. But everyone was sure that one or the other of the Strettons had something to do with it.

Upwych was once more split into factions; factions that had never really disappeared since the recent unfortunate matter of the sabotage of Annesley brine pipes.

Besides, not one of the workers wanted to lose his nor her job, and a careless word anywhere was dangerous. Both Strettons and Annesleys held the workers' fate in their hands. With the damage to Annesley Works, Strettons were their only hope, and there were already jobs starting on the new bore hole on Stretton land.

Yet there wasn't a man, woman, nor child in Upwych who hadn't heard the story of the young mistress's kindness towards Sally Shrike on her first visit to the works. Nor one who didn't hope she'd be found safe and become the saviour of their jobs, and the reviver of Annesley fortunes.

Yet what would happen if the young mistress was never found?

It was too horrible to think of. However, whispered gossip was rife and unfounded; could it be possible that Miss Liddy, faced with insurmountable problems had had enough of country life and had decided to run off back to London? Or was she really lying dead or drowned somewhere - speculation which was supported by the hysterical outburst from *The Journal's* eager editorial. The fact that her mare had returned was evidence enough to suggest a terrible accident. But no body had been recovered from the river, nor from the canal. Nor found. Which could only mean Miss Liddy had either been spirited away or decided to take off voluntarily. Capricious she might be, was the general opinion, but not so unfeeling as to leave her dear aunt grieving.

Indeed, Annesley itself couldn't bear a hint of any tragedy and it was whispered that Miss Liddy's maid, Sarah, had had complete hysterics in the kitchen, and had been carried off to her *bedroom* by Blanchard, the only Annesley servant trying to hold on to common sense.

Yet the truth was, Blanchard had been more afraid she'd disturb Miss Elizabeth who had been prescribed a sedative draught daily since Miss Liddy's disappearance. He'd actually dropped the hysterical maid on the bed and left her in the care of the housekeeper, Wilson.

All he wished was that he'd been with Miss Annesley when she'd ridden off. He'd seen that look in her eyes before, but being just a servant, he could do nothing about it. But of one thing he was sure: she'd had a bone to pick with the Strettons. Which one he didn't know, but he suspected it was something to do with Mr Caleb.

And Blanchard was well aware of town gossip. It was said little Jemmy Yarwood had been one of the last to see Miss Liddy. The lad had been skulking about two miles from Raven's Mill in the hope of lifting some bream from the Salwarpe, when he'd seen the young mistress on Sophie - or so he said. But he was very young and his word couldn't be trusted. Besides the Yarwoods were likely to say anything which might bring in a few pence, given their poverty-stricken circumstances. Jemmy had been questioned by the bailiff and had been so frightened he'd burst into tears, especially when the constable was mentioned. Then Miss Elizabeth had sent for him and he'd shuffled into her bedroom rightly overawed, and spun out another cock n' bull story about seeing both Mr Caleb and Mr Charlie in the vicinity about the same time.

His great, round eyes staring from his pale, thin face showed he was evidently given to fancies. Even Miss Elizabeth, who could be exceedingly frightening most times, would have failed to wrest the truth from him, the lad was in such a state.

Nevertheless, the matter was now in the law's hands. Miss Liddy had been missing since Saturday and both Mr Caleb and his idle half-brother were under suspicion. The constables had made extensive house-to-house inquiries too, which had been related in turn to every lady who visited the butcher's or the sweet shop or the milliner's. Investigations had been instigated, and it was rumoured that even Raven's Mill was to be searched.

And everyone seemed to have an opinion as to who might have seen Miss Liddy Annesley last. There had even been bets taken in secret. Charlie boy or Caleb? Or even Sammy Shrike?

As for sober Blanchard, he was afraid of Mr Caleb's angry moods, but he respected him too. If it was to be either one of that Stretton brood - and if he could have afforded it out of his wages - he'd have put his money on good-for-nothing Charlie. Blanchard would have wagered his year's wages that Caleb Vyne would never hurt Miss Liddy.

* * *

Caleb could set his mind to nothing. Feeling vulnerable was quite out of his experience. He was, he believed, impervious to hurt given the taunts and scorn with which he'd been treated since boyhood. Caring about such was non-existent. But this was too much to handle. Lydia Annesley was missing and he was a main suspect.

His interview with the constables had been particularly humiliating. As a master he expected obedience, and during the questioning, he'd been constrained to answer correctly or face the rebuke of the law. No Englishman was above it. This he knew. But not only this. He was, for the first time in his life truly afraid, not of his questioners, but in case someone had harmed her. Not for Caleb the anguished threats of Elizabeth Annesley, but a fierce, dark anger which consumed him totally.

Whoever had stolen Liddy away would pay for it. He blamed himself for leaving her to return alone to Upwych. It was one of the worst things he had done. And she had seen Sally Shrike.

As soon as the news broke that Miss Lydia's mare had returned home riderless, he had ridden over to Sally's and been told secretly about her meeting with her mistress. Sally had been the last to see her. He and the female salter had gone over the interview several times, with Sally swearing that when Miss Liddy left she was happy and relieved.

How shocking it was to think she'd not returned home. It was a complete mystery to Caleb. He had told Sally not to breathe a word of her visit, and the girl had agreed gladly. Later, if she was interviewed, then the truth must be told. Caleb had some qualms about hiding any-thing from the constables, but at least, he knew Sally had nothing to do with Lydia's disappearance.

Not only he, but also the police had questioned the men who worked on the coal barges and in the yard. The latter could have no suspicion that Miss Annesley had ridden past there, but Caleb knew it was on her way home.

He was coming to the conclusion that she had been abducted. By whom? And how? She would have put up a fight, he knew that.

A cold feeling came over him when he thought she might be lying murdered somewhere. Upwych had a reputation for desperate acts, and could Miss Liddy be the victim of another?

Then he thought of Charlie and suspected him. But his half-brother seemed as cut up as he was. Caleb had told him that if he had harmed Miss Annesley he would break his neck - and Charlie knew he meant it.

In fact, added to such terrible feelings of exacting revenge was the painful knowledge he had come under suspicion. He had to be. Wasn't he a Stretton and her sworn enemy in the eyes of the public? By them, he could only be judged as guilty. And he could tell nothing that had passed between him and Lydia.

As Caleb lay on his bed, dressed only in his breeches, his head was aching. He had no alibi. It had been a great blow when the knowledge broke about Jemmy Yarwood.

In fact, he had quite forgotten seeing the boy. Early on Saturday Caleb had reined in his horse quite near to where the little rascal was fishing. If he had been anyone but a child Caleb would have sent him off from the Stretton stretch of the river with a box on the ear. But Caleb liked children, however grubby and deprived. Each reminded him how he'd once been. He liked Jemmy Yarwood's toddling desperation, and his courage at five or six to confront the foaming river with a hook like a barge pole.

He had been lucky not to have fallen in and drowned. That was a common enough occurrence for the salters' children, who were warned constantly but who were hungry enough to venture a fish for breakfast.

He'd given Jemmy a hand and landed four flat wriggling bodies into the boy's bag. The child had been wild with joy, ready to kiss his boots. But Caleb's embarrassment had been hidden by stern warnings: "Get off home now, Jemmy Yarwood, and if I catch you here on Stretton water again, I'll take my belt to you." The boy had shrunk back then, a desperate look on his face, small, thin hands clinging on to the precious catch. "And don't say who gave you the fish," Caleb had added. It wouldn't do for anyone to know he was aiding and abetting a poacher. But it did him good just to see the boy's expression.

It was natural enough that, under such pressure, Jemmy had told the constable he'd only *seen* Caleb in the vicinity. He could never have told the child to lie for him.

Caleb could hardly seek Jemmy out and ask the lad if he had heard *what* had passed between him and Lydia Annesley. If he had, and imparted the same, then the constables would have had a real suspect.

But, as for Jemmy's insistence on seeing Charlie too, that was different. Caleb himself had not seen his half-brother skulking, for which he was very glad on his own account, hating his slyness as he did.

But not on Lydia's. If Charlie had been watching them together then. . . Caleb bit his lip. He knew anything was possible, given Sheridan's tastes.

Caleb swung his legs off the bed and started to pull

on his boots. His brain felt near bursting. If Charlie had touched her, he'd kill him. But where could she be?

Perhaps she'd taken fright and gone off to London after all. Perhaps she'd had enough of the miseries of Upwych. But then he was remembering that determined chin and clear look; those green eyes appraising his and blazing into accusation. No, not Miss Annesley. She was far too proud to go skulking off like that. If she was prepared to do so, she would have set her plans in the open.

He could see how she'd blamed him for the cutting of the Annesley pipes. She'd made that clear enough. That she had blamed him instead of Charlie was more upsetting. He could never understand why women could see no further than a handsome face. Charlie was an out-and-out rascal, and Miss Annesley had been just as susceptible as Sally Shrike. That's why Caleb had told her the truth and sent her to the salter.

But there was something else behind it too. *He needed her good opinion.* Although his experience with women of his own class was little, he was sure she was moved by the things he'd said. He cursed himself for holding her hand in case she despised him.

But he'd felt her hand tremble under his. Had he frightened her? She'd called him boorish.

Caleb went over and over their meeting again, looking for clues as to why Lydia could be missing.

Then he shook his head and swore out loud. Life had dealt him a poor hand of cards and, once again, Charlie was holding trumps. But in this case, the game was going to be finding the lady.

He glanced briefly at his watch. He'd be late for the appointment. All of him ached to know what Sam Shrike had to say. He had always trusted his friend and the salter would never have asked for a secret appointment if the news had not been important.

Caleb sensed it must be about Lydia. Sam had sent one of his younger brothers with the message *that Mr Caleb should come to Sam at the church after bell-ringing.* Sam's brawny arms were assets to the vicar of Dodderhill, and he had an ear for rhythm.

Besides, Caleb was sure there would be no constables combing the churchyard, which was high and inaccessible. No one took the steep path gratefully.

However, the reward for reaching the top was a view of Upwych stretching its expanding way to all points of the compass, with the outstanding marks on the landscape being the gracious hotel, the mixture of houses, the Covercroft chimneys and, always, the ribbon gleam of the Salwarpe on its slow way to join the rushing Severn.

Caleb fastened his cloak about the neck and drew a brush through thick tangled curls. A sombre reflection stared back at him from the mirror. If his salters had seen him that day they would have kept away. His expression was stern and unrelenting. That was exactly how he felt when he considered that rapscallion, Charlie, who Fate had destined to be his half-brother.

Once, he'd thought him just young and heedless. Now Caleb knew that he was ruthless and very dangerous.

* * *

Caleb left his horse tethered outside the lych gate. On his ride to the foot of the hill, there had seemed nothing but bells in his ears. It was Sunday, of course, and Caleb hadn't graced Divine Service with his presence. The fact would have been noticed and Caleb was wary about meeting the vicar.

He knew there had been prayers that morning for Miss Lydia's safety, and the hypocritical Sheridans had accompanied his mother to church. He disdained the sham of their worship. He preferred the love of natural things, but in his heart he was praying for Liddy too.

Caleb stood quietly in the dusk, his body half-obscured by a great gravestone, which towered towards Heaven. Was it a bad omen to meet in the churchyard? He hoped with all his might that he would be attending no funeral soon. The thought drove him mad.

There was excited chatter as the bell ringers came out, dressed in their best. At least, on Sunday, they were accorded some little rest. He could see the spare frame of Sam come out into the porch, the lantern light glinting on his fair hair.

Beside him was the vicar, a hawk-nosed man carrying too much weight for his own good. Caleb watched Sam make obeisance, then don his cap. The vicar went back inside and Caleb heard him drawing the great bolts of the church door.

Sam stood uncertainly for a moment, looking round. A small group of salters were lingering, waiting for him, but he was calling: "Go on without me. I've a might of things to do."

"And what would those be?" giggled one of their Stretton girls. "Come down with us."

"Get you off home, Daisy," shouted Sam, "or I won't be answerable."

Doubled up with laughter, the girls ran off, followed by the rest of the town's ringers. When they were safely out of hearing, Caleb stepped out.

"Is it you, Mr Vyne?" said Sam hoarsely.

"Who else? I got your message. What's up?"

"Come," said Sam, looking all round. "Over here."

They made for the massive hollow trunk of a tree, which years ago had been struck by lightning. In its protection, Caleb listened.

"How do you know this, Sam?" asked Caleb, the only light in his dark eyes reflected by the moon.

"Ain't I one of your workers, Mr Vyne? And haven't I sworn to keep an eye on Mr Sheridan's tricks after what he done to my sister?"

"I'm sorry, Sam, and believe me, I can't doubt you. God knows I wish I could. Have you told the constable this? Have you told the constable, Sam?"

"I've not, although I have a murdering wish to do so. I wished to speak to you first, master."

"Don't call me that, Sam. I may be master, but I'm your friend as well. . . So, you saw Miss Liddy and Charlie?"

Sam nodded, his face a serious mask, chapped and worn from years of crusted salt. "Not *together,* sir, but he was riding some distance after her past the coal yard. I had no idea she'd been to see Sally. I was bringing back the bag with the provisions. Mother and the nippers were lagging behind. She didn't look in no trouble. She's a fine rider and at first . . ." Sam hesitated, "at first I thought it be you following her, sir. For I have seen you two together."

"And have you said that?"

Caleb's face flushed at the thought of what had passed between him and Liddy. If that was told, then those who judged him guilty would have had grounds for thinking so. But the thought that Charlie had been following behind was monstrous.

"I have not. And if I did it would carry no weight, sir.

182

None of us thinks you would harm Miss Liddy." Sam put a long, thin hand on Caleb's arm.

Caleb nodded gratefully. "Thanks, Sam. I'm touched at your trust. And you are right. In no way would I harm Miss Lydia if she were the most dangerous Annesley in the world."

"But what of Master Sheridan? Could he have done so?" Sam's face twisted into an ugly grimace. "Both you and I know, sir, where his pleasures lie."

"Aye, we do, but he would be mad to touch her. And she has never encouraged him." Caleb said it firmly. He breathed in deeply and was very glad when Sam answered:

"Nor will she ever care for him, Mr Vyne. She's a real lady. Look what she done for our Sally."

The men stood quietly. Then Caleb drove an angry fist against his other hand.

"God, Sam, what will we do if she has really disappeared? Could that wild fool have cajoled her into belief of any of his lies? I swear that if he has I will break his neck with these very hands." Caleb ground his fists, one against the other as if he had Charlie between them.

Lydia had gone to Sally and heard her corroborate Caleb's words. Perhaps Charlie had waylaid her and she, having charged him with his crimes, had been cajoled into thinking Caleb and Sally were lying. And then what happened? Had she run off? He could hardly believe that might be so, but he knew Charlie's power over young women.

He was thinking about the day he'd first seen Miss Annesley framed in the window of the train - and how she'd looked at Charlie.

He dispelled the memory immediately, not questioning why it had come to his mind; jealousy was something Caleb did not yet understand about himself.

He dropped his fists. It was no good working himself up now. He'd take another crack at Charlie later.

Caleb looked Sam straight in the eyes. "You and I must find Miss Liddy, Sam, whatever else we do." Then he glanced up at the church tower and breathed a silent prayer.

"Yes, sir, we will. I've made up *my* mind anyway."

"What to, Sam?"

"To speak to Master Sheridan about my sister's position, sir."

"Now, Sam, do not. You'll only get into another fight, and what good will that do her or your mother? It will break their hearts. And if you are charged then you could find yourself before the Bench. Who'll get the bread then? No, man, leave it to me. He'll tell me the truth. By God, he will."

He said the words so forcefully that Sam Shrike knew *he* would have no wish to be standing in Charlie Sheridan's boots, young master or not.

* * *

Chapter 10

Surprisingly, Charlie was at home by the fire. His boots were lying on the rug and his powerful legs were stretched selfishly across the hearth, taking the fire from his father, who'd lapsed into a drunken stupor. His mother was blue with cold.

Caleb unfastened his cloak, his tall body throwing a looming shadow over the mantelpiece. As Charlie snarled a curse at him, Caleb caught sight of his mother's frightened eyes. He didn't want to cause her more pain but, somehow, Charlie Sheridan was going to tell him what he knew about Lydia's disappearance.

Caleb went over to Lavinia and put his cloak about her shoulders. Her eyes were full of tears.

"Thank you, Caleb."

"Very touching," sneered Charlie, pulling out his watch and checking the time. "Where the hell's that maid, I want my supper."

"As do we all. And what's more I have relieved Hannah of her supper duties," replied Caleb.

"What? Why?" Charlie stared, catching the cool, measured tone.

"Therefore, mother, would you be willing to take yourself into the kitchen and seek out some cheese and bread, while Charlie and I have some small conversation?" Caleb glanced at his mother meaningfully.

In spite of her fear they would harm each other, Lavinia was up and away like a frightened partridge in the covert. Billy Sheridan snored on oblivious to everything, while Caleb stared steadily at Charlie.

"What's brewing, Vyne?" growled Charlie. "Spit out what you have to say!" His thick, drawling, insolent lips were ready for splitting. And Caleb would have done that, had it not been for his mother.

"That I intend to do," said Caleb, his tone harder than his half-brother had ever heard it.

"Carry on," countered Charlie, his face an uneasy sneer. He was still sprawling in front of the fire, but jumped back as a sparking branch tumbled out and flamed in the heaps of mounting ash.

It was then Caleb had him by the arm. The younger tried to wrest himself out and away from his hard grasp.

"Leave go. I don't have to stand your bullying. If I wake father he'll have you out of doors in a trice."

"Billy can't help you now," replied Caleb, and Charlie cowered instinctively at the decisive tone. "You're coming with me." In one powerful cat-like movement, he had his hand over young Charlie's mouth and was dragging him struggling out into the night. "I've wanted to do that for a very long time."

Caleb threw his half-brother down on the ground, while the dogs jumped around, barking frantically. And, from deep inside the house, he heard his grandfather's weak shout of protest at the noise. Caleb saw his mother hovering in the doorway, but then she scuttled away.

"I'll have you for this, you rogue," cried Charlie, trying to pick himself up. But Caleb's boot was against his chest, thrusting him back, its spur dangerously near the cleft in his open shirt.

"And you call *me*, rogue?" Caleb added. "Take care, Charlie, I'm not finished yet."

Charlie's eyes were darting about for a means of escape, but the dogs were still frantically leaping about the couple. He sat back on his hands, looking at Caleb's boot print on his chest. He was trying to brave it out, his eyes shifting to and fro.

"No, I'm not finished until I hear the truth," repeated Caleb. "What have you done with Lydia Annesley?"

"I've done nothing," shouted Charlie into his brother's face. "I know *nothing* of her whereabouts. How dare you treat me like this, Vyne? I promise you, I'll pay you back. This assault is unforgivable."

"As are you, sir," said Caleb, dragging him up by the collar. "Now, where is she, you blackguard?"

Caleb knew his eyes were flaming and he could feel blood on his lip where his own teeth had struck it. He also realised that Charlie knew desperate situations demanded desperate remedies. At that moment, he could have beaten his brother into submission - but he needed the truth from him.

"I swear it, Caleb, I know nothing of Miss Lydia's disappearance," blubbered Charlie.

Caleb heard his protestations with disgust. He had heard it all before.

"Like you swore you'd never touched Sally Shrike? Your remorse for that act has been little enough. Where is the recompense you promised Sam on behalf of his sister? I should have let him beat you, sir."

Then he floored him again with the accusation: "As for Miss Annesley. You were seen riding behind her. Where were you bound? *What did you do?* Answer me, you dog. Can you not curb your lust? If you've harmed her like Sally Shrike, caused her to run from here, I'll see you put behind bars for ever - that's if you live that long."

His violence was working. Charlie was like all the Sheridan breed, a coward. The scum to which Caleb had been so unwillingly allied, only understood violence.

"Let me go - and I'll tell you. But only what I know." Charlie ducked. "I didn't touch her. I promise. I only followed after I heard you and she . . ."

"So!" Caleb's breathing was very fast. "You were spying on me."

"I was not." And Charlie was twisting his body away to escape, but Caleb was there again barring the way into the house.

"Then what did you hear?"

"I heard you quarrelling. And it was bad, sir, was it not? If I was to tell the constable . . ?"

"Then I would ram *this* down your throat." Caleb showed him his fist and the other subsided. "You'll say nothing. Miss Lydia Annesley alone has the power to charge any ill on my person. It's her prerogative and I am too much of a gentleman even to speak of it."

"But she gave it you hard, didn't she, Caleb?" spat Charlie. "God save her brine pipes." He shied away at Caleb's look.

"Miss Annesley knows I had nothing to do with such a crime." Caleb had no intention of letting Charlie know Lydia had heard the truth about Sally Shrike from him. Otherwise, if his half-brother hadn't harmed her now, he would if he were the first to find her. Caleb's hard voice continued, "If she is found, and God help us all if she isn't, I will make it right with her and her aunt. The man who cut Annesley's pipes will pay for it. I promise you that."

"How noble!" sneered Charlie, whose face was hearth paste white.

It was all Caleb could do not to lay him out on the floor, but he hadn't found Lydia yet.

"On the other hand, Caleb," Charlie's colour was returning, "when she *is* found, let us see which of us Strettons she believes. I know who it will be."

Caleb's eyes narrowed as Charlie waded on saving his skin. "I spoke to her, I grant you that. She was mighty upset, Caleb. Whatever you imparted had caused her great pain." Caleb hated his mealy-mouthed mien. "I fear she hates you, brother. In fact, she was quite strung up when she protested her wish never to see a Stretton again."

Caleb stood stiffly, listening silently while Charlie added, "She is bound for lawyers too. She told me that she intended to leave Upwych and sue damages for the cutting of her pipes. She thinks she will prosecute her case in London more successfully. She wants vengeance on us, Caleb. She blames the Strettons for her aunt's illness and for the ruin of her business."

Caleb regarded Charlie. That could be true, but it was unlikely. *Unless Miss Annesley was only pretending to believe what he had told her.*

"This is a glib story, Charlie," he said, "and God help you if it is all lies. Who cut the brine pipes anyway? Where were you that day, Charlie? Out riding, if I remember." Caleb's eyes glinted.

"But I couldn't have done it alone, could I?"

"True, but there are others who would help."

He was thinking of Billy Sheridan.

"Not with you behind them, Caleb," cried Charlie, sensing that he was winning. But his triumph was short-lived; Caleb was shaking him again.

"Less of your lip. What next about Miss Annesley?"

"Whether she intended to leave straightaway or not, I cannot tell, but one thing, I must say, was how enchanting she looked with those green eyes flashing fire." His wide, cunning mouth was twisted into a taunt. "Am I hurting you, Caleb, by telling you that?"

Caleb's temper erupted. Next moment Charlie was sprawling on the ground, nursing his jaw.

"You deserved that," growled Caleb. "And a great deal more. Not only I, but the constables will be checking up your story. Remember. And you will have us both to answer to if it's proved false."

Caleb Vyne, passion at last overcoming his reason, left his whimpering cub of a brother and strode out and off towards the stables.

* * *

Lydia realised she was lying flat. Uncomfortably, she opened her frightened eyes and closed them again quickly. She felt sick, dizzy and nothing but the dull ache of bruising in her limbs. Her head was throbbing and her stomach turned dangerously. About her she could smell strong drink.

What had the monster done? Her terrified eyes stared down at her bodice, at the three-cornered rip in her riding habit and, with horror, saw her skirt had been torn from waist to thigh.

She must have collapsed from pure exhaustion and terror when Sheridan made his filthy attack on her person She'd fallen off Sophie and he'd attempted her. She could hardly believe the enormity of the crime. The man was pure brute, not fit for decent society. *And she had thought Mr Vyne cruel once*. Then Lydia began to

190

cry, not as ladies do from vexation, but great gasping sobs of hurt. Where was she? He must have
imprisoned her.

In panic, she tried to rise suddenly but nearly fainted
with the pain. It seemed like her rib was bursting
through the skin. She couldn't even put a hand to her
side to help her to breathe more easily. It was pure
agony.

How could he have treated her so inhumanely after
such an accident? And when did he? Had she been out
of her senses for long? Perhaps the fall after Sophie
bolted had caused the damage? What crime had he perpetrated on her person? And what had happened to her
mare? Had she gone home? Or had Sheridan done Sophie
some mischief too?

Lydia continued sobbing and hiccoughing until the fit
of frightened self-pity was over and she was pulling herself together. Her eyes were becoming accustomed to
the dimness.

Lydia looked around her small prison, scared that
the rancid air, smelling of the farm, would putrefy and
smother her. She needed a drink badly. Had he left her
to die of thirst?

She appeared to be in a box-like room with not even
a window. The walls were rough stone and there was
no furniture save for the narrow straw sacks on which
she lay, and a heavy old chair and table. On the table
was a candlestick, its blue enamel bowl full of wax. But
there were no matches. Where was the light coming
from? She looked up. The ceiling was slatted narrowly
in one corner.

A hatch.

A shudder ran through her. She was under the ground.
Would he kill her now she knew his secret? Charles

Sheridan had no scruples. She was his prisoner - and his enemy. She was the one who stood between him and a salt fortune. If the Strettons were rid of her, then the way was clear.

But it would be murder.

The brute couldn't keep her like this for ever. She must escape before he had the chance. Lydia struggled to rise, but the pain prevented any hasty movement. Her hair, which had been forced out of the restraining net, cascaded over her shoulders and her forehead. She brushed it back, again feeling pain as she moved her arm and shoulder muscles.

But, suddenly, the Annesley spirit was returning, replacing fear with anger. How dare he do this? He'd pay for his crimes. *She would make him.*

Once on her feet and swaying dizzily, she looked round for a way to reach up to the slatted opening in the ceiling corner. At least, if she climbed up there, she could breathe in fresh air.

Determining not to panic again, she began to try to push the heavy table under the skylight. But she wasn't strong enough. After several anguished minutes, Lydia collapsed once more on the narrow bed and lay staring up, her mind blanked out with the horror of it all.

Controlling her fear again, she began to think about who else could save her. Surely the whole of Upwych must be looking for her by now? And what of Aunt Elizabeth? Lydia's heart lurched at the thought of the pain her abduction would cause. The shock might even be fatal. And with Elizabeth gone - and the heiress too? Lydia put her hands over her eyes in frustration at the implications of Charles Sheridan's plot. She had to get out of here. He couldn't hold her for ever? *But what else could he do?*

Suddenly, Caleb Vyne came into her thoughts. It was at that moment she regretted every cruel mistaken accusation she'd thrown into his face. She had misjudged him very badly. Could he ever forgive her?

Lydia went over and over it all in her head. She had believed Caleb to be the villain, not Charlie - and she was paying for choosing the wrong man as her protector. All those empty promises Sheridan had made. What a fool she'd been to believe him.

Inside, both her reason and emotions told her Caleb would find her. And he was the only one who seemed to have control of that wicked man, his brother. If Sheridan had it in mind to keep her imprisoned for ever, to starve or beat her to death, Caleb would discover it.

Weary and shocked by her ordeal, Lydia closed her green eyes, rolled on her side on the straw sack and prayed to be rescued. And, somewhere, inside her head, a small persistent voice was urging her to raise her spirits and to believe that someone would come to release her very soon.

* * *

The salters' union committee dribbled out of the tavern, along the cobbled pathways of the notorious Vynes area of Upwych, towards the meeting called by Masters Billy and Charlie Sheridan and Mr Caleb Vyne. They had made their own decision through pure need. Now all they had to do was to listen to what Strettons offered.

It had been a noisy gathering, as many had been bound in loyalty to Annesley Works for years, as had their fathers before them. Upwych salters were proud of their heritage. Some said they could traceit back to the Norman Conquest when the salt had been carried up the old Saltway by pack horses through Feckenham Forest, north and east, south or west; even as far as Ireland. Others claimed kinship with one of Upwych's most famous sons, Richard, Bishop of Chichester who, when the Great Pit had dried up, had been the saviour of Upwych. After blessing the Pit, the brine had begun to flow again and the townsfolk's livelihood was safe once more. They needed another saint now to help them.

As they looked up at Dodderhill Church clinging to the hillside, it seemed to the poorest salters a symbol of Heaven, far removed from the heat of the salt pans that made a hell of their working days.

Sally Shrike, who had been waiting with most of the women in the room beside the inn where the salters had been meeting, was hurriedly pulling her shawl over her head and trying at the same time to keep up with her brother, whose long legs strode on grimly.

"Slow down, please."

He waited, having almost forgotten that his sister wasn't as healthy as he.

"Sam, you have to do something. The men'll listen to you. Don't take Strettons' offer on. Not even for Mr Vyne. I can't work for Sheridan, you know that."

Sam pulled her into a doorway so that others could pass on the narrow path.

"You ain't workin' now, Sally, in your state of health. I'll keep you until the baby comes."

"You can't. There are too many mouths to feed."

"I will - and that's why I have to go along with Mr Caleb. He'll pay me bonuses."

"But, Sam," she said, "you can't stomach working for

194

that devil, Sheridan, either. What will you do when you have to take orders from him?"

Looking down into her eager face, Sam yearned to tell her that she wasn't the first of Charlie's conquests, nor would she be the last. He hated the wild young wastrel with all his heart.

"I shall be civil to him, but he'll know how I feel in secret." He put his arm round his sister's shoulders and they walked on slowly across Chapel Bridge. "We've agreed to manning the Stretton bore hole. Most of us anyway. 'Tis not surprisin' that folks will change their mind when their bellies are empty. And Mr Caleb will keep his promise and look after us, Sal."

"He's a good man, Sam," said Sally and her brother nodded in agreement. "If only Miss Annesley were found. I just can't believe she's run back to London, but I can't bear the thought of what might have happened to her either. She was so kind to me."

"Don't worry, Sal. Mr Caleb'll find her if anyone can. And there's constables looking and . . . and everyone," finished Sam lamely. He hadn't any idea where Miss Annesley could be, but he was praying she would be back soon or else her fortune might seep away into the ground like her salt.

* * *

The town was at work again. Miss Annesley's pipes had been drawn up the canal, but there was some doubt at present as to who would pay and, therefore, they lay idle.

It was rumoured that Lord George Tulham was negotiating with the bank and the salters, loyal to Annesley, were prepared to wait a few more days. These consisted mainly of older men and boys, who had not so much to lose in their wage packets.

Most of the married men had turned to Stretton in spite of their misgivings. At least, they knew they would be paid, however much they disliked the Sheridans. They were being worked extra hard by those devils, as old Mr Stretton knew he had precious little time to capture all the profits and, therefore, was making the most of Annesley misfortune.

But, on every site and in every part of town, folks were talking about Miss Annesley. Miss Elizabeth was pitied greatly not only because her chimneys were idle but because of the loss of her lovely young niece.

The elderly George Tulham had visited every day to comfort the old lady, and had put up a reward for knowledge of Miss Lydia's whereabouts. And the search continued.

The beginning of the week brought about a meeting which Sam Shrike could never have imagined. They were bringing in the heavy machinery to get ready to sink the bore into the new brine seam, when Charlie Sheridan arrived on site to oversee the works. Fifty hostile pairs of eyes stared as he dismounted and walked up and down the diggings.

"Sam Shrike?"

"Ower there, sir."

Sam had been detailed by the foreman to supervise the levelling off of the ground. He looked up from his work into the staring blue eyes of Sheridan. He didn't take off his cap but stared back.

Sheridan thumbed in the direction of the foreman's hut. "I want a word with you, Shrike. It shouldn't take long."

Sam hesitated, but had no option. The man was

master and he dared do nothing in reason to cross him. He followed Charlie into the wooden structure, very conscious of his dirty face and blackened hands. The other, dressed immaculately in bottle green coat and well-cut breeches, was sitting down at the makeshift table.

As Charlie settled himself Sam was preparing himself to be told he had no place with Strettons, being a reminder to Sheridan of his misdemeanour. It would be a disaster for the Shrike family but, inside, there was still some comfort as he knew Mr Caleb would overrule this puppy in Sam's favour.

The salter was full of contempt for Sheridan as he waited. His master looked up, and if Sam hadn't known his real character, he would have judged those eyes honest.

"Well, Sam, you've come over to us after all. How's Sally?"

Sam's mouth opened in surprise. The last thing he expected was Sheridan's inquiring after Sal's health. He pulled himself together. The rogue wouldn't catch him off guard that way.

"Aye, Mr Sheridan. I've come over because I've mouths to feed. But unwillingly." He waited for the outburst but none came.

"And Sally?" repeated Charlie.

"Why are you askin' after my sister? You know well how she is," accused Sam.

"And that is why I'm asking you, man. Although . . ." Sheridan looked down at the table, then up again, "we have had our differences in the past, I . . . I should like to make amends . . ." Sam stared at him uncomprehending. ". . . for the evil I have done Sally. It's not in my nature to hurt."

Sam stood quite still, trying to work it out. What was going on? He studied the young master's face. It was bruised all right. He'd taken some punishment! And then it began to make sense. Mr Caleb had had it out with him. Frightened him to death. Sam was glad for it, though he'd yearned to do it himself.

"If you say so." There was no way Sam could be civil.

"I do, and therefore, I've a proposition to make you, Shrike. If this had happened to your Sally by any other man, what would you have asked?" Sam took a step nearer the table, clenching his fists.

"I'd have asked what any natural brother or father would; that the lad married her honestly."

"Married, eh?" replied Charles Sheridan, staring in front of him.

"The decent thing, but only if the lass was well and willing. There be no shotguns in our family, Mr Sheridan; and if there were then mayhap ye wouldn't be sittin' there so safely now. 'Twas a terrible thing you did to our Sal. She and I used to set in that stable without a care in the world. She wouldn't go near there now for anythin'. D'ye know that?"

Sam was very close to Charlie and he could see the fear in the blackguard's eyes. "But if ye're willin' to make amends, I'll put it to our Sal and see what she says." He moved back, fearful of the violent feelings Charlie Sheridan brought up in him.

"So be it, Shrike," said Charlie. "And . . . I am willing to do something for your family too." Sam thought what a beating Caleb Vyne must've given his half-brother. "This spring we have found. . . The engineer says it's deeper than first thought. The boring could be a lengthy business. On account of your Sally, I'm willing to give you the job on the bore, for twice the usual pay."

"The dangerous job, you mean?" asked Sam, his heart accelerating. "How deep will ye go, Master Sheridan?"

"As deep as it takes, man. Are you afraid?"

Sam shook his head. "No more afraid than any other man with hunger in his belly. Oh, I will take yer offer for the sake of my family, but I'd have been happier if it had been offered by a master with his worker's true interest at heart."

Sheridan flushed as he stood up. "It will be my last offer to you, Shrike. And my last admission of repentance. Take it or leave it."

"I'll take it, but not with a glad heart. And, if our Sal says she will have nothing from you, then I shall abide by her wishes. You understand?"

There was no way that Sam intended to grovel. To him, salt men had always been gentlemen, but this one was not of that breed. He also knew in his heart what his sister would say. And he was the one to pay the price for Sheridan's repentance. Working close to the bore could be very dangerous indeed, hence the high price. If the brine broke through and up the bore, a worker could be flung up in the air and maimed for life, if not have the life taken from him.

But the pay - that was another matter.

Sam's face was whiter now and not only from crusted salt. He wondered what Caleb would have said if he'd known what Charlie had offered. But he wasn't going to, as the Shrikes needed the extra and Sam wanted no more charity from Strettons, even if it was Mr Caleb who dispensed it.

* * *

Charles rode past the coal yard late in the evening when the tired workers had gone home. In the pitch dark he quietly led his own horse inside the condemned stable and prepared to let himself down into the little room he'd discovered, which had been first, an excellent place from which to spy upon Sally Shrike, and second, a hiding place for Miss Lydia.

After her fainting fit, he had taken the whisky flask and poured it in her mouth. It had done the trick. The fall and the drink had put her out for hours.

It had been a capital idea to place her in there. The noise of the distant machinery would have strangled her screams. In any case, she'd be so hungry and thirsty she'd comply with any wish of his, however ignoble - and he still had to decide what was the best to do with her. He knew that he couldn't keep her a prisoner for ever, and he was sure that, finally, she would agree to a compromise.

Charlie still had it in mind that his efforts in persuading her on his behalf would be successful. What young lady would want the world to know she'd been ravished by a young man whom she'd taken a fancy to? And who would believe a girl as high-spirited and self-willed as Lydia not to be rash enough to take a shine to Charlie Sheridan? A young woman who wandered alone in the park unchaperoned and rode where she would?

He was quite *au fait* with the story of her mother's sojourn in London, having gleaned it from local sources. She'd been a wild young thing herself by all accounts, and taken off at nineteen with thirty-five year old Bertram Annesley without either parents' consent. A love match they said, to cover their crime.

Like mother like daughter, thought Charlie as he removed the grating, leading to the feed chamber. *If it*

*hadn't been for her mother dying and her aunt's failing
health, the heiress would have still been in London living
the high life.*

Indeed, her *abduction* could be construed as an
elopement. Although he had not interfered with her, he
would let her think so. Doubtless, Miss Annesley was a
virgin and had had little experience of men. He would
tell her what he wanted her to know and she would do
as he said.

* * *

Lydia had been in the dark so long that she screamed
out loud for help when she saw light coming through
the slatted trapdoor, then a man. She had imagined her
ordeal was at an end, but when he dropped through into
the room she went quiet and, shrinking back, stared at
Charlie with horrified reproach in her eyes, puffed up
from tears.

"The eyes speak for you, ma'am," he said, putting
down the lantern on the table, adjusting his coat and
swiftly scanning her body with his. He went over to her
and she tried to escape him, pressing herself against
the wall.

"Devil, you devil," cried Lydia wildly but her voice
broke in a crack. He pulled her back onto the straw
mattress then smiled down at her.

"Devil I may be, but would you care for a nip?" He
pulled out a silver hip flask and held it to Lydia's lips.
She spluttered at the hot spirit. Retched! "There. That's
brought colour to your cheeks. You have a fondness for
strong drink."

She beat at his chest in anger.

He held her off.

"Yes, ma'am, you took your whip to me yesterday, did you not?" asked Charlie, holding her tight.

"You brute. Let me go. I'll have you hanged for this." cried Lydia. "Where am I? Have you no pity?"

"I have, in a tolerable amount. This was the nearest place to bring you that was safe for both our purpose."

"You call it safe?" Lydia's eyes blazed in her white face.

"Yes, safe with me," said Charlie. She stared at him in horror. "If we're to be married, then we must know each other's vices."

"Married?" she cried.

"*United*. I mentioned the idea earlier. That was when you picked up the whip. Remember? Causing the mare to bolt."

She could only stare at him in horror. The thought of marriage to someone like Charlie Sheridan was pure degradation.

"You're staring, Lydia. You find me handsome then?"

"Repulsive," cried Lydia with a shudder. "You're mad." She had scarcely felt ill in her life, now she was sick in the stomach.

"You didn't think so after I brought you here?" said Charlie in a silky voice. "Why you held on to me with your arms and allowed me the most marvellous freedoms. I would say you were the one out of your mind."

She couldn't speak.

He continued, "And, yet, I had hopes."

"Hopes?" Her voice was dull.

Had he touched her? Probed her innocent body with those ugly blue eyes? And what else? It was too horrible to think about. *If only she had never met him!*

"Hopes that we may be more than friends. I, for one,

will never speak of how we behaved but . . ." he paused, "it could be a scandal if folk were to know we spent the night alone here."

"What do you mean?"

"Have you no watch, Miss Annesley? The night hours passed and we were alone together. As lovers."

"No, it's not true. I would have known," cried Lydia.

"I think you did," answered Charlie suavely, "for you were only *almost* out of your mind when you allowed me to bring you here and caress you. We drank . . ."

"Stop!" cried poor Lydia, thinking of the taste in her mouth, "I don't believe you. I was out of my senses. I remember nothing."

"What a pity, Miss Lydia; but it was a very pretty scene which I shall always remember," he answered smiling.

Lydia turned over on the straw sack and sobbed.

"I have food for you, ma'am."

She didn't reply.

Charlie stood up.

She continued to lie still.

"Then you won't have it."

Not a sound except a muffled sobbing.

He looked down at the motionless figure of the girl he'd desired since he met her in the park. "Crying will do you no good, Miss Annesley. What's done is done. I suggest you think on what I've said and have an answer ready for me when I return. I won't leave you food, but I've brought you a bottle of water. No more strong drink, ma'am, it's no good for the female constitution."

Suddenly, Lydia was up and, with cries of pain and frustration, was hitting out at him for all she was worth. He held her at arm's length, grinning.

"That's better," laughed Charlie Sheridan. "I like my

women with spirit. Caleb saw it too, didn't he? . . . Yesterday. . . Outside the Mill."

"Caleb?"

"Ay, my damned half-brother. And what did he tell you about me?"

"Enough to realise every word was true," replied Lydia hotly. She'd had enough of caterwauling. If she lost heart now, she'd be done for.

"And you saw that trollop, Sally Shrike. Yes, ma'am, don't look so white. I was following you all afternoon. Whatever the female told you wasn't near the truth. She's a confirmed liar."

"And she's with child!" shouted Lydia.

"Bold words for a young lady," sneered Charlie. "And she has charged it on me. Oh, no, I shan't take that blame. But, like the good young master I am, she and her bastard will be provided for one way or another."

"I know all you're saying is lies," pursued Lydia courageously. "And you won't keep me here much longer. My aunt will find me. I know everyone in Upwych will be looking for me." She dared not mention Caleb Vyne unless the monster standing before her did him some harm. "And they will find you," she added. "And run you down. You're not going to break my spirit, and . . ." she was breathing heavily now with pain and exhaustion, "whatever you've done to me you'll pay for. I don't know what that is, in spite of your foul lies, but I know I'm innocent." She was gasping. "If you'd put your dirty hands on me I would never, never have submitted to you if you were the last man on earth, Charlie Sheridan."

She fell back on the straw sack as Charlie lashed out in fury, striking her on the cheek.

He could see she meant it, that she had no intention of changing her mind. But he couldn't let her

go. Not now. He'd give her some more time to think.
When she was hungry enough she'd come to her senses.

Charles, for all his villainy, was suddenly realising
what he'd done. Once more his lust had got the better
of him, and this time it wasn't to be satisfied. His plan
wasn't working. He'd have to think of something else,
and quickly. However, at that moment, staring at the
bruised cheek and the terrified green eyes, he felt no
desire for Miss Annesley at all.

She withdrew her hand from her cheek and stared
back haughtily. "You cannot keep me here for ever.
Someone will find me. Come to your senses and let me
go. If you do . . ." she swallowed with difficulty, controlling
the panic in her voice, "I'll give you some time to get
away from here, to make your escape. If only you let
me go." She was clutching at any means of escape -
before he murdered her.

"Would you indeed, ma'am?" he laughed. "Well, I'll
think on your offer," he added with a sneer, "but, I tell
you, Miss Annesley, I have other plans for you now I
have tasted your beauty." He was close and she shrank
away. He straightened his jacket and riding stock.

"I offered you food," he went on, "and you refused it.
See what Monday evening brings and how you feel then.
Perhaps you may have seen sense."

"Are you leaving me a light?" Lydia cried, conscious
that without his lantern she would be in the dark again.

"A match maybe," he said. "But one, and only one. So
don't waste it. . . Nor your candle." Taking a box from
his jacket, he withdrew a single stalk and laid it on the
table.

Keeping her head, Lydia realised that once Charles
Sheridan withdrew she wouldn't be able to see to light
her candle. He laughed as she struck the match against

the candlestick, fingers trembling. It flamed first time.

"Well done, Miss Annesley, but how long will it last? Not until morning. Now think on what I've said. United, we could do much. Otherwise . . ." he shrugged.

She watched him, hate in her eyes. As he was pulling himself up and through the slatted trapdoor, she was imagining herself with a pistol, shooting him through the heart. But then she would be as bad as he.

His ugly face peered down at her.

Looking up, she cried, "At least tell me where I am. And think of what I said. If you let me go . . ."

Her words were curtailed as the trapdoor thudded in place. Panic rose in her once more. How long would he keep her under the floor? If she didn't agree, would he murder her? She heard his hateful voice.

"You're in the condemned stable."

She shivered. What did he mean? What was it? Where was it? She had to keep up her spirits, not let go. Somehow she must try and outwit him - even if it meant agreeing to his terms now and reneging later.

But what would he do to her if she consented? Indeed, what had he done already. She looked down at her torn and blackened dress. Surely she would have known if he'd ravished her? The thought of what he'd said, and Charles Sheridan's vile length on her body, made her retch.

As Lydia stared at her pathetic half-burnt candle, all she could do now was blot out her mind to him and concentrate on the hope that, again, someone would discover her prison and release her.

* * *

Chapter 11

There were folks in Upwych who had been eagerly waiting for Monday to dawn, but Sally Shrike wasn't one of them. As she stumbled out the back to the privy to be sick, clutching her shawl about her, she wondered why she had been made to suffer so.

The privy was a small brick building with a wooden seat which opened over a bucket. The latter hadn't been emptied on Sunday and was full of excrement, the sight of which turned Sally's stomach even more, making her heave over and over again until the tears came.

Understandably, she could face no breakfast in the shape of bread, but she took some milk. Her mother and Sam were ready for work already and Sally begged to go, but one look at her face confirmed her state. Therefore, she was to be left alone while John, Tim and Mary went to their charity school down the Vynes. Sam was hoping that they'd learn something there before they were swept into the factory like the rest.

Mrs Shrike took the baby and Tommy, the youngest brother, to work with her. The baby would be looked after by a child, only a few years older who, herself, was tied to a post by a string so she couldn't wander off nor become entangled in the salt works machinery. But Tommy was old enough to run errands for the men and Dobson, the foreman especially. Tommy and Jemmy

Yarwood, thick as pigs in muck, were running round all day, which kept them out of mischief.

However, now the brine flow had ceased at Annesley Works, those who'd elected to stay or been forced because of their physical condition, had been found a variety of jobs to do, financed by money personally from Miss Elizabeth Annesley and Lord George Tulham, in the name of the missing heiress.

But how long would it last, and even more important, was there enough to pay for the new pipes to be laid. It was rumoured that work would be underway later that week but all was in uproar because Miss Annesley was missing.

Sam was off to Strettons that morning and hadn't been looking forward to Monday either. He'd had a bad night and dreams of disaster. In fact, there was a gloom about the whole family as Sally dressed the shivering children in the hard pink of dawn.

"Now, lass, don't ye get doin' too much," said Sam, pulling on his boots. Since he'd spoken to Master Sheridan, he was morose. There was no way he'd tell his mother, nor Sal, where he'd be working that day.

"I won't," cried Sally, "but I feel so useless doing nothing. I might come down to you later." But then she remembered where he was working. "Or to see you, Mam?"

"Don't come near us," said her mother, picking up their daily bundles. There was resentment in her voice. "If Dobson sees you, he'll think you fit for work."

Throughout her pregnancies, she'd been shown no care, except from her husband who was powerless to do anything but slave, shovelling coal under the pans. But their Sally had Mr Caleb and Miss Annesley as champions.

"All right, Mam, I won't then," said Sally, dreading another cheerless day. "Will you leave me the baby?"

"No, her's happy with the little wench," said her mother, picking up the baby. "There's plenty to do here anyway."

"And I've cut your wood," said Sam. "Remember."

"Thanks," said Sally, kissing him on the cheek. Her brothers and sisters exchanged glances. They were frightened of him, but Sally could twist him round her finger.

Later, a disconsolate Sally leaned against the lintel as her whole family, led by Sam, tramped off down the towpath, crunching with frost.

The last she saw of her brother was as the tall figure turned to wave to her at the bend, and she waved back.

* * *

Caleb Vyne was worried when he saw Sheridan's plans, but both stepfather and grandfather were determined to overrule him. He'd remonstrated with them but they wouldn't hear of any change.

"I estimate the brine is too deep for us to sink the bore safely," were the last brief words he said. At least, he had negated his responsibility. It was up to them now. If they were able to penetrate the gypsum, who knew what force of brine stream ran below?

They laughed at him. Billy Sheridan's piggy eyes were gleaming at the thought of new bushels of salt.

"Shut your mouth, Caleb Vyne. I was trained as an engineer and I know how far we can go. We have to tackle the seepage, or our profits will diminish."

"Your profits are increasing," retorted Caleb, "as you take advantage of Annesley. And why can't we attend to the seepage? I've heard the new master of Stoke makes seepage a priority. It is said his deep shafts will be lined with iron, and sealed."

"Nonsense," quavered old Mr Stretton. "We haven't Corbett's cash. All we can do is discover new brine and *it is there*, flowing under the earth, waiting to be tapped."

Caleb's warnings had, as ever, gone unheard. The damned Irishman who'd married his mother had put such notions in old Stretton's head that no one could shift, and his oldest grandson was sick of the lot of them.

He had to attend the boring but he intended to get away as quickly as he could to continue his search for Miss Annesley. He knew now he didn't believe Charlie's words. He had decided that whoever had abducted her had been local, and that she would be found in some building in the town. Like the constables he'd enquired at the station. No one had seen her leave. He'd been to the livery stables and she hadn't hired a horse. He'd checked cab drivers and every kind of conveyance leaving Upwych that Saturday, and it had come to nothing.

Caleb was sure Miss Annesley had been hidden or, for some reason of her own, had gone into hiding herself. Yet the latter he didn't really believe either. From what he knew of Lydia, she wouldn't cause her aunt such pain. And the old lady was crazy with worry, so Blanchard said. Caleb was determined to find her, as was Sam.

It was a bad business that Sam Shrike was back working for them against his will. It must have been death to him to accept work from Charlie. But the beating Caleb had given his half-brother might make him wary in the future when he was thinking of ravishing young women.

Caleb hoped Sam hadn't carried out his threat to confront Charlie. It would do the salter no good. But he was a good lad and always heeded Caleb's words.

As Caleb hacked along on his bay to the site, he passed the coalyard and the deserted stable nearby where Charlie had perpetrated the worst of his crimes. The place needed demolishing soon. He'd promised Sally Shrike that, at least.

Its half-door was swinging wide open in the wind, revealing the empty expanse inside. He glanced up to the loft window where the crime had taken place, and shivered. Whatever woman Caleb had taken, had always agreed. There was no way he could ever constrain a woman.

He hacked on, wrapped in his riding cloak, with the noise of heavy machinery battering his ears. If he hadn't been a Stretton, what would have been his fate? Might he have travelled in Europe like other fashionable young men and seen the sights of the world?

But Caleb's education had come mostly from his own reading; the school to which he had been sent had been inadequate, full of the boorish sons of country squires and self-made men. Salters were gentlemen in the shires, but could not compare with the oldest gentry.

Yet, in Upwych, Strettons and Annesleys were the masters and, being one of them, he couldn't throw away his heritage. Given his mother's unwise marriage to Billy Sheridan, every day brought that moment nearer when he would be disinherited in favour of that scoundrel, Charlie Sheridan.

As Caleb rode on to the site of the boring, he was telling himself should that day ever come, he would pack his bags and leave Raven's Mill for good. Or even England. But it was then he thought of his sick mother in her faded green gown. The only way he could say farewell to Lavinia was when she said goodbye to this earth finally. He couldn't desert her to be abused by Billy Sheridan.

In the distance, Caleb could see his stepfather giving orders, accompanied by Charlie. He drew in his breath, stifling a sigh. He could see no way out of his predicament, into which he had entered entirely without blame, as a young and innocent boy left with no natural father to protect his interests.

Then, breaking into a gallop, Caleb Vyne headed for the meadow where Strettons were about to sink the deepest bore hole yet seen in the Upwych environs.

* * *

The site was a maelstrom of huts, which stood precariously on ground that had been churned by the hooves of the shire horses, dragging in heavy tackle. The frost had hardened the great ruts of muddy ground and men walking along them swore as their boots broke the glassy ice, crunching it into splinters.

Many of the workers wore jackets, too thin to protect them from the weather, but also too warm to keep on wearing under the pressure of hard labour. So even on that biting morning, men were stripping off as they sweated with the spade and shovel, filling carts and receptacles with tons of soil from the diggings.

The bit for boring was in place, ready to be driven into the ground. And beneath it men were disappearing into the great pit which had been started over the last few weeks. The pump house was criss-crossed and circled by workers, who carried on each of their tasks in the manner of ants engaged in frenzied activity.

Around were trenches being laid for new pipes, full of workers with their spades. Soon, Caleb was amongst all the monstrous mess, which accompanied the drawing of the newly-discovered brine to the surface, from where it crawled sluggishly along in its underground river pathway. Sam Shrike and a few other courageous salters were working frantically at the very mouth of the shaft. But Caleb didn't see him. He had other things on his mind, like looking for Lydia Annesley.

He didn't dismount, only nodded absent-mindedly in the direction of the salters, whose back-breaking task he did not envy. He kept looking in the direction he had come, past the coal yard and over towards the Shrike cottage.

Then he would look at Charlie, who was, as usual, lording it over everyone, including the foreman of works. The young puppy thought, like his father, that he knew everything about engineering. He was striding about in a claret-coloured coat, his fair hair tied back   with a silk, and his unpleasant voice roaring at anyone he fancied.

Had he committed some evil against Miss Annesley, or was his story of her flight plain truth? Caleb doubted it for the hundredth time. But how could he make him tell?

It was then Caleb began to feel the strangest emotion he had ever known. *He wanted to see Lydia again. He could not bear it if she was lost to him.* It was suddenly very clear. Miss Annesley had become more than just a pleasant acquaintance. He had admired her for her courage, beauty and tenacity before, said he wished them to be *friends*.

He remembered her loveliness as she stood, framed

213

in the window of the train; by the great fireplace at Annesley when he'd offered her his help. And now he was mad to see her again - even to take her in his arms and . . .

He came to with a start as the gang of salters began to drive down through the surface of the earth. He was trying to act as overseer, but Miss Annesley's red-gold hair and green eyes were so fixed in his mind that he couldn't rid himself of the image. He was surprised at the depth of his feeling, remembering that he had no knowledge of young society women of only eighteen years. What kind of man was he becoming?

As the shouts below rose into the air encouraging the gang at the centre of the bore pressing down into the earth's heart, he was thinking of his own, fast-beating. Her memory had brought up such feelings and he begged for their relief in the finding of their author.

Could she care for him? He was her sworn enemy and she had ridden to Raven's Mill to accuse him. Had his explanation to justify himself been enough? *She had allowed him to hold her hand.*

That villain Charlie had intimated she preferred him to Caleb. If past signs were anything to go by, then the liar could be speaking the truth this time. No woman seemed able to resist him, willing or unwilling.

Caleb had no fancy words and phrases for women. He spoke only what was in his heart. Perhaps he would never see Lydia again; never get the chance to be near her, or talk peaceably with her instead of wrangling? The thought was agonising.

He had to find her.

* * *

Sally Shrike had felt unnaturally worried for hours after her brother and the rest of the family had left. Coupled with her sickness, the morning hours were most unpleasant. Between visits to the privy and lying on the sofa, Sally decided she needed some fresh air.

She'd also made up her mind to go over to Strettons new site in spite of her fear of Charlie Sheridan. She was worried about Sam. She'd not liked the look on his face the moment he'd got up that morning. She was sure something was wrong with him. He'd threatened to have it out with her attacker and she was afraid what would happen to him.

As she hurried towards the site, her breath coming short and fast, the machinery noise was already increasing which meant that they'd commenced with the boring of the new shaft. . .

* * *

In her underground prison, Lydia Annesley had been trying since dawn to reach the trapdoor above her. It didn't help that her body was so cold and weak from lack of food, but she was still attempting to escape. If only she could move the rectangular wood block, which was making her a prisoner. Another terrible night could be in store if she didn't succeed.

She had dragged the table finally into the corner and was standing on it. But she had no strength, nor was she even tall enough to reach the hatch if she had.

Climbing down painfully, she commanded her fuddled brain to respond. What else could she do? With her riding crop in her hand, she managed to get the chair upon the table. *Now she could reach. But was the trapdoor chained on the outside?* She prayed then that it wasn't.

Every effort to reach that precarious position of

standing balancing on the chair was agony. If she overbalanced, she might break her leg.

Carefully climbing down from the table again, she took off the torn skirt of her riding habit and her petticoat and stays. Then, clad only in drawers from the waist down and bodice on top, she climbed up again, sweating freely with the exertion. Her hair hung about her like a wet cloak, as Lydia prised and pushed at the trap with her riding crop and hands, screaming out for help in short bursts. She could see daylight above crown level, but she knew in her heart that no one could hear her cries, as the noise of daytime machinery in the distance was growing even louder. On the other hand, there were *people* out there who would help her if only she could alert them. She kept pushing and pushing frantically, then pausing to rest with her eyes closed.

* * *

The boring continued to go well but was driving dangerously deeper. The tackle had struck exceptionally hard rock and there was a question they could go on further. But Billy Sheridan wouldn't stop. He intended to suck up the brine below and line his own pockets handsomely from the bushels of salt it would produce.

"Harder!" he urged. "Deeper, men, deeper!"

Accompanied by Charlie, he was standing at a safe distance, using a megaphone. And, meanwhile the patient horses strove on, carting the soil away.

Finally, the gypsum gave and the bore struck the brine seam, which wasn't sluggish but was a lethally fast-flowing river. Sam heard it first, a roaring, rumbling and thundering below his feet. He nor the others had any time to retreat as the brine came rolling up like a

216

tidal wave. It burst through the earth with a savage roar, taking the men with it who were working closest to the shaft, and tossed them like empty husks high in the air.

Sam felt little then, except for a great rush and gurgle in his lungs and ears as he fell from the nothing of air and was struck by a searing red-hot pain, which agonisingly but mercifully took his senses clean away into an eternity of blackness.

Caleb's startled horse bucked like the others around, and it was only its rider's presence of mind which prevented him being thrown. Panic and confusion followed. With his injured men's cries in his ears, Caleb spurred towards the bore, where the brine was gushing out.

They found Sam Shrike lying senseless some fifty feet from the scene. He had fallen onto a wooden stake, jutting out of the ground. It had speared him through the stomach. Caleb's horrified eyes took in the copious amount of Sam's blood seeping away, and the immediate knowledge that his friend, the salter, was close to his end.

There was nothing anyone could do. Another small knot of men collected about every casualty, and a worker had been dispatched to fetch Dr May. But everyone knew he couldn't help Sam Shrike.

As Caleb Vyne's hand lay over Sam's, the salter let his last breath out of his chest in a juddering gasp.

"He's gone," said Caleb, looking up at the rough faces around him, some of them streaked with tears. "Sam's gone." He shook his head, hopelessly.

Caleb couldn't say even a prayer for him. He was too full of hate for his stepfather. If the man had listened Sam mightn't be lying dead now. He got up off his knees, straightened and threw his cloak about him. There was no sign of Billy Sheridan. What about the rest of the men? A swift search revealed three in a serious state and one luckily unscathed, but badly shocked.

Then Caleb saw Charlie. With wide, steady strides, Caleb negotiated the mud holes, now full to overflowing with brine.

"What was Sam Shrike doing down the bore? You know he had children to feed. Answer me!" And he was shaking Charlie like the man's own terriers had torn away at the badger's set. The salters looked on dumbly.

"He needed the money, Caleb. He was willing."

Then Billy Sheridan came running from the foreman's office and fastened himself on to Caleb, trying to prise his arm away. And still the salters watched their masters struggling, their silence slowly growing into a dull muttering.

Caleb shook off the Irishman and threw Charlie down in the mud.

"Wallow in your brine," he shouted. "What you've done to the best man in this town can only compare with what you did to his sister."

It was then they heard screaming.

Sally had begun to run when the explosion happened, arriving on the site just after Sam's fatal fall. She'd found him and was lying beside her brother's body in a paroxysm of grief. Her shawl and dress was stiffening with his blood and she seemed like a bundle of rags as Caleb Vyne ran across frantically, pulled her up gently and hid her face against his shoulder.

Then she was turning from his arms and picking her way through the soaking debris towards Charlie Sheridan.

Caleb Vyne and his men followed her silently and did

218

not try to detain her. Like a wild cat, Sally was up and at him, battering him with her fists.

"What was Sam doing at the bottom of the shaft, you murderer? That was what you wanted, wasn't it? You wanted vengeance on him for laying my shame upon your shoulders."

Her strength almost gone, she fell back with the other workers, who had made a circle about the couple and, hunching her thin shoulders, she screamed: "This is the culprit who needs shaming. This is the man who plucked my virtue in the stable over there. Who raped me on Christmas Eve. *In a stable*. Think on it! And, now, he has killed my brother. . . Sam! Sam! My dearest brother!" She was rocking to and fro with grief.

And it was Caleb who broke through to comfort her, but she pushed him away with her small hands.

"No, Master Caleb. Listen. . ." she was walking round at the ever-deepening circle. "Listen all of you. The bastard inside me is Charlie Sheridan's. And Caleb Vyne is innocent of any charges laid against him. He only did good for me and my brother. My brother, my brother." She shook her head in disbelief.

It was then a woman broke through the circle too and cradled Sally's body to her. Charlie, stark fear on his face, was trying to find a way out through the grim, silent salters when there was another surprised murmuring from the back which, suddenly, rose to a roar.

"Look, look!" The men broke the circle again as Caleb strode out. The sight was more than he could have imagined. "Look! The young mistress! Over there!"

Their voices died away in shock as Lydia Annesley, copper-coloured hair straggled and clinging to her shoulders, dressed only in bodice and drawers of pure thin silk, came running crazily through knots of amazed salters. As she lurched towards them and freedom, arms outstretched wide for help, Caleb caught her and covered her indecency with his cloak. Then, gathering her in his arms, he carried to her a low dray that had been carrying straw and laid her down tenderly. He didn't even look round as Charlie Sheridan broke frantically through the surprised salters and, grabbing the nearest horse, vaulted into the saddle and took off in the direction of Upwych.

"Lydia, for God's sake what has happened to you? Where have you been?"

She stared into his anxious face and broke into the wildest weeping. "Charlie Sheridan, Caleb. He imprisoned me and kept me in the stable. Over there."

Every man and woman heard the young mistress's accusation, spoken in a cracked and broken voice. Then the muttering hum of surprise rose into one mighty roar against a man whom everyone hated.

Soon, the salter woman, who'd cradled the weeping Sally in her arms, was now supporting her at the spot where Sam was lying. One of the salters had covered him with sacking; others turned and helped the injured, while some set about making the brine seam safe under the guidance of the foreman. All the time, however, they kept glancing at the strange picture poor Miss Annesley made, crouched under Mr Caleb's cloak, and their hitherto stern master, taking no notice of anything about him, but only bending over her protectively.

"Miss Lydia," he whispered, "can you forgive me? If I hadn't let you ride on to Sally Shrike's alone, this wouldn't have happened."

Her eyes studied his face, the dark curls falling over

his brow and his shoulders, which seemed broad enough to carry any burden. "Are you your brother's keeper?" was all she whispered. But she couldn't smile at him; it hurt too much.

"Stay quiet," he said kindly, "until Doctor May comes. We have sent for him." He put out his hand and she grasped it tightly.

"What was that terrible noise, Caleb?" she murmured, staring into the smoky grey sky. "I heard it before I found you."

"Nothing for you to worry about, Miss Annesley," he said. He would not add to her misery with his own tale of tragedy. "Now close your eyes and draw up in my cloak. For you will soon have your carriage here and your maid to comfort you."

Obediently, the weary Lydia closed her lids and, as Caleb looked down on her fragile face, which reminded him of the pale and beautiful snowdrop bunch he had plucked beside the river near Raven's Mill, a sense of foreboding cast itself over him like a black veil.

Lydia was injured now and weak but, later would she really forgive him? He shared the blood of the villain, who'd caused her so much pain. And what had the coward done to her?

Caleb shuddered violently from mental pain and anger. The only thing he felt sure of at that moment was he would make Charles Sheridan rue the day he had ever touched Lydia Annesley.

* * *

Chapter 12

Caleb Vyne was not given the chance to vent his hostility upon his villainous half-brother because, by the time the law was on to him, Charlie had packed his bags and left Upwych for good.

The events which had led to his departure were the talk of the town. Every cubicle in the Royal Brine Baths was awash with gossip, every invalid discussed it during treatment and *The Journal* was read so avidly, far and near, that the editor's column became famous for its anecdotes on Upwych family connections and predictions of Charles Sheridan's future doom when apprehended.

It was rumoured that the culprit had fled to Liverpool and then on to Ireland; that he would soon be caught and brought back to face trial. A history of the lawless Stretton family followed, and the clan's misdemeanours were spread far and wide.

Lavinia Stretton's past unfortunate meeting in London with Mr William Sheridan was recalled, and the latter's Irish pedigree examined. Even the unfortunate Harry Vyne's death in a riding accident was resurrected. However, Mr Caleb Vyne, *The Journal* reported regretfully, had declined to be interviewed and, together with his mother and grandfather, the ailing Mr Stretton, was pursuing his business in the salt trade from his home at Raven's Mill.

The newspaper then examined the Annesley fortunes at length, with the result that many carriages pulled up outside the gates of Annesley House, their occupants peering through in the hope of seeing a glimpse of the abducted heiress, whom, it was reported, was still suffering much from her incarceration.

However, the column rejoiced in the fact that Miss Elizabeth Annesley was restored to health and had again taken the reins of the salt works, aided by Lord George Tulham who was well-known as a kind and generous benefactor to the town of Upwych.

A more lugubrious addition dealt with a description and sketch of the infamous stable, where Miss Lydia Annesley had been imprisoned, being razed to the ground by Stretton workers. Its demolition was attended by upwards of one hundred inhabitants.

Added to this was another complete feature on the visit of Mr and Mrs Brodrick Fortey of London, who had hurried to inquire of Miss Lydia's health, and who were also in Upwych to take the brine.

Miss Annesley's stepfather, with his new bride, a society beauty, had been staying at the Royal, from which they had journeyed to Annesley House to be entertained for a short time by the Misses Annesley.

* * *

Lydia put down the paper in annoyance. She felt quite well physically, although her aunt had insisted she lie for one hour each afternoon on the day bed, which her aunt had had placed in the drawing-room.

However, she often had nightmares and still suffered from panic attacks if she felt at all confined.

As she lay on the pretty walnut bed, with its elegant

cabriole legs and well-shaped back, her pale blue gown brought out the delicacy of her skin and the contrasting auburn of her hair. But the gown, reflected in her eyes, was now a sombre green.

"Aunt, when will they cease to publish such scurrilous pieces?" she asked seriously. "Can nothing be done?"

"I fear not, Liddy," said Elizabeth, sighing over her embroidery. "Newspaper men have always sought freedom of speech. And, as brinemasters, we are the property of the public."

"But to report my stepfather's coming with that vulgar woman."

It had been an ordeal to welcome the couple into the house. Although it was a mercy Brodrick had chosen someone like himself to share his hearth. At least, the new Mrs Fortey would not be made miserable like Liddy's mother had been.

"I thought it quite amusing, dear, that he has met his match at last," commented her aunt drily. "But, yes, I feel for you. You look extremely pale today, Liddy, and I'm quite worried."

"Please don't be, aunt. I feel well and want to be ordinary again." She looked at the newspaper with a sigh. "Why do folks take notice of such slight writing?"

"Out of curiosity, my dear," said Elizabeth wisely, "but it will all be over soon. Now, shall I ring for Sarah to bring in the tea?"

"Yes, aunt," sighed Lydia.

But she knew it would never be over for her until Charles Sheridan was caught and punished. She had not mellowed to him, could not even bear to think of the violence he had offered her. Her time at his mercy was dreadful to think of and she was still unaware of what freedoms he'd taken while she was out of her senses. The fact had caused almost her breakdown, and Lydia would never forgive him.

On the other hand, she dreaded Charles Sheridan being taken, on account of the harm to her own feelings and those she loved but, at least, he wouldn't be able to wreak his callousness on any other girl who took his fancy. He was a danger indeed to all young women and should be brought to trial as quickly as possible.

Lydia was also thinking of Caleb. She had not seen him since the day of her escape from the stable and she wanted to a great deal. He must be feeling as much as she about the reports daily on his family and circumstances.

At least, in the Annesleys' case, the articles were sympathetic. But the castigation of the Strettons had been savage. *And mostly well-deserved*, concluded the injured Lydia, *except in the case of Caleb Vyne, and probably his mother.*

Of Lavinia, she knew nothing, except her son thought a great deal of her. However, there was no possibility of another meeting with Caleb. The last was too fresh in her mind. Her days of riding out unchaperoned were over, and she could not stomach the thought of approaching Raven's Mill, nor even the other side of Upwych yet. Perhaps when she was better.

But the thought of his hand over hers as they sat on their horses - and the tender way he'd wrapped her body in his cloak and carried her; his words as he begged for her forgiveness. As her aunt worked peaceably on her embroidery frame, Lydia yearned to hear Caleb's voice again.

Just then Sarah brought in the tea and disturbed her reverie. The girl was smiling brightly as she bobbed a curtsy.

"Beggin' your pardon, ma'am," she said to Miss

225

Elizabeth, "but I see'd Lord George Tulham on his way up the drive. Shall I bring in another cup?"

"Yes, do that, Sarah," answered Aunt Elizabeth with such alacrity that Lydia smiled.

Lord George's frequent visits were now much appreciated by her and, more evidently, by her aunt. His entry into the drawing-room seemed to bring with it a glimpse of the outside world. He looked well, hearty, and certainly not as elderly as Lydia had thought at the time of their first meeting in the bank. His moustache had been carefully trimmed and he was wearing a spotless starched collar with ribbon tie.

Aunt Elizabeth was already patting the chair nearest to hers and he sat down obediently. "What news, George, now from Upwych? Liddy and I have become quite nunlike, although we deal with salt matters every day. And remember we want the *truth*, which is more than we can glean from that." She pointed to *The Journal*.

"Madam, do you doubt my veracity?" he joked. "So I must tell you nothing of the works - except that the new pipes are holding well and we're in full production. In fact, I'm quite enjoying myself, deputising for you both. I'd become too accustomed to the pursuit of leisure, like a horse unharnessed, and thanks to you ladies I've come to feel useful again." He beamed at them both.

Lydia would dearly have liked to ask for news of Caleb Vyne, but it would have been indiscreet. Her aunt had said quite forthrightly that the name of Stretton should never be mentioned in her presence again.

And Caleb was a Stretton.

"Thank you, George, for your great help," replied Elizabeth, and they stayed staring at one another for a few seconds.

Lydia had suspected rightly that Lord George's feelings for her aunt had not waned with time. It was a pretty sight at their ages.

He turned, his white beetling brows drawn together anxiously. "And, Miss Lydia, how are you feeling today?"

"Well, thank you, my lord," she replied.

"And are you ready for news too?"

"Lydia's persistent curiosity overcomes mine," quipped her aunt.

"Even if it should concern the Strettons?" He looked keenly at Elizabeth, who frowned, her black silk rustling impatiently as she shifted in her chair.

"George, I've forbidden their name in this house," she reproved.

Lydia was preparing herself. "Have they found . . . Mr Sheridan?"

"I have heard they are near to it," replied Lord George gravely. "The bloodhounds are out in County Kerry. And, Elizabeth, forgive me if I speak plainly. Miss Lydia will have more to face if the young scoundrel is brought to trial and, therefore, I think . . ." he looked at her aunt, waiting for the signal to proceed. She nodded briefly. ". . . that we should speak of the Strettons sometimes - but only rarely."

Lydia was fanning herself, and Lord George rose from the chair and pulled the up the sash window letting in air, with a hint of spring behind it.

He turned. "I only advise this amongst ourselves. We have heard enough tittle-tattle already." He crossed the room and sat down, lifting his tails as he did so. "I have received more than rumours concerning Billy Sheridan. From the office of Mr Smith. . . In confidence, mind."

"The bank?" asked Lydia.

"Indeed. It seems that Billy Sheridan has been withdrawing large amounts over the last few weeks, and . . ."

"Spending it on more new machinery?" Elizabeth's voice was cold and hard.

"No, indeed, *not* spending it. For my part, ladies, I feel that Mr Sheridan is about to quit Upwych. I'll vouch he has wind of his son's impending arrest and does not wish implication."

"In what, Lord George?" Lydia asked quietly.

"The cutting of the pipes, ma'am. So far no one has been brought to justice, and if I was a betting man I would say that the young devil couldn't have accomplished such without help. And from who else but his father?"

"But what of old Mr Stretton?" Elizabeth looked sharply at her niece, whose pallor was frightening.

"He is too far gone to bother with salt now. All that is left to Caleb Vyne."

As Lord George uttered his name, Lydia was feeling quite faint. She stretched out her hand for her tea cup and sipped the sweet liquid.

"And Caleb Vyne will order his matters well. But what of Lavinia?" asked Elizabeth briefly.

"Sick and mad with anxiety. What will become of Strettons is a conundrum. Mr Vyne is a hard taskmaster but some of his men are muttering that he, too, has lost interest in the business. Not that I blame him the way he was treated by his kin."

"They've been fools," muttered Elizabeth gruffly. "With a son like Caleb Vyne, their fortunes were assured."

"Quite so, Elizabeth," answered George briefly.

Lydia was remembering their earlier conversation when Lord Tulham had spoken of the past. What had he said? *Miss Elizabeth had fallen head over heels in love with Harry Vyne but he had married Lavinia Stretton.* If Aunt Elizabeth had married him, then Caleb might have been first cousin to her. A near blood relation. It was a thought Lydia did not wish to entertain.

"The young man has been severely wronged and he has much to suffer still. Saddled with a sick mother and an old man, wandering in mind. On top of that, a dissatisfied work force and a hated name."

Lord George and Aunt Elizabeth looked so severe that tears started in Lydia's eyes when she thought of poor Caleb and what he was suffering.

* * *

Caleb had done nothing to hinder Billy Sheridan's evident plans for departure. He knew he was gambling with his mother's marriage, but not her happiness. If that was love between her and Billy, then Caleb would never love anyone. It was best if the rogue was gone.

Mr Smith had called him into the bank a month ago and told him in confidence of the withdrawals on the account. He knew the astute manager wished him to charge Sheridan with his actions, but Caleb did nothing. He cared little for money anyway. It made men into grasping, greedy fools. As long as he had a roof over his head and the salt continued to flow through the pumps, Caleb could survive.

However, his grandfather was proving to be more of a headache. The old man, who had always been a victim of violent whims, was now behaving in an insufferable manner. The very day that Caleb had seen Sheridan packing his bags, old Mr Stretton had ordered Caleb to his rooms at the top of the house.

Even Lavinia never entered there now and Stretton

only allowed his own manservant to be in attendance. It was well known though that his favourite, Charlie used to frequent his rooms twice a week at least. Caleb could never understand old Stretton's fondness for his half-brother. The old man had been a shrewd business dealer in his time and should have seen through Charlie's blustering.

The top floor of Raven's Mill was even gloomier than below. As a small child Caleb had been afraid of apparitions, and if ever he had seen one it would have been near Grandfather Stretton's apartments.

Caleb had no knowledge why old Stretton shunned him. He'd supposed as a boy that his grandfather disliked children. Indeed, he seemed to have no natural feelings for Caleb but, when Charlie was mewling and puking about the house, his grandfather had called for him to be brought up to his rooms and admired.

Caleb had long ceased to question the fact. He was unloved, with the exception of his mother. All he had done for Stretton he had done for her, not for the severe old man who'd retreated upstairs with advancing age. He'd always been a tyrant.

Caleb could hardly remember his natural father, but when anyone spoke of him it had been with fondness; so Caleb had grown in the knowledge that he was a true Vyne and disdained to be a Stretton. But his mother had instilled the notion in him that he was a grandchild and the Stretton inheritance was jointly his. She had never explained his grandfather's aversion to him, and since a child he had never asked. It remained as big a puzzle as was Stretton's preference for Charlie.

Caleb walked along the landing, his boots making the floorboards creak. He had to acknowledge his feelings had been mixed at the summons, being sure it was something to do with the flight of Charlie. The old man was lying in his bed. All the curtains of the four poster were drawn except for those facing Caleb. He stood stiffly in front of the old man, who had made his personal life a misery, but he was already realising that most of the anger he'd felt in the past was draining, leaving Caleb empty of feeling. Who could hate such a frail old stick, whose head, clad in the tasselled night-cap, shivered like a grass by the river?

Caleb had been expecting the hostile look that usually characterised his reception, but that day it was absent. The old man's face was vacant and devoid of feeling. He appeared to be gazing *through* Caleb, not at him.

"You sent for me?" asked Caleb briefly. He had much on his mind.

"Harry Vyne!"

Caleb shivered as the keen wind blew along the corridor and under the door.

"Caleb," he corrected, walking nearer.

He'd suspected for some time that the old man's mind was wandering.

Stretton was staring at him from cunning eyes, which had almost disappeared under wrinkled pockets of skin. He'd been a hard brinemaster in his time and it still showed.

"You wanted me?" Caleb repeated.

"Keep away from her," his grandfather hissed.

Caleb stood back from the bed, surprised by the violence in the tone. "You are mistaking me, grandfather, for someone else."

But the old man was shaking a palsied fist at him. "Keep away or it'll be the worse for you. Keep away from Livvy, I'm warning you." The old man's breath was fast and the veins were standing out on his forehead.

Caleb was unsure whether to remonstrate or not when the door of the bedroom opened and his grandfather's servant entered without even a knock.

"How long has he been like this, Preece?" questioned Caleb. "He doesn't even know who I am. Yet he sent for me."

The manservant went over to the bed and felt for the pulse in the old man's wrist. "Racing. We should call Dr May."

"You take much upon you, Preece," barked Caleb.

"Aye, master, that I do. But he's ordered me to call on the doctor whenever I will."

"Then do so, Preece, but leave me out of it," retorted Caleb. "Inform my mother so that she may come to him. For myself, I have better things to do than be insulted in my own house."

Caleb had not shown his temper to anyone since his last disagreement with Charlie, but there was something in his grandfather's tone which was particularly irksome. Old and crazed he might be, but Caleb had had enough of sneers. He was aware that his own hasty temper was his most unpleasant trait but, at that very moment he was ready to let it fly. But he managed to control himself and strode out of the room.

It was only later, when Dr May and his mother were still upstairs with his grandfather, that he was relenting. It was quite likely the old man had taken him for his father. In the one portrait of Harry that remained hanging in Lavinia's closet, Caleb recognised every feature as his own.

When the doctor came down alone, his expression was troubled.

"Come in, doctor, and take some wine. It's cold outside and you have other calls to make." Dr May didn't

232

remonstrate but took the goblet from Caleb with enthusiasm. "I take your expression to mean all is not well upstairs?"

"Far from it, Mr Vyne." The doctor looked round and sighed. "This house has seen some trouble in its time and will see more. His heart wearies, sir, and my diagnosis is that he has not much time left. And he should not be excited."

"I infer from that you mean my visit?" challenged Caleb. "Believe me, Dr May, I was unwilling."

"Caleb, Caleb," said the elderly doctor, "I brought you into the world, remember. Do not be sore with me."

"But he mistook me for my father."

"Did he, by Jove?" The doctor stroked his beard thoughtfully. "Small wonder, I suppose, seeing you are so like him."

"He hated him, did he not? As he hates me."

Caleb drained his own goblet then poured himself another. The two men regarded each other silently.

"Have you . . . ever spoken about this to your mother?"

Caleb was astonished at the question. "Then you agree I'm much maligned? I can tell you, doctor, I have not. My mother and I have never spoken ill words to each other - and I have borne enough of those on my back in this house." He gazed around gloomily.

Then, recollecting himself, he added decisively, "And now, I suppose I must speak my mind. . ." His eyes narrowed. "My wastrel of a half-brother is hiding out somewhere in Ireland, and my brutish stepfather is about to follow him." The doctor looked startled. "Oh, yes, Dr May, he is busying himself for that. And I will not lift a finger to stop him."

The doctor could see Caleb's fine lips quivering with the hurt he was feeling.

"I prize my mother's love, doctor, and soon it may be mine alone. Do you grudge me that? You understand the Sheridan character very well and know his worth. She is better off without him."

"Caleb, I realise that you mean every word you say and, doubtless, you are right. But you cannot make your mother's choices for her."

"I can, and I will in this matter, doctor. She is unwell and his behaviour towards her daily is sending her to her grave." Caleb spoke so passionately that Dr May laid a restraining hand on his arm.

"She is certainly not well and getting weaker. She has never recovered from bearing Charlie so late in life, albeit twenty years since. She always had a delicate constitution." Privately, the doctor wondered how Lavinia Sheridan had lasted in the atmosphere at Raven's Mill. "I fear," he added, "that she can take no more shocks of the kind to which she has been subjected of late. And, now . . . if deserted . . ."

"She'll not be deserted," retorted Caleb. "I shall be here to care for her."

"And what of your grandfather?"

"I cannot tell," Caleb replied, shaking his head. "I don't know what he wants from me. I have worked hard for Strettons all my life and given him not the slightest pain, and this is how I stand. Why does he treat me so?"

The doctor looked into his goblet and drained it. "I can tell that neither. But you have nothing with which to reproach yourself. I suggest you speak to your mother." He put on his hat. "I have prescribed a seda-tive draught for your grandfather - and something for your mother. She has retired to her bed. Go up and see her soon. And, Caleb, as a friend rather than your doc-tor, I urge you not to interfere in their marriage."

"I will take your advice as a friend," Caleb replied, "but I won't see my mother hurt any more by that scoundrel."

He ushered Dr. May to the door and watched him ride away. Then with a deep sigh, Caleb Vyne closed the heavy door of Raven's Mill and went upstairs to his mother, but she was already sleeping.

* * *

Believing it to be his secret, Billy Sheridan rode off just before midnight. He had a ticket booked on a Liverpool package boat, and intended to be in Ireland post-haste. He took with him large sums of money and most of Lavinia's jewellery. With the proceeds of this, he intended to meet up with his son and cross to Holland as soon as possible, in the hope that he and Charlie could lose themselves in the wildness of the Continent.

Caleb listened to the horse's hooves thudding away. He was letting the thief creep off with a glad heart. Billy Sheridan's departure represented more to him than the plunder of the Stretton bank account. It symbolised the stealing of his youth. It was worth the loss of any money. Caleb had endured twenty-one years of slights at the blackguard's hands - almost as much as his mother. He might have to account to the shareholders, but that was a little matter set against the benefit of the Irishman's absence.

Throwing on his robe, he walked along the corridor with his candle wavering in the draught. His mother's door was closed; she and Sheridan slept together no more, nor had they done for years.

Then, under the stern gaze of his Stretton ancestors, Caleb walked quietly on to the chamber his stepfather had occupied. The door was ajar. Caleb looked in. The man had made a good job of it, emptied the wardrobes and drawers, taken everything he thought he owned. Caleb set down his candle, sat on the untouched bed and, closing his eyes momentarily, sighed in relief.

After a while he descended the dusty staircase and, entering the echoing drawing-room, stretched out his long legs on the faded rug in front of the fire that was banked up with slack for the morning. Charlie's once favourite spot was now his.

In the quiet of the night, with the wind blowing about the eaves, he reflected on his unnatural behaviour, but it was still a pleasant feeling. Caleb was allowing himself to savour being the only master left.

It was then he rehearsed telling his mother. It must be gently. She had suffered so many blows - his father first, her illness, Sheridan's cruelty, his slights, and the knowledge of Charlie's evil-doing.

But now she was free. And she would know nothing of the trial, when it came about. There was no doubt Charlie would be brought to justice. Caleb hoped also it would be before Sally Shrike gave birth. Since poor Sam's death the whole family had been plunged into gloom and would have gone hungry if Caleb had not sustained them. Whoever judged Charlie would, at least, make him admit to fathering her child and charge him for it.

Then Caleb started to come to his senses. The rooms around him were huge and cold, their glory faded. The doctor had just given him bad news of his mother's health. How could he tell her that he hadn't tried to stop Billy Sheridan leaving? And what would be the effect on his ailing grandfather with both Sheridans gone?

Caleb was twenty-eight years old and had no woman's love to sustain him, except for past brief liaisons for which he cared little.

Lydia Annesley, whom he admired with all his heart, was most surely lost to him. How was she faring? He had heard gossip about her sufferings and of her imprisonment. She, too, would have read of Strettons' misdemeanours and know them to be true. What did she think of him now?

The precious day she had come running into his arms was long gone indeed when he had wrapped her in his cloak for comfort and laid her on the dray. The thought of that moment made his loins ache as much as when he had first seen her at Fern Hill Heath.

Suddenly, Caleb dropped his head in his hands and closed his weary eyes. Surely, wasn't living at Raven's Mill more than any ordinary man could bear?

* * *

Chapter 13

Lavinia Sheridan greeted Caleb with a smile. He was glad of it; she had smiled little since her son, Charlie had been branded a cowardly criminal and had taken off to Ireland. Caleb knew she had prayed for his worthless half- brother; he had seen her kneeling one night and heard the words of pleading. His rage had boiled up then and he'd vowed once more to make Charlie pay for hurting all those who were dear to him.

"Good morning, mother." Caleb kissed her on the cheek. "I've brought your chocolate, instead of Hannah."

"Wonderful, my love." She glanced at his day attire and a slight frown chased the smile away. "But why aren't you at the salt sheds? There has been no mishap, I hope."

Caleb sat down on the bed and took her thin white hand in his. He was saddened to feel her fingers so roughened by housework.

"No mishap, but . . ." he hesitated, "you should brace yourself, mother, for some news."

"What news?" Her face was paler than ever. "Bad? I can tell by your looks, Caleb. They've found Charlie."

"Would that be bad news, mother, after what he's done?" He was sorry to utter the words.

"He's still my son," she cried, "whatever felony he's committed."

"I know, mother, I know." He put a strong arm about her. "No, Charlie is free still," he sighed. "But Billy is gone."

"Gone? Billy?" Lavinia was holding on to him tightly. "Where? Have you sent after him?"

"I have not, mother."

"Why not?" Her eyes were studying his face. "Is it for long?"

"I don't know, but he's taken everything. I think he plans on a sojourn somewhere other than Raven's Mill."

He held her to him, wondering if it had been the right way to tell her but, as a forthright man, he knew no other way. After some time holding her, Caleb felt his mother's body relax against him. They sat on the bed for a while in silence and then he lifted her face up to his. Tears were coursing down her cheeks as she sobbed silently for Billy Sheridan.

"He's left me, hasn't he?" Her voice was dull. "He won't come back."

"I think so, mother . . . but you have me still."

She put up her hand and stroked back his dark curls. There was pain in her eyes. "Caleb, Caleb, what you mean to me is more than I can tell you but . . . Billy going . . . it's a terrible thing to be a deserted wife."

Her breaths were short and Caleb remembered Dr. May's words the night before that she could take no more shocks. *"It's worse to be abused,"* Caleb broke out. "Mother, think of what you're saying. Every day he has done ill to you. I've seen it, remember. All of it."

"Don't be angry, Caleb," she begged. "If *you* rage at me what will I do?"

"I am not," he said, rising from the bed, "but I cannot understand your concern for the man. He was a villain. You've been in fear of your life."

"Only when he was drinking."

"And that has been always."

She lay back on her pillows, trembling, and closed her eyes. Then she opened them with shock. *"My son and my husband.* Folks will say I drove them away."

"Then folks would be mad. And, mother, if they had not gone, I should have."

She was looking at him with frightened eyes. He hadn't meant to say such cruel words, but his exasperation was great. If his mother still *loved* Billy Sheridan, then it was the worse for her. She was wrong in this. The man was a fool, a bully and a blackguard. And all those traits he'd passed down to his son.

Caleb was losing patience. He loved his mother greatly but a woman's reasoning was beyond him.

"You'll not leave me, will you, Caleb?" Next moment, she had the hem of his coat fast in her fingers.

He reached down and released then from the cloth, sat down again and held her to him. "I'll never quit Raven's Mill. Nor you. I promise. And you must not leave me."

She sobbed again and he heard her muffled words. "You hate this place, don't you? For they were bad to you. All of them. 'Tis not your fault, Caleb. 'Twas mine."

He disengaged her from him.

"How yours? No, mother."

"Your grandfather does not favour you. That is my fault."

"How so?"

"Oh, Caleb, the story is long. I've never told it for fear of hurting you. Your grandfather favours your

240

brother - and I admit Charlie has such little good in him. I know you have wondered why."

Caleb waited, his patience returning. At least, he was doing as the doctor bid him. Hadn't he told him to question Lavinia?

"Your grandfather was hard set against me marrying your father, Harry Vyne. To think, the whole of Upwych loved him, except my own father. Harry had given him no cause to be against him. There was only one impediment." Lavinia's breathing was shallow. "Grandfather wanted me to marry someone else."

"Who, mother?"

"Bertram Annesley."

"Grandfather wanted you to marry an Annesley?"

"Yes. He wanted Bertram for me. He had a notion that a great salt fortune would be made. It was the only chance Annesley and Stretton had of friendship. The only time they were agreed on anything.

"Indeed," she added, frowning, "your grandfather tried to force me into it. But I ran away. . . With Harry Vyne. . . And he's never truly forgiven me. Nor you."

"And my father loved you?"

"To distraction. Better than any woman was ever loved before. I could not come home after until Bertram himself eloped with another. And then my father and his father saw that the match would never have worked. . . Bertram didn't want *me* either," she added. "I suppose in our hearts we were still Stretton and Annesley. There were too many generations of hate between us. They say he was happy with the girl, as happy as I with Harry. And we had a son."

"And Bertram?"

"A daughter. The one whom Charlie - but I shan't speak of it. It's all too shameful."

241

"Lydia."

"Ay, Lydia Annesley, whose coming here has caused as much pain as all of us to each other."

"It was not her fault, mother, no more than it was mine. Nor yours, either," defended Caleb,

"Maybe you're right," replied his mother, "but between our two families there has been too much suspicion. And all because of salt.

"Your grandfather shuns you, Caleb, because you remind him of Harry and the denial of all he planned for me." Lavinia stroked back Caleb's hair, underpinned with streaks of red. "Harry had hair just like yours and the face to go with it. Charlie looks like the Strettons. He has my features and his grandfather's ways. How nature conspires to seal our lives." She shook her head, sighing. "When your grandfather heard of the new young heiress, doubtless it was in his mind again for Charlie."

Caleb's heart lurched at the thought.

"Lydia Annesley was not for Charlie, mother. He has treated her foully. She's a girl of spirit and beauty, who any man could be proud to pay court to in the proper manner."

"Well, my son," said Lavinia, her eyes dry at last and staring at him curiously, "the feud will go on until one day, when the old folks are gone, some good will come out of it. But not in this time of mine. And you are paying for my sins."

"No, mother, no sin in what you've done. But sin in letting yourself be ruled by a man like Sheridan. Listen. I promised you once when I brought you the snowdrops that I would take you out," he smiled. "This we shall do. You'll be seen in Upwych again. Things will be different here. You'll have nothing to fear. And you'll feel a new woman." He smiled at the thought of cosseting her.

But Lavinia had a look on her face that he did not understand. As though she were a great distance from him.

"Now drink up your chocolate," he said, "before it goes cold." He handed her the cup but she didn't notice.

She was staring up at the window. "You know, Caleb, you can hear the water from here."

"Oh, ay," he smiled, agreeing with her. "Over the noise of the machinery."

"In the night you can," she said softly. "Where did you pick the snowdrops?"

"By the Salwarpe. There was a pretty clump where the water eddied about some sticks. Near the bridge. A lonely spot."

"They always grew there," she replied, "when I used to walk out in secret with your father." She closed her eyes.

Caleb put down the cup and kissed her. "Sleep now," he said. "I'll see you at dinner. I must get off to the sheds."

As he strode down the corridor, away from his mother's bedroom, it was with a sense of relief at what he'd learned. And telling her had not been as bad as he'd feared. She had not taken hysterics nor a seizure. She seemed to understand he would look after her.

As he entered his bedroom and found the garments for his working day had already been laid out by his valet, his strong fine lips curled into a smile. Now he was master things would be different at Raven's Mill. And his mother had nothing to fear any more.

* * *

"There will never be peace in that house," cried Aunt Elizabeth, handing the newspaper to Lydia.

"Which, aunt?"

"Raven's Mill. But I pity the boy." There was a soft look on old Miss Annesley's face.

As Lydia scanned the column with anxious eyes, she blanched. "What a misfortune, aunt. How terrible for Caleb Vyne."

"Ay, that it is," replied Elizabeth sincerely. "What life has Lavinia enjoyed? Except when she ran off with Harry Vyne."

"But to die so," cried Lydia, thinking of Caleb's distress. "What can we do to help him, aunt?"

"Naught as far as I can see," replied Elizabeth, "but we may attend the funeral as a mark of respect. Lavinia and I were acquainted in our youth. She was always a restive, weak thing given to fancies. She wouldn't have suited our Bertram. I hope she may rest in peace."

"Amen," said Lydia, pushing *The Journal* from out of her sight. Her heart was full of sorrow too. Not on account of Lavinia Sheridan, whom she had known only by reputation, but on her son's, whose devastation must have been, by then, utterly complete.

* * *

The chimney smoke which hung over the town of Upwych had cleared for a few short hours and the day was not even the Sabbath. The shops were closed and the tolling bell reminded brinemasters and salters alike they had a funeral to go to.

Indeed, most of Upwych turned out for the funeral of Lavinia Vyne. On account of the evil reputation the Sheridans had brought to the town, the brinemaster's daughter was spoken of in the name they knew best. The Sheridans had been newcomers, and in a place like Upwych such were viewed with suspicion.

But the salters had known and loved Harry Vyne and it was his name they spoke as they mourned for his widow. They came too as a mark of respect for his son, Master Caleb.

There had been many who bore the Strettons ill-will, and had stated publicly that they wouldn't be seen anywhere near Dodderhill Church, and who, afterwards, relented. They were not there, they said, out of respect for old Stretton, who looked likely to be in his own coffin soon, but for Miss Lavinia who'd followed her heart all those years ago and made a good choice.

Sally Shrike, now well on in her pregnancy, stood with her family beyond Chapel Bridge. She was the eldest Shrike now and no use to the others. Her mother was sole breadwinner, and if it hadn't been for Caleb Vyne the nippers would have starved. Her legs ached as she faced that blustery day, which sent the rooks tossing like feather dusters through the sky. But on the hillside beneath the church there was a bloom of green on the bushes already.

The salters stood, hatless, as the cortege wound by. Old Stretton had distinguished himself by his avarice, but he was almost out of his wits, seated, nodding in the carriage behind the hearse. They had heard that he wished to deny his only daughter a decent burial, but Mr Caleb and the Stretton shareholders had the persuasion of it in the end, and were giving Lavinia the magnificence never accorded to her in life.

The glass hearse pulled by six spirited horses, sporting plumes, dragged slowly up the hill, followed by a score of carriages full of mourners. Gentlemen in sober black suits, with scarves of black crepe worn across one shoulder and with hatbands to match. There were no close Stretton relations in womankind, but the wives of the town's luminaries were wearing black dresses and black gloves.

And, in front of it all, the local undertaker and his top-hatted men had learned the dead march well.

There were many whispers as the Annesley landau, driven by Blanchard, passed through the workers.

Sally's mother turned to her next door neighbour. "That her's come is some surprise."

"Aye, after what that rascal done to her. Young heiress is a good-lookin' lass though."

"True enough. And Miss Elizabeth was allus a fair one. And her carried the torch for Master Vyne."

"Aye, and ain't his son like 'im. The very image. But 'e ain't got the smile."

"Hush, ma," warned Sally. She'd have no word said against Mr Caleb. Sam had loved him and so did she. He'd been the world to them both. And what had Mr Caleb to smile about anyway with burying his mother?

Sally pulled her garments close to her to huddle against the wind. It was a strange thing that the baby coming was kin to Mr Caleb. But she knew that, although she hated its father, she would love it for his brother's sake.

* * *

Caleb's head was bent as he sat in the narrow pew. He stared at his knees and the cold stone floor, then up at the stained-glass windows. Anywhere but at the coffin where Lavinia lay.

Finding her was something he'd never forget on the

very day after he'd told her she was safe with him. . .
He'd been called from the salt sheds by Hannah. The
maid's face was worried and red from running. She held
her side, sore from a stitch. "Master Caleb, Master
Caleb!" He'd managed to get some sense out of the girl
finally. His mother had been talking all morning to her
about wanting to send someone to look for Mr Sheridan.
She had some notion he'd gone into Upwych and would
be taking the drink.

Finally, Lavinia had sent for Caleb's valet. But the
man had gone into Upwych himself to the tailor's. She
had seemed most distressed that there was no one to do
her bidding and had retired to her room.

Some little time after, she went up to old Mr Stretton,
from which interview she'd emerged weeping. Calling
Hannah, she'd ordered her to the kitchen to prepare
lunch and, in the girl's sight, she had taken Dr May's
prescription.

After eating, Hannah had left Mrs Vyne lying on her
bed, and it was not until near four that she went up to
her room again, to find Lavinia gone, her clothes, still
hanging untouched in the closet. Hannah and the valet,
who'd returned by then, had searched the house and
even old Mr Stretton's rooms. But she had disappeared.
In panic, they decided to turn to Caleb.

He sent Hannah back to the house and, taking some
of the salters, began to search the buildings, his fear
increasing as time passed. His mother never left Raven's
Mill, even accompanied, except to church; never mind
alone and undressed.

In his head, Caleb went over and over their
conversation and the even earlier one with Dr May.
The medical man had been right, not Caleb. He should
never have assumed anything about the marriage;

247

should have done something to stop Billy Sheridan's flight.

It was then he had thought of his mother's longing look at the window and her talk of spring and snowdrops. Caleb's heart was banging as he raced along the bank of the Salwarpe to the spot below the wooden bridge, where the fast-flowing river had divided itself into a silent pool, dammed by sticks.

His stomach sickened as he went over the scene again and again in his mind. A shred of the old green robe his father had bought her from Birmingham was hanging from a bough. It had torn as she fell in - or had tried to save herself by hanging on to the branch. But, then, his horrified mind could only fix on the bundle of drifting silk, its green blackened by river water, which had jammed itself on the edge of that natural pool, frantic for the current to take it on down to the Severn and the sea.

Inside it was the white, bloated body of his mother, Lavinia, whose troubles were at an end and who was truly free at last.

She would not have meant to throw herself in. It was not suicide, although there were rumours of her shame and misery. Caleb had promised to take her to the spot where he had plucked the snowdrops and where, now, the primroses were already dying. Caleb blamed him-self for failing her.

He prayed on, head bowed. With his mother gone, now there was certainly nothing left for him at Raven's Mill. If his grandfather could not forgive him before, he would not forgive him now.

Caleb had also learned from the bank manager that unless production kept increasing by the provision of new methods, Strettons could cease to make a profit, given the development of richer brine fields under other ownership. And he'd rashly allowed Charlie and Billy Sheridan to take off and rob him of his birthright.

Caleb, who had always been so cautious in business, was now to blame for the company's demise too. And all of it had come about because of his personal animosity. If he had been more like his grandfather and Charlie Sheridan, he had no doubt the Stretton fortune would have continued to increase unhindered.

* * *

Lydia made as pretty a picture in black as in anything else. Her sombre hat and veil only made her auburn hair and green eyes a more delightful contrast.

She and her aunt stood as Lavinia Vyne's coffin was carried towards the church door. The bearers, who included Caleb amongst them, had rested for a moment in the airy space where the four aisles of the church met in the shape of a cross.

She had stared at the slump of Caleb's back as they prayed and his stoically erect bearing when they sang. In fact, as the weary service continued, Lydia's heart had gone out to him.

When he turned at the end, she could see there were tears left on his cheek. It was then she wanted to comfort Caleb. To hold him in her arms.

It was an urgent need which made her tremble.

She was thinking of it when his eyes met hers as he stooped to pick up the coffin. Her stomach fluttered at the beseeching look in those dark eyes, then sobered again. Slowly and painfully Caleb passed her, carrying Lavinia Vyne away to the Stretton family vault that Aunt Elizabeth had said was the only place poor, silly

Lavinia Vyne could ever expect to find the peace she'd been searching for all her life.

* * *

There seemed to be no end to Caleb's troubles. Some weeks after Lavinia's funeral, the family lawyer, Dandy, was called to his grandfather's bedside. Caleb, who'd had no words with the old man since the fateful evening before his mother's death, suspected Mr Stretton was about to embark upon some scheme from which he was to be excluded. His grandfather's frailty was increasing and the whole burden of Stretton Salt Works was, as usual, heavy upon his shoulders.

As he waited for the lawyer to descend the staircase, Caleb glanced cursorily at his reflection in the mirror over the mantelshelf. He decided he had become quite haggard over the last few weeks. And there were stray grey hairs emerging amongst the dark. Feeling even more morose, he sat down on the high-backed chair, its solid seat and high turned front stretcher seeming the only stable things in Caleb's present unstable world.

There was worse to come.

He could hardly believe what Mr Dandy was telling him. His grandfather had ordered the firm to hire an agent to sell. Not Raven's Mill, but the Works.

"This cannot be," he said.

The lawyer looked particularly miserable. He liked Caleb Vyne and saw him as the means of keeping *Dandy & Son* in victuals for a good while yet.

But if Stretton was sold . . .

Mr Dandy sighed. Another family firm swallowed up by the new men coming in. Upwych would be poor if

Stretton became part of a mighty salt union, and even poorer if Annesley shut down or joined as well.

Whether old Stretton was of sound mind was another matter. But attorney would have to be applied for and that wouldn't be easy, given that there were other relatives to be considered. On the run though!

Mr Dandy, like the rest of Upwych, waited eagerly for news of the apprehension of Charlie Sheridan. A good case at the Assizes would do either a power of good to Stretton or to Annesley, both of which *Dandy* represented. But he had to admit feeling sorrow for Mr Caleb.

"I fear it is, sir. Your grandfather has it in his head that selling out will restore his fortune, given that . . ." he paused, choosing his words carefully, "given that he feels - only *feels*, mind you - that there is no one to inherit."

"No one?" Caleb ground his back teeth. He wasn't going to lose his temper before Dandy. He was no churchgoer, but the parable of the Prodigal Son was readily springing to life. Indeed, if Charlie returned and was acquitted, which would be unthinkable, then and only then would his grandfather rue the day he'd sold off Strettons. Caleb didn't deserve to be treated in this way. He was finished with it all.

"I can see I've put you out of temper," interposed Mr Dandy suavely. "But, Mr Caleb, although this may be indiscreet of me and, bearing in mind your grandfather is not one to change *his* mind, my advice would be to bide your time.

"Your grandfather is a sick man. He has lost his only daughter *and* the young man he doted on, however unwisely. The latter has absconded and may not be found. If he is, he will be condemned. And should your grandfather die, then you will inherit."

"He has not changed his will?"

Mr Dandy shook his head briefly. There was no way in which he could tell Mr Caleb Vyne he had been cut out already. But Dandy knew that should old Mr Stretton die and Mr Sheridan be transported for his felonious deeds, then Mr Caleb could sue for his rights. It was thus best to keep on the young man's right side.

"Thank you for your advice," retorted Caleb. "But, Mr Dandy, at this moment I could not care less what happened to my *inheritance*. If I loose the reins of Stretton, then it will fail, I tell you that, and many men with it. If my grandfather has made up his mind to sell," he added decisively, "then so be it. But I'll not stand by and watch. It seems the greatest portion of my boyhood and all of my manhood has been wasted looking after Stretton interests and, now, with the small amount of monies my mother left me, I shall quit England for freedom and travel abroad. That will be my decision - if I'm left destitute."

The lawyer laid a cool hand on the impetuous young man's arm, thinking how much like his father he was and how similar had been the situation when Harry Vyne had come to him to beg his help in his suit for Lavinia Stretton. But that was all history.

"Have courage, Caleb," he added. "Things have an unexpected way of turning out and, I, for one, would rather see you master of Stretton than anyone."

"Thanks, Dandy," said Caleb. "I need good friends around me now."

* * *

Charlie Sheridan was taken by the authorities finally in a small Irish boarding house on the edge of Bantry Bay. It was believed he was about to set sail for America, but always being a coward, he gave up without a struggle and arrived under police guard in England at the end of May.

There had been an inquest into Sam's death after the accident at the boring. Because there were questions remaining as to how Shrike found himself in the most dangerous position in the pit, given the scandal of his sister's rape by Sheridan, the inquest in the Coroner's Court was adjourned until after the criminal proceedings.

They made much of this in Upwych, where it was talked of copiously and rumoured that not only would Charlie stand accused of abduction of the heiress and the rape of a female salter, but also he could very well be tried for manslaughter.

Added to this was the fact that the Sheridans could both be to blame for the cutting of Annesley brine pipes. However, Billy Sheridan had disappeared completely, having probably taken flight when his son was apprehended. Indeed, there had never been a greater criminal in Upwych than Charles Sheridan. All his misdemeanours, from leading hounds on to the railway line to ensnaring young ladies, were examined; no more as boyish pranks, but as evidence of his wicked and profligate nature.

His trial at the next Assizes was something Lydia Annesley was dreading.

* * *

Caleb's heart went out to her as she was examined by the prosecutor. The trial had continued at a rattling pace; the judge determined to see there would be no miscarriage of justice.

There were no witnesses for the defence and my lord was delighted. Indeed, there was no one at all with a good word for Charlie Sheridan. He'd always been bad, and bad he would remain.

Caleb fixed his eyes on Lydia's face as she told her dreadful story. The public gallery was packed and the horrified faces of the spectators bore witness to how everyone felt about his crime.

The abduction of any woman was serious but that it should be the young heiress to a salt fortune seemed heinous. Aunt Elizabeth, her face set like a stone, watched in misery as Lydia recounted her ordeal, having had to be brought water several times.

Several of the court officials, well used to felony, coughed and fanned themselves as she spoke, obviously moved by her words.

Caleb was raging inside as he heard what his damned half-brother had done. The man was seated in the dock, head hanging down. All Caleb could think of was that his mother had been spared such horrors.

But he, himself, was pointed at and sneered at by strangers as the half-brother of the criminal. When he had walked out of the Assize court the day before, someone had flung a stone at his carriage. And, although it missed, Caleb's shock at being connected with his brother's crime was utterly painful.

And now Miss Lydia Annesley was suffering. Her pale face, under the sober dark green hat and veil, wore a strained expression and she looked near to fainting. She had to be supported from the witness box and taken to her seat.

How Caleb wished to stride forward and carry her off to some quiet place where they could both be free. Once or twice their eyes had met and, given her look, he hoped and believed that she would hold him responsible for only doing good to her, rather than think his blood tainted by his brother's crime.

The evidence which Sally Shrike gave was equally damning. Surely a more despicable villain could not be found? To take advantage of a helpless young woman in a stable on Christmas Eve was horrific. One look at her body was enough to add enormity to this worst of crimes - and the evidence of Dr May, confirming her pregnancy, added weight to her story. Sally Shrike's good character was supported by Mr Caleb Vyne who spoke well of her and her brother. That he was the defendant's half-brother and was giving evidence against him, gave even more weight to the jury's opinion of Charlie's guilt.

And Charlie was questioned as to his motives in ordering Sam Shrike to the nethermost parts of the bore hole. Although he protested the salter was willing, no one believed it, especially after having heard from witnesses who had seen Sam and he sparring outside 'The Talbot' in Upwych.

This time, thought Caleb, as he saw his brother's arrogant looks and impudent blue eyes chastened by the fear of his sentence, *I cannot save you any more. Nor do I wish to, Charlie. For you are the biggest scoundrel I have ever set eyes on, even though the same blood runs through our veins. God have mercy on you.*

The charge laid upon Charlie of severing the Annesley pipes was more difficult to prove, given that no accomplice could be found. But, even though this was not laid at the Sheridans' door, there were many in the public gallery who believed the charge was yet another to be added to the growing list of felonies.

And, all through the rest of the trial, Lydia sat, eyes fixed anywhere but on Charles Sheridan. Instead, she glanced many times at Caleb Vyne, whose face was set like a mask, as the Stretton name was consigned to the mud. She was sorry for him. Indeed, her heart went out to him, and she longed to tell him she bore no ill-will. But the hurried walk from court to carriage, when they were forced to pass through waiting crowds, precluded any conversation with Caleb.

In any case, it would have looked bad for Annesley should she be seen speaking with a son of Stretton. And the torture continued until the judge's summing up.

"The offences against persons here have been presented fully and competently," he said, turning to members of the jury. He was fully aware of the pressure he was under to make the right decision, but could not be swayed by public opinion. "I urge you, therefore, to bring about a verdict which has taken into account all the charges, and which shall make full use of the penalties at my disposal."

While the jury was out, rumour was rife. There was no doubt in anyone's mind that Charlie would be found guilty on all counts, except for, perhaps, the crime against Annesley's brine pipes. The editor of *The Journal* had his quill sharpened and was ready to throw his own peculiar slant on the daily reportage of the trial. In 'The Talbot' bets had been taken on whether Charlie would get transportation or hard labour.

"Both!" snarled one of the regulars, whose antipathy towards Stretton was well-known.

"The black cap," averred another, "for that man murdered Sam Shrike as sure as I stand here today."

* * *

Lydia found it most difficult to get her breath after the foreman of the jury stood up.

"Have you reached your verdict?" asked the judge sternly, and the court was as silent as the stones on which it was built.

"We have," was the reply, "and we find the defendant *guilty* on the first charge, abduction; on the second, rape, *guilty*. On the third charge, the manslaughter of Sam Shrike, *not guilty*, and on the fourth, the severing of Annesley brine pipes, *not guilty*."

Lydia looked at Elizabeth Annesley, then closed her eyes as she felt her aunt clutching her arm sympathetically. When she opened them, she stared deliberately at the ceiling as the judge was sentencing Charlie to be detained at Her Majesty's pleasure for a twelve year sentence of hard labour.

There was wild cheering from the public gallery, and a dazed Lydia looked across at her tormentor being led away, head still hanging down, flanked by two constables.

Then she was conscious of someone staring at her. Across the courtroom she could see Caleb Vyne putting on his hat. He bowed to her courteously, but his white face wore an expression she was hard put to to recognise, given her knowledge of him. It was pure pleading and, she knew, a begging for merciful thoughts.

Suddenly and instinctively, she smiled, to let him see that whatever a Stretton had done to her, it had nothing to do with how she felt about Caleb Vyne.

* * *

With the Sheridan business finally resolved, Upwych returned to some normality. On the advice of Lord George, Elizabeth had appointed an overseer for the works, which rid her of much responsibility and, quite understandably, improved her health. She had taken up bridge and whist again and was less of the stern mistress she'd been. Fewer duties also gave her more time to spend with Lord George and Lydia, whom she found an ever-increasing joy.

Lydia, too, had found Charles Sheridan's trial a great ordeal. But one afternoon at the end of May, when justice had finally been dispensed, and around the Upwych lanes the hawthorn blossoms were turning brown from an extra spate of rain, she had promised herself she must ride out on Sophie to quench any fears that still remained within her. There was need for her to take courage at last. That day had arrived.

She surveyed herself in the hall mirror, which stood on a well-proportioned table with three side drawers where Lydia kept her gloves. There was little to criticise in the exquisite dark-blue of her new velvet riding habit. Aunt Elizabeth had taken her on a shopping spree to raise her spirits.

Lydia was satisfied with her outer vesture. But, what of inside? Pursing her lips, the young mistress of Annesley reflected on that very fact.

When Lydia had come first to the little town, it had impressed her only with its ugliness. When she had started to learn about the salt trade her first impression of that had been mistaken too. Her knowledge had not come from books. She had seen everything at first hand - the mixture of misery and joy in the common lives of the salters; and had gone on to experience a great deal of sadness herself. She reflected that, since the day the hunt had halted the train at Fern Hill Heath, she, Lydia Annesley, had *grown up*. Her green eyes stared back candidly from her reflection in the mirror. They saw the same person on the exterior but, inside, Lydia felt different. She was seeing life from a different perspective.

At first, in London, she'd been content to help her mother about the house, like any daughter. She'd dreamed of romance and marriage, worn frivolous bonnets, and before her mother became ill had enjoyed musical evenings and dancing. She had also been forced to fend off Brodrick Fortey, which had been a shock to her constitution. From this she was rescued by Aunt Elizabeth and, in Upwych the third chapter of her life began. . . She sighed.

Then Lydia tried on her fashionable riding hat, securing it with the broad blue ribbons. It was becoming. As she put it back upon the table she was thinking of all that had happened since. She had fallen foul of Mr Sheridan, not through her own fault but because of her rash behaviour.

She could see now why young ladies need chaperoning, and why her aunt had felt such anxiety when she'd given Blanchard the slip.

And she was quite ashamed that she'd misjudged Caleb Vyne. He had been keeping her from harm and she'd never known it. One of the first things her aunt had uttered should have been ringing in her ears. *Salt men are gentlemen.* The exception had been Charlie Sheridan. If she had listened to Caleb she would have known. She really had no need any more to doubt it.

There was nothing to fear from Raven's Mill now Charlie was gone. Lydia also realised that her self-examination was tempered with curiosity. She wanted to know what the house was like inside. Had done so ever since that first time she'd come across it by accident. It must have taken on an entirely different character with Caleb as its master.

He had looked so stern and pale throughout the trial, a stranger even - and she had so much wished to know him better. But she had smiled at him. Perhaps they could still be *friends*. She had wrestled with herself over what he had meant by that word many times since the day Charlie Sheridan imprisoned her.

And the small persistent voice in her head had continued telling her ever since, that such friendship should be treasured. But how was she to meet him now? He never rode into town, had become as much a recluse as his grandfather and his late mother. She had heard that he still attended the Stretton salt works every day; his enthusiasm for business evidently had not abated but, afterwards, gloomy Raven's Mill appeared to swallow him like a hermit. He never took the waters, nor visited the Assembly Rooms. He was not seen at concerts nor parties. In fact, it was quite clear to Lydia that Caleb felt an outcast on account of his kin's behaviour. Another bond! She had felt the same on account of his half-brother's.

From this had stemmed the desire to seek him out. In fact, several days before, she had penned him a polite letter saying she wished to visit him at the Mill, accompanied by her maid and coachman; and mentioning her time of arrival with Blanchard. Although she received no answer, she had still decided to go, sure that pressing business had prevented him from replying.

She remembered the last time she had attempted to visit Mr Caleb Vyne and on what a different kind of errand. But, this time, she would make amends. And would come to no harm.

When she had told Sarah where they were going, the girl had been terribly frightened, begging her young mistress not to take her on the visit to Raven's Mill. Well aware of Sarah's hysterical disposition, Lydia relented at last. And, as there was now no need to take the carriage, she had ordered Blanchard to saddle up Sophie after lunch in readiness for a tolerable ride.

However, her new-found wisdom had not allowed her to inform her aunt as to the meeting. Although Elizabeth had expressed her sympathy for Caleb's misfortunes frequently, Lydia was still undetermined as to how she would feel about the impending visit. So, just in case her aunt was to forbid it, she intended to keep her own counsel.

With all these things in mind, Lydia responded to the summons of the gong to the dining-room. She knew she was going to find it very difficult to continue the subterfuge and make polite conversation through luncheon, because the thought of meeting Caleb on his home ground made her stomach flutter and her heart beat exceedingly fast.

* * *

The dining-room at Annesley House was very grand, looking over the Italian garden. Aunt Elizabeth had a penchant for oak and the furniture reflected her taste. The table had been in the family since the reign of George the Third, as had the prim set of six single and two elbow spindle-back chairs.

"My dear," said Aunt Elizabeth, looking Lydia over. She was seated at the head of the table on one of the carvers, a very doyenne in grey silk and feathers. "Your new habit looks magnificent." She settled back in her chair as Lydia seated herself at the table.

"Thank you, aunt, for buying it," said Lydia. "And I must christen it this afternoon. I'm all set on my outing with Blanchard."

"Excellent. I'm glad you have decided to take up riding again. But don't overtire yourself by going too far."

Her aunt was busying herself with the meat. She declined having servants wait on her at lunchtime, preferring to serve herself. Lydia followed with a small portion. She had not yet quite regained her full appetite.

Their conversation dealt with matters of salt first, then Lord George who, added Lydia teasingly, was becoming such a frequent visitor he seemed to belong at Annesley. But, then, Aunt Elizabeth lapsed into silence, only glancing briefly at her niece.

"Is there something the matter, aunt?" asked Lydia, taking a morsel of cheese and butter.

"Not directly," Elizabeth replied, "but, I suppose, it does border on us business-wise."

"Have prices fallen then?" asked Lydia, conscious that, throughout the last weeks, she had not taken quite enough care over her inheritance.

"No, prices stay steady, Lydia, and with Lord George and the new overseer at the helm, we have little to worry about at the moment. Although . . ." a slight frown wrinkled her brow, "this new salt baron who has taken over Stoke has plans for Upwych too, I hear."

"Mr Corbett?"

"The same. But let us not talk of him. The matter to which I'm referring is rather delicate."

Lydia was beginning to suspect it had something to do with Sheridan as her aunt was hedging so much.

"Then I'm ready to hear it, aunt," she replied, attempting to sound trivial.

"I've received some disconcerting news about Strettons." Then Lydia had been right. She braced herself. "It seems old Stretton has decided to sell."

"What? Sell the works?" Lydia's inelegant questions sprang from an immediate desire to know its effect on Caleb.

"I fear so. And its implications for us are huge. Although competition will decrease, there will be salters on the market. We cannot furnish them with jobs. And, worse, who will come after Stretton?"

"You mean Mr Corbett?"

"Perhaps. And with such an acquisition, a new salt empire would be formed which would extend to near monopoly in the market. Not a particularly pleasing prospect."

Lydia was thinking suddenly of another, even less pleasant; the further blow to Mr Caleb Vyne. Had ever a man been so unfortunate? What would happen to him, deprived of livelihood?

"You look pale, dear. Please don't be anxious. Our profits have been excellent of late, and Annesley has another ten years left in the new seam discovered last month. And after that, who knows what a decade may bring?"

"I'm quite all right, aunt, except I was wondering what might happen to . . . to Mr Caleb Vyne."

"Ah," said her aunt, adjusting her lorgnette. She sighed. "That is the other part of my news." Lydia's heart fluttered. "I've heard he is bound for Europe. He may have left already."

"Europe?"

"It's rumoured that Mr Vyne has had it in mind to

make a tour for some time. He was, I believe, left a fair inheritance by poor Lavinia. What a scandal that Sheridan should have run off with her jewellery. She had some lovely pieces. Used to wear them as a girl."

Lydia was in no mood to hear her aunt's reminiscences. All she could think of was Caleb going to Europe, and that she might never set eyes on him again. That was probably why her letter had received no answer. Suddenly, she was conscious of her aunt's keen look.

"You'll not forgo your rest on the day-bed, Liddy? You need it before your ride. And don't take fright at my news. Think rather that we shall have nothing to fear from Strettons after such an amount of years." Her aunt folded her napkin in a decided manner. "Lucas Stretton was always a greedy man," she concluded drily, "and I would not have expected him to improve, given his state of health, either in the management of his works or in the treatment of his grandson." Aunt Elizabeth shook her skirts free of crumbs, adding vehemently, "I would call both shameful. But his is the loss."

Lydia's heart lurched again. As she suspected, her aunt was sympathetic to Caleb. She pushed back her chair.

"I shall go and rest now, aunt, so I'll be fresh for my ride." Her aunt was studying her face as if she hadn't seen it before. She folded her napkin as she stood up.

"My dear, you're taking Blanchard?"

"Of course. I've learned my lesson, aunt."

"Then you will be safe - wherever you're bound." Her aunt's eyes were angry no longer; in fact, there was the twinkle of a smile lighting them.

"Of course."

Lydia was about to add, *Where do you think I'm going?*

but thought better of it. Whatever happened that afternoon, she intended to ride out to Raven's Mill. And she was praying she wouldn't be too late.

* * *

Chapter 14

Riding out of the gates later that afternoon gave Lydia the feeling which had often come to her the morning after dreams. That she was acting out some drama she had played in long before.

Beside her was Blanchard whom, once again, she had not enlightened as to their destination; and before her flowed the river which led straight to it.

No difference in anything except, she believed, her personal self. Different, and so much wiser. It was difficult being a woman. One couldn't frame properly the questions which propriety forbade.

How easy it would have been to communicate to her aunt or her coachman that Raven's Mill was the place Lydia craved most, and for what reason. But it would have been unbelievably *improper*. It was enough to think she had written Caleb Vyne a letter which might be returned to its sender, or even fall into the wrong hands.

Lydia's face burned as they trotted along. She would not like to be accused of any impropriety after her assault by Charlie Sheridan. Her walk in the park unattended, alone could have been sufficient reason for her abduction to be treated as near consent, had not Caleb Vyne taken the witness stand and testified that Lydia, a stranger to the town, had been lost, thus incriminating his brother.

She trotted on in silence, unaware of the large water-filled potholes in the road, come from too much rain for the time of year.

They were approaching the brow of the hill. By now, Blanchard must have suspected where Lydia intended to ride; but he was a servant and must follow.

She reined in at the top. A panorama of fields and gentle hills lay before them. In the near distance, across several fields, was the green darkness of a small spinney leading on to the wild river valley, which hid Raven's Mill in its heart. Neither mistress nor groom spoke as Sophie and his horse champed at their bits waiting for orders.

"We shall go that way," said Lydia, pointing with her whip.

"Will we, miss? But not too far. The rain has swollen the river and the path is likely flooded."

"Surely not in June?"

"Near June, miss," corrected Blanchard. "It gets bad down there in the winter and, begging your pardon, miss, this spring has foretold a poor summer to come."

"I didn't realise you were a herald of the weather, Blanchard," quipped Lydia lightly. But her heart was far from happy.

If the Salwarpe was flooded, how would she reach the Mill? It was something she was not prepared for. And soon she must tell the groom about her visit. They rode on until they reached the high bank which overshadowed the river valley. Reining in once more Lydia gasped at the sight that presented itself through the trees. The little Salwarpe was higher than she'd ever seen it. Even the wildness of winter had not increased its fullness to such a depth. The strong current made it froth and boil and its angry surface seemed to fill the narrow valley through which it wandered aimlessly in summer.

"See, miss," warned Blanchard. "The path is near gone. One slip and we'd be in."

"No, Blanchard, it isn't covered yet. Only in places." The man looked worried. Lydia hesitated. It would be only fair to tell him. "You see, I intend to go down there. To the house."

"To Raven's Mill, miss?" His mouth remained open.

"Yes, Blanchard. I am expected."

He was silent and Lydia knew he was trying to decide on a course of action. He was, she supposed, weighing the danger. As a faithful servant of Miss Elizabeth he was bound to try and stop her. Lydia gave him no chance and was already urging Sophie down towards the path.

He was following dutifully.

"Miss, come back, I beg you."

She pretended she was deafened by the fast-flowing river. Besides, it gave her a feeling of exhilaration. It was so near - like a fluid animal, racing along.

He caught up with her, but was prevented from riding by her side because of the overflowing waters. They continued in single file.

Soon, when they rounded the corner, they would see the bridge that led to the house.

It was a wild sight. The swollen river had almost filled the arches. Above, the sky was dark enough to presage a storm and, below, the clumps of may blossom were darkening brown. But in their stead, early dog-roses and moon daisies starred the rough banks making the gorge a place of eerie beauty.

The house lay in a mist of damp. In the distance, she could see the water wheel and salt sheds, behind them the chimneys lying next to the towpath of the canal.

She shivered momentarily thinking of her last ride that way.

Then she returned to the present. She had believed that with Caleb as master the house might have lost its forbidding looks. But was mistaken again. As she stared in silence, she was still resolved to approach. If Caleb was gone, then he was gone. At least, she would know.

She could feel Blanchard's reproving eyes on her back. And, suddenly, her cheeks felt a smatter of wet.

"I am going over the bridge, Blanchard," she said. "Besides, I don't wish to be caught in the rain."

"Over the bridge, miss?" he questioned. She knew she'd won; the groom could not stop her. "But it doesn't look safe," he added.

She ignored his words and trotted on. Sophie's nimble feet were picking their way through the fringe of swirling river water when, suddenly, a streak of sizzling lightning split the sky. As she controlled her startled mount, Lydia's apprehension increased. And then it was raining; running down her face, hurling itself at her body in furious stinging slashes as the summer storm increased in force.

"Hurry, Blanchard," she shouted, urging the mare towards the wooden span of the bridge.

There could be no hesitation now. The rain was forcing her on to seek shelter from whoever remained at Raven's Mill, and however unwelcoming.

* * *

Caleb had been checking the sheds where the salt was stored in readiness for transport. He was satisfied. The salt, high on its wooden pallets, was safe from the river waters which had risen higher than he had ever seen for the time of year. Owing to his grandfather's final deliberate decision to sell, he was conducting one last service for Strettons. He had no need, except that his mother would have expected it of him - and there was no one else.

Besides he had the men to think of. Strettons' sale was to be in entirety, workers and all. Once the contracts were signed, the salters' labour would be the property of the new brinemaster, whose ambition was to restore Upwych to its former great importance; importance that it had not enjoyed since the abolition of the salt tax, some thirty years before.

Caleb's decision to leave Raven's Mill and travel abroad had not been taken lightly. If his grandfather was to relent, he still might stay to claim his inheritance and set himself up, not against the new trends in salt production, but to run Strettons alongside.

As he gloomily surveyed the stock, he was wondering what else he was fitted to do in the world. If his grandfather had not been a domineering old tyrant, then Caleb could have tolerated him. But his interfering practices were so unpleasant that it was impossible.

The thunder cracked above the shed as Caleb finished his task, jammed his hat down on his head and muffling his face against the rain, prepared to run back to the protection of the house. . .

Suddenly, he heard shouting above the noise of the storm. The sound was thin and distant, carried downstream by the wind. Squinting against the rain, he could hardly believe his eyes. A rider was trying to cross the bridge. It was madness. He had forbidden his workers even to try, though taking the long way round was a pain. What fool was attempting to cross the river? Running out and along the sopping grass, he sustained a further shock. The rider was a woman. And her companion was trying to follow, shouting all the while.

"Stop!" shouted Caleb. "Stop! Get off the bridge. You'll never make it. Stop! Are you mad?"

And his breath almost ceased in his body as the horse, terrified by the current and the nearness of the water, reared, unseating its rider, who was gone in a moment. Her hat fell off, leaving her bright hair spread for a moment on the surface before it disappeared beneath the flood.

Without any care for himself, Caleb ran to the edge, threw off his coat and, arching his arms over his head, dived into the Salwarpe after her.

* * *

The waters closed over Lydia's head as she was dragged down by the river current. Strangely enough her only thought as she went was what her aunt would say.

Then came the shocking feeling of desperation and helplessness, combined with the pain of water pouring into her ears and mouth, drowning her cries. She prayed in her mind, which was crystal clear, and no longer seemed any part of her at all. Past events in her life flashed by and, then, she was struggling to the surface for one brief moment - to see the world above the river, slanting crazily in a sliver of light - before the blue velvet habit, weighing like lead, pulled her once more into that unknown white nothingness.

She didn't feel the strong arms about her, nor the firm hand under her chin. All she could do was kick and struggle as Caleb Vyne fought to save the woman he loved from drowning like his mother.

The current carried them both downstream past the Mill and, all the time, Caleb continued to strike for the bank. The frantic Blanchard was left, unable to proceed further, his way blocked by the flooded path. It was then he turned and spurred back towards Upwych for help.

All Caleb's boyhood years of familiarity with the Salwarpe were paying off. He knew the course the river ran and where it was least dangerous. Still holding Lydia's chin, but tiring badly, he managed to avoid the deep channels, full of choking weed, and tow them both into the shallows.

His feet slipped on the slimy bottom as he dragged her towards where the bank should be, making for the only landmark he could recognise, the elm, which had been struck by lightning several years before.

He struck out for the branch that was half-submerged, then he was pulling them both out and up into the steaming world where the rain had ceased and the small, pale roses were nodding their heads on the bushes beside the Salwarpe.

Caleb's shoulders rose as he gasped air into his lungs. Then he was staggering with the shock, and almost fell back in but, remembering there was no time to lose, collected himself enough to pull Lydia's sodden body clear of the water below, using the branch to guide them both to safety. Soon, he had laid her body across the old tree's wet roots. He called her name over and over as he pressed his hard palms against her chest, rhythmically fighting to expel the river from Lydia's lungs.

* * *

She could hear a distant voice bringing her out of a twilight world where the sky seemed black and there was a great rushing noise in her ears.

Her arms and legs wouldn't do as she bid them; they had given up the struggle and her mind perceived she was dead already. Then coughing racked her body, the pain breaking her in two. But, after that, she found that her desire to return to life was growing.

Water rushed from her mouth as Caleb turned her on her side. There were weeds on her face and in her hair. He brushed them away as he cradled her body in his arms to warm her, which was the next most important task now she was breathing again.

Cold though he was, that body contact warmed them both. She could not remember what he said, only that he held her, murmuring into her almost deaf ears little words of love.

* * *

Blanchard and his helpers, carrying boat hooks to pluck the bodies from the water, were forced to ride and run along the path at the top of the valley and look down on the river from a distance. Not a man spoke on the way, but just kept peering down through the thick bushes in the hope of catching sight of either corpse.

Jemmy Yarwood's father, who knew the valley well, was sure where the bodies would come up. In the past, he'd been right many times. He made for the same place as Caleb had done earlier, where the river wound over and across the summer shallows.

When the party caught the glimmer of white, they knew they'd found either the young mistress or master. There were tears running down Blanchard's face as he and the men carried the makeshift stretchers down the bank, falling and rolling through the deep wet grasses and hollows towards the fallen elm.

It was difficult to believe their eyes. They knew it was a miracle. Mr Caleb Vyne was alive and seated on the broad branch of the half-submerged tree, which was drooping over the water. He was holding Miss Annesley close in a tight embrace, her long, red hair, wrapped around what was left of his white shirt.

"Come on, lads," he said, his voice husky. "Bring the stretcher over. She's alive, thank God. And so am I." He looked up at the sky as if to reassure himself and, next moment, Caleb was lost amidst the group of his salters, who were congratulating and blessing him, then shaking his hand over and over again.

* * *

Lydia started out of sleep conscious that someone was beside her. Opening her eyes, she saw the worried face of her aunt bending over her. It was at that moment she began to cry.

"Lydia, dear, you are overwrought after your terrible experience. I have thanked God every day that you were spared."

Lydia looked around blankly at the dark red hangings of her four poster as if she didn't recognise where she was. It had been the same since she had been brought back on the stretcher to Annesley. She had raved in a delirium brought on by damage to her lungs. But, today, she looked slightly better and Elizabeth had hopes for her recovery. Dr May had attended every day and there had been a stream of visitors ranging from her aristocratic neighbours to her poorest workers.

Everyone wished to know how she had fared after her miraculous rescue from the flooded river.

"Aunt, I'm a burden to you," whispered Lydia, her voice still hoarse from coughing.

"A burden I can bear, my dear. I am only too happy. And I speak for everyone in Upwych."

Lydia nodded her head and collapsed back against her pillows. She felt light-headed now although she didn't wish to sleep again.

It was then Sarah brought in some egg nog, and honey and sugar for her cough. She bobbed to Lydia and her eyes were full of tears. Lydia was so thankful she'd not persuaded Sarah to go on the journey as she'd first intended.

Suddenly, she realised that it was the first time a straight thought had come into her head since her rescue. Of it, she could remember little, rather the pain when she was drowning.

She shivered and Elizabeth Annesley reached over holding a light woollen shawl, finely embroidered at the edges, which she drew about Lydia carefully. Then she sat down beside her. Lydia was mortified. Here she was in her bed and her aunt waiting upon her. It should be the other way round.

"I am a great trouble to you, aren't I?" she repeated. "And you're not well. I've caused you so much pain through my own stubbornness."

"Shh," cried her aunt. "If I'd lost you 'twould have been the greatest calamity. But you're home and safe."

"I was rescued by Mr Vyne," said Lydia as if to make sure it was the truth. Suddenly, she was afraid. Perhaps he'd left for Europe and she'd never thanked him.

"Yes, my dear, and he has my grateful thanks."

"Was he injured, aunt?"

"No, but I believe he's taken some cold. However, it seems that he's up and about again."

"Then he's still at Raven's Mill."

Aunt Elizabeth's face was severe for a moment and then she relaxed. She was in no mind to scold Liddy ever again, so grateful she was to have her back. It had crossed the mind of the elderly Miss Annesley that it was time her niece had some stronger restraining influence in her life to prevent her from such hasty and ill conceived notions as trying to ford a river in flood.

"I shouldn't have done it, aunt," said Lydia suddenly. "But . . . I had written a letter to . . ." she drew in her breath.

"To Mr Vyne," finished her aunt.

"How did you know?"

"Mr Vyne told me." Lydia's eyes were wide and her aunt thought how lovely she looked. "It seems he did not receive your letter in time to prevent you visiting him."

"But I sent it in good time." Lydia clapped a hand to her mouth.

"Yes, Lydia, but it did not reach him." There was the hint of a smile about her aunt's lips. "It seems that Lucas Stretton had commanded all mail to be brought to him, and seeing your letter from Caleb, ordered it to be destroyed."

"But that is monstrous," cried Lydia.

"No more than many other wrongs that have been wreaked on Mr Vyne," said Aunt Elizabeth. "It is only a mercy that Caleb was still at Raven's Mill on account of the flooding. Otherwise, my Liddy might not have been here now."

"And is Mr Vyne still leaving?" Lydia hoped her tone would not give her away. She was remembering herself waking from black nothingness to the sound of his voice, whispering sweetness.

"I think that may depend on certain matters over which he has no control," was her aunt's surprising reply. She looked keenly at Lydia.

"What matters?" She saw her aunt frown. "I'm sorry, Aunt Elizabeth, but . . ." Suddenly, Lydia sat up from amongst the pillows. "Mr Vyne's well-being is a matter of great interest to me, given that he was my saviour."

"He will be glad to hear that, Liddy." Her aunt rose from the bedside chair and twitched her skirts about her. "And you may tell him so yourself."

"Tell him so?" repeated Lydia.

"My dear," replied her aunt, looking down, "Mr Vyne has been seated in the drawing-room each day since you've been sick. It seems that your health is of great concern to him too."

"Is he out there still?" cried Lydia, her heartbeat quickening.

"Still, indeed," her aunt answered drily.

"And may I see him?"

"Yes. And, although I consider it entirely improper, you may see him alone." Elizabeth's Annesley's eyes were twinkling. By the look on her niece's face, Mr Caleb Vyne was the kind of medicine Lydia needed to make a full recovery.

"Thank you, aunt." She was longing to see him and speak with him.

Lydia caught her breath as Caleb walked in, his dark tail coat and elegant woollen breeches showing off his athletic figure. The fine bone structure and the dark crop of strong curly hair that she had first admired, were still evident to her, but now there was so much more.

In his eyes she saw concern tempered with eager-

277

ness, and in his expression a graveness in keeping with her vulnerable position. Her aunt's words to Brodrick Fortey, *Salt men are gentlemen*, were fresh in her mind as he bowed courteously.

"Please sit down, Mr Vyne," she said, indicating the chair beside her. Those hard lips, which she had fancied had scolded her too much, curved into a smile of relief.

"Miss Annesley, it's so good to see you." Caleb's eyes searched her face for any reciprocal sign of fondness. "Are you feeling much better now?"

"Much, thank you, Mr Vyne." Lydia was conscious of his eyes upon her face and that she was wearing only her night attire. She blushed.

"I am so glad to see you," he repeated.

"And I, you."

"Your aunt has given me leave to talk with you for a while," he added. "And I'm grateful for it."

"I heard you had taken cold, Mr Vyne?" asked Lydia solicitously.

"Only a brief spell," he replied. "I have other more pressing matters than my own health."

"Are there such?" she asked, wishing to add his health was of great concern to her.

"My grandfather was taken seriously ill three days ago."

Her heart lurched. "Then you will be staying at Raven's Mill?"

"I will."

"Ah."

Lydia lay back against the pillows. It was what she'd needed to hear. She was not to lose him yet. Then she was longing to say what was in her heart.

"Am I tiring you?" he asked anxiously.

"Oh, no, Caleb."

Her familiar use of his Christian name was a signal of her feelings. Her every nerve was straining for him to act. If he would only take her hand. And Caleb must have understood for, next moment, he bent his head and, taking her hand in his, kissed it tenderly. Lydia flamed inside, closing her eyes briefly. When she opened the lids, she met his steadfast gaze.

"Then we are *friends*, Miss Liddy? I have wished it for so long." He did not release her hand and she could feel fire in his touch.

"Friends, Caleb? Always," she replied, hoping for more protestations of his concern. "And, thank you for saving me."

"If you had drowned, then . . . then I would have not wanted to live on without you." Caleb had risked all to say it, not knowing if she truly felt for him what he felt for her.

Lydia's heart was singing. She wanted to hear more. And she was remembering again the sweet things he'd murmured as he brought her back to life.

"If you had left me," he continued, seeing her loving look, "my world would have been an even darker place."

She put up her other hand and stroked his hair. "I have misjudged you, Caleb. Can you ever forgive me for my foolishness?"

"With all my heart." His voice was muffled with emotion. "From the moment I saw you on the train I was . . ." he raised his head, looked into her eyes, ". . . in love with you."

"Ah," said Lydia, knowing that was all she needed to hear.

"And I have some hope?"

"Oh, yes, Caleb. But will you still go away after? From

me and Raven's Mill?" The thought of that made her tremble.

"I never wished to go, but there seemed nothing for me. Now I have the greatest reason to remain." She knew well what he meant by the look in his eyes. "Grandfather was determined to sell off Stretton." Caleb looked anxiously at Lydia while she held his hand tightly. "But the day before yesterday, when he took the seizure, I knew I had to stay. And, just this morning Dr May says he may not recover, or if he does, be more of an invalid than he is already. He can neither speak nor hear."

"Oh, Caleb," said Lydia, "how terrible. So many sad things have happened to you."

"My grandfather has never cared for me, Liddy, but when he goes I shall be master of Stretton." His words were forceful now. "Many years ago, he didn't want my mother to marry a Vyne. He had someone else in mind." His dark eyes roved over her face.

"My father," said Lydia. "Aunt Elizabeth told me the story. It had been the only chance for Annesley and Stretton." Her green eyes were shining, thinking of what was to come.

"But now, matters have come full circle," said Caleb, and there was no mistaking his meaning.

He kissed her hand again and, rising from the chair, dropped down beside the bed onto his knees so he could be close to her.

"It is time to resolve that feud - if you are willing? Are you, Lydia?"

"Yes, Caleb, I am." She had never been surer of anything in her life.

"Then you will marry me, Miss Annesley?"

"Yes, Caleb." She lifted her face to his and he bent

and kissed her. In that sweet moment, she thought of the day she had left London for Upwych wondering if she would find romance there. She clung to him breathlessly.

He said: "Now I must tell your aunt. She's seated outside for the sake of propriety." He smiled. "And I don't think our news will be received with surprise. But, certainly, with alacrity." Caleb got up from beside the bed and, taking her hand again, kissed it. "I must linger no longer," he said, "but tear myself from you to enlighten Miss Annesley." He had a look of utter love in his eyes as he prised himself away.

As Caleb's strong, tall figure disappeared around the door, Lydia lay back against her pillows, thinking of the first day she had come to Upwych and seen Caleb Vyne. Even then she must have loved him and didn't know it. She was also imagining something equally exciting. That Caleb Vyne was hers alone, and that soon, Lydia would not only be heiress of Annesley, but also his bride and mistress of Raven's Mill.

* * *

Chapter 15

Maria Shrike looked up from raking the salt. She knew she couldn't last much longer. She was getting too old to toil in the intense heat, and the wage she received for such punishing work was quite inadequate to feed the family.

Now Sally was near her time and there'd be another mouth to feed. If it hadn't been for Mr Vyne's kindness, they would have surely starved or ended up in the work-house at Worcester. But it was justice. The young master had promised Sally he would provide for the baby; why should he not provide for them all as it was of his blood?

But Maria had never wanted charity. If her son hadn't died they'd have survived on their own. Sam's death had been such a blow. Husband and son killed as they worked. And all for salt.

Maria hated the pure, white crystals which, like snow, hid darkness underneath. But there was now a way of escape which Maria had never had to consider before, but had been the way of poor women for many a year. She had no man any more, but she was thinking of taking another. She also had no adult son left to think ill of her, and the little ones had no notion of wrong.

She started to rake the salt again and, as she did so, pushed back her grey hair and smiled at the grizzled, middle-aged man who worked and sweated beside her, stoking the pans. Her soft spot was for Albert, who had taken on the job when her husband, Joseph, had fallen.

Though he worked a full six days and she had the nippers to care for, they'd snatched a few brief moments already down Gurney's Lane. After that, she'd fetched him his snap a fair few times and Maria was now of a mind to place him in her affections. There was nothing he didn't know about her; she worked bare-breasted beside him; and he had no wife.

Where he'd come from seemed as far away as the moon in the sky. They had salt works too in Cheshire, but they were miners there instead of pumping up the brine. He told her over a glass of gin that he'd been a bargeman on the canals before he'd taken to salt mining, and thought it was a fair exchange.

He'd had some woman up there, but she'd let him down badly, so he'd taken to bargework again and travelled to Upwych to work on the new canal. But then his employer had let him go, and he went back into factory work.

But Albert still missed up north and had told the nippers, who had taken to him too, all about Cheshire on a Sunday.

His voice was broader than theirs, like his shoulders, and she couldn't understand what he said sometimes, but when he took her in his arms, it was like having Joseph back again, although they weren't man and wife.

As she raked the salt near him, he winked. "What's thinkin' of, lass?"

"Our Sal and the baby."

"Don't fret. Tha'll be all reet! And bread for ye, lass."
The idea had been forming in Maria's head for

some time. On Mr Caleb's money, they could all up sticks and go back to the Cheshire mine with Albert.

* * *

The cradle was ready in the corner. It had been made back in the 1700s from Upwych elm, and each of the Shrike babies had laid in it.

Sally was proud of the polished wood. It was the only decent furniture they had, except for the dresser that had belonged to her grandmother. But she hadn't wanted to put a bastard into it.

How she was going to love Charlie Sheridan's baby she didn't know. It had been put into her unwillingly, and unwillingly she was having it. It was not the nipper's fault, but how different things would have been with a lad she loved.

But after what had happened to her in the stable she doubted she'd go with a man again. When her mother had brought Albert Younger to the house, she had almost died from shame. But he'd just smiled in his gap-toothed manner and asked what Sally was going to call it. He didn't seem to take any notice, nor think bad of her.

But females whispered and pointed her out. She hated that and longed with all her heart that she could pack her few bits and never see Upwych again. Besides, everyone knew it was Charlie Sheridan's and had a felon for a father. Thinking of that and still mourning for Sam, Sally used to sit down every day and cry, which did her no good at all. How she was going to wait another month before it was born she didn't know.

However, that particular summer morning, she suddenly felt brighter. Although she was very heavy, the weight of carrying the child didn't seem so much of a burden. The weather was warm and the cottage smelled foul. It needed a good clean-up.

Sally looked round, sighing. The Shrikes were better off than salters in Upwych as they could draw pure spring water from the well at the bottom of the garden. But it was still very difficult keeping the house clean, living so near the coalyard. There always seemed to be a film of black dust over everything.

And today she wasn't alone. Usually, having one of her brothers and sisters around annoyed her because of her tiredness. But being in such a good mood evoked a smile at little Tommy, who was outside whittling wood with a knife. Their mother had left him at home in case Sally needed anything. Indeed, if the baby was coming, he could run off for help. When she went to him and asked him to go and draw a bucket of water so she could wash the floor, Tommy groaned but obeyed with a good will. He could stand Sal's biddings more than the foreman's.

Sally was feeling quite energetic and even pitied the little man as he struggled up to her with the pail. Warming up the water was more difficult, but she and Tommy managed to get the big kettle full to the brim. While she was waiting for it to boil she had a go at dusting the whole house while he got up on a chair and put the feather duster in the corners. Sally was very pleased with the effect and couldn't wait to get started on the floor, which hadn't been washed for ages.

Later, when the water was ready and in the pail, she took the big bar of soap and placed it beside it. She was nearly ready. Reaching down the scrubbing brush from the outside of the scullery wall was an ordeal, but she managed and, soon, the grateful Tommy was sent outside again and Sally was on her hands and knees tackling the floor. She felt almost light-headed, her belly relieved of the weight as she bent forward carefully. She mustn't pull and push too much, but she was determined to have a proper clean-up before the baby came.

When she'd accomplished about three feet of filthy floor, she found the sweat running down her face. Sitting back on her heels, she raised an arm and wiped her brow.

Then the pain hit her, rising so cruelly that she screamed out.

Tommy dropped the kitchen knife and ran inside. His sister was doubled up on the floor, the scrubbing brush and bucket beside her.

"Sal, Sal, have you hurt yourself?" The little lad tugged at her arm.

When she looked at him, it was through terrified eyes. "Tommy," she whispered hoarsely. "Get off to Upwych and tell our Mam the baby's on the way. And call into Minto's and tell his wife I need her."

The frightened Tommy nodded and, with one last look at his sister, he scuttled out of the cottage and ran madly off along the towpath in the direction of Upwych.

* * *

Caleb Vyne was returning from a visit to the coalyard when he saw young Tommy Shrike dashing like a rabbit down the path.

"Hold on there, Tommy," he said, reining in. "Is the cottage on fire?"

The little boy's face was red and it took him a few seconds to answer. "Can't stop, master. Our Sal's started

286

wi' the baby and I have to fetch me Mam and Mrs Minto."
Touching his cap respectfully, Tommy shot off.

Caleb sat for a moment, controlling his restive bay.
How would it look if he went to see Sally Shrike? He
had no wish to offend anyone. And the girl was in this
position on account of Charlie. And alone. She might
need help until her mother came. Although it was no
place for a man, he would just look in for a moment.
After all, he'd supported the Shrikes for a long time
and, anyway, he owed it to Sam.

Sally had never *known* it hurt so much. She knew all
about having babies as she'd been there at her mother's
confinements. But when it came to oneself it was
different.

Besides, now her happiness had worn off, and she
was cursing Charlie Sheridan for making her suffer so
much. Never had such dreadful words passed her lips.
She was near to fainting as she lay down on the corded
bed-stock. She was very frightened knowing the child
was early, but glad, too, to think she'd soon be rid of it
inside.

How long before Tommy got to Minto's? She needed the
midwife quickly. Panic was setting in. What
happened if no one got here in time? But then
reason took its place, telling her it was the first and wouldn't
come quickly. She groaned as the contraction rose.

Caleb was about to knock, then heard her scream.
He was sweating as he opened the door. He'd never
attended a birth before. It wasn't seemly for a man. But
he cared for Sally and couldn't see her hurt. She would
have no father to be overjoyed at the birth. And it was
part of his blood and his mother's. He stepped into the
room, avoided the discarded bucket and scrubbing brush
and rushed over to her.

When he saw the look in her eyes, he was glad he had.

"Sir, you shouldn't be here," she cried, trying to make herself decent before him.

"I met Tommy. I'll stay until the midwife comes."

He pulled up the sacking and held her thin hand.

"Bless you, Mr Caleb. Bless you, sir." She was out of her mind when the pains came.

What thoughts ran through his head as he partook of her pain. He was realising then how a woman suffered having children, and he thought of his Lydia when Sal's eyes were closed. Soon they'd be wed. And she was the loveliest woman he'd ever met. He would always be kind to her. And he never wanted to lose her.

Then he thought of Sam. The salter had been his true friend and this was the least he could do for his sister. When the baby came, Caleb would go on helping the Shrikes for his sake.

He smiled down at Sally, who was wakening again and she was still holding on to his strong hand gratefully.

Caleb Vyne was the kindest master in the world and Miss Lydia was lucky to have him. His dark eyes bred confidence in her, and Sally thought if the child had been his and not that devil, Charlie's, she would have borne every pain with never a sound.

* * *

Lydia had learned from gossip that Sally Shrike had had a son. She asked Caleb if he knew as she and her aunt entertained him to dinner. Their other guest was Lord George, who was seated beside Elizabeth Annesley looking positively happy, as if it was his rightful place already.

Caleb smiled. He could keep nothing from his bride-to-be.

"Indeed I did. I was riding along the towpath on the day in question when I met the girl's brother running for the midwife."

Aunt Elizabeth looked shocked. The fashion for plain speech was coming in, but this conversation was not quite proper.

"Dear Liddy, you think this discourse is fit for the dinner table?"

"Please, aunt," replied Lydia directly, her chin tilted. "The girl is one of our workers, and I have them all at heart. Of course Caleb must tell me. We are about to be married."

Aunt Elizabeth, with a brief glance at Lord George who shrugged in return, wiped her mouth with her napkin and continued her dinner.

Lydia's green eyes opened wide. "Now, tell me. Has the girl everything she needs?"

"They lack everything in that cottage." Caleb was thinking of the squalor. "But I have helped them before, and I shall help them again. For Sam's sake."

"The salter was a favourite of yours?" Lydia wanted to know everything about Caleb.

"Not just that but a very good friend. We were boys together."

"Yes, I remember it," added Lord George. "I used to meet you both sometimes fishing in the Salwarpe."

Caleb nodded. "I stayed with Sally. . ." Elizabeth Annesley's eyebrows were raised further. ". . . until the midwife came." He waited for the reaction, but he had complete trust in Lydia.

She was looking particularly beautiful. Her deep lace collar fell off the shoulders fashionably, showing off her beautiful neckline and arms. Simplicity and youth were qualities Caleb had hardly known in a woman before, but she personified it. Her wonderful auburn hair was caught in a chignon at the back of her neck, and she was wearing the dainty posy of summer flowers he had brought her, pinned to her berthe. He had rarely seen her in white before, but her perfection put him in mind of an angel.

"But that was very good of you, Caleb. Was the girl in much pain?" Lydia's eyes showed anxiety now.

"The child was premature, Liddy. And, it is said, came faster than expected."

Aunt Elizabeth tut-tutted at this and helped herself to more meat. Lord George busied himself with his dinner and then spluttered into his handkerchief.

"Remember, I only stayed for a little while until Mrs Minto arrived." He smiled. "I didn't think it *proper* otherwise." They laughed together glancing at their elders. "I have heard Sally and her boy are doing well. They say he's a beautiful child."

There was a moment of silence as the quartet continued with their dinner. Each seemed lost in thought, and Lydia, especially, was fighting to put to the back of her mind remembrance of Charlie Sheridan and her ordeal. Caleb must have understood because he put out his hand and closed it over hers.

"And what are you going to do for them now, Caleb?" asked Lydia. His hand on hers was bringing her those riotous and wonderful feelings she'd been experiencing ever since they had met.

"Strange you should ask that, as an opportunity

to do them a bit of good has just presented itself."

Aunt Elizabeth laid down her knife and fork to listen.

He glanced at her. "Although it could mean losing one or two salters, I think that Sally Shrike's happiness and well-being could be of importance to us."

His audience were agreeing in their hearts already.

Elizabeth Annesley could see it would be difficult for the young couple with Caleb's brother's bastard growing up a salter, and perhaps beside their own. Lydia, too, knew that each time she saw Sally Shrike's child she would be thinking of Sheridan.

Caleb continued, "I'm referring to one, Albert Younger."

Aunt Elizabeth was raising her eyebrows again.

"Strange name," said Lord George.

"He comes from the North of England, my lord. He used to be a barge man before he took to the factory."

"You seem to know more about my workers than I do," Elizabeth said drily. "But I have let go the reins of late and left it all to George."

My lord smiled, patted her on the hand and continued with his dinner.

"Maria Shrike and he are walking out."

"At her age?" Elizabeth looked suitably shocked.

"Why not, aunt?" cried Lydia mischievously.

"Indeed," said Caleb. "Besides, the woman is lonely, having lost husband and son. The man is a straight fellow and is evidently hankering for home."

"Where's that then?" asked George.

"Cheshire."

"Ah, I thought so. I have cousins up there. Something to do with the salt mines."

"Even better," said Caleb. "Then you can give the Shrikes an introduction. . . Even a reference."

"Wonderful," said Lydia. "You mean then, Caleb, to send them into Cheshire?"

"But they're to be married, mind," said Elizabeth, drawing her cashmere shawl about her. "Loose living is the scourge of the salt trade, and my workers have always been encouraged not to partake in such foul practices."

"Quite so, Elizabeth. Bravo!" cried Lord George.

"I believe it is their wish," answered Caleb, looking Lydia full in the eyes. "Then you will support their move, Miss Elizabeth? Lord George?"

The elderly folk nodded.

Elizabeth finished her dessert and waited for Lydia. Then she tweaked her purple skirts about her.

"Come through to the dining-room, dear, and leave the men to their port. I'm sure they've a great deal to talk about."

With a covert and loving glance at Caleb from under her dark eyelashes, Lydia rose from the table and followed her aunt.

"Wonderful-looking young woman, Caleb," George said. "Makes me quite envious."

"I love her to distraction, George," he said. "I don't think I've been happier in the whole of my life. Lydia means the world to me."

"Well, old chap," said George, "you both mean that to the whole of Upwych. You've had your bad times, now enjoy your good. There's not a salter in Upwych who does not wish you well. I, for my part, are just glad the feud is over. Your grandfather shows no sign of coming to his senses?"

"No, he is badly stricken. Just how long he will last none of us know." A frown passed over Caleb's brow at the thought of the tyrannical old man who had tried to blight his future.

"Then he must be pitied," said George, pouring himself port. "And you shall be master now, both of Annesley and Raven's Mill."

"And what of you, sir?" Caleb's eyes twinkled. "You have been doing well yourself on that front, have you not?"

"I have been merely *playing* at brinemaster, Caleb. But soon, if I play my cards right, it will be bridge and hunting again, with perhaps a lady to keep me company. Of course, that's if she'll have me this time."

"Then I wish you good luck with her, George."

Caleb laughed and shook hands with a true gentleman who, although near to seventy, still had plenty of time to make up all the living he had missed.

* * *

They had chosen after Christmas for the wedding. Lydia thought it was a good time. She had come to Upwych in the winter and a fresh year seemed a good time to begin their new life.

She had never been happier than on New Year's Eve when she woke and realised she was to be married to Caleb Vyne. The whole house was in uproar like her heart, and even Wilson, the housekeeper, was singing a song as she went about her duties.

Lord George had been asked to give the bride away and had arrived already and was preening in the morning room.

Lydia had risen late and the hairdresser had come and gone. Her auburn tresses were smoothly obedient and her head crowned with a chaplet of flowers, ordered by Caleb especially. There were ribbons twined around them, which kissed the back of her neck.

When she looked in the mirror she hardly knew herself. Her new stays, although constricting, had drawn in her waist to seventeen inches. The circumference of her hoop, about which she'd worried in London, was amply fashionable and, after stepping into the dress held by Sarah, she wondered how Caleb would even get near her, so wide was the skirt.

But the dress itself was wonderful, looped and scooped with bows; the crinoline, in purest white, was the dream of any young bride. Lydia had never worn any jewellery but simple pearls before, and when Aunt Elizabeth had presented her with the Annesley emeralds, she'd gasped. They matched her eyes almost exactly, and when Sarah clasped them about her neck, the girl had cried out in pleasure, "They'm wonderful, miss!"

They were indeed, and fitting for the heiress of Annesley. They had been kept in Mr Smith's vault since her grandfather, Herbert Annesley, married.

A trifling frown passed over Lydia's face as she thought of how her mother had not been deemed worthy, but it passed. She would think only of happy things on her wedding day. And her father had made a true love match.

She remembered the day she had sat in her chair in the London bedroom, and wondered if Upwych would yield romance. What things had happened to her since? But now she had Caleb and all things had come right.

The thought of her handsome husband-to-be made her catch her breath and her cheeks flame. Tonight could not come soon enough for her. Her heart beat fast. She had had no one to tell her about love, Mama having died, and Aunt Elizabeth quite prudish. She was ignorant of a man's needs, but had much belief that Caleb would have the experience. She determined she would never think of his half-brother again who was slaving under hard labour. He had been lying when he said he'd touched her. But would Caleb know?

* * *

On her way to the church, Miss Elizabeth Annesley remembered her thoughts on looking at Liddy in her wedding gown. No such ravishing bride had been seen in Upwych for years.

As an old maid, it made her heart lurch to see the girl she had brought back from London - and to count her own single years as loss. But then fond thoughts of her old friend arose. Lord George had been a treasure. But, as the carriage pulled up at the lych gate, she was thinking of Caleb Vyne, whose father, although unattainable, had meant so much to her. Each time she saw his son, she fancied that he could have been hers. But an old maid must take the opportunity nearest home.

Lydia smiled as she waited for Lord George. He came in, looking remarkably smart in his wedding frock coat, and carrying a wonderful top hat, brushed to perfection.

"I beg your pardon for staring, Miss Lydia, but you are beautiful."

Sarah handed her the bouquet and stood back.

Lydia looked around the pretty bedroom that had been hers in Annesley House. Soon, she would be a wedded woman and sharing a new one with Caleb. A thrill ran right through her then.

He was taking her back to Raven's Mill. In the months they had waited for the wedding, he had not allowed her to enter the house, saying he was making changes - all for her. Thus the current state of the mill precluded a visit.

His grandfather had full time nursing and would be no trouble to her, he said, given the size of the place. But he'd arranged for the old man to be moved to the Royal to give them some privacy at first.

Once Caleb had offered to buy another home for them both but she had declined, knowing her fascination for the strange house by the river. And it was his by right. So he'd agreed. Before they set off on their wedding journey, they would spend the night under its roof. The thought of being with Caleb there made Lydia tremble.

Allowing Lord George to take her arm, Lydia, emeralds glittering about her neck and holding her beautiful bouquet, passed out of Annesley House to the waiting carriage, towards her wedding at Dodderhill.

* * *

The Shrikes, now re-named Younger, had agreed they wouldn't leave Upwych before they saw Mr Caleb and Miss Annesley married. But they needed to be in Cheshire for New Year. Maria chivvied the children as they hurried over Chapel Bridge. Albert was carrying the youngest, while Sally came behind with her baby, James Caleb.

She'd fed him earlier so he wouldn't be squalling throughout the service. There'd be no room for salters in Dodderhill church itself, but the vicar had allowed them to stand in the churchyard to watch. It was cold but fresh for New Year, and they didn't mind the weather as they all had hope for better things to come.

Both Maria and Sal were thinking about Sam and Joseph as they passed the grave where the broken bodies lay. The family paused to say a prayer, while Albert stood back in his good-mannered way, cap in hand.

"Aye, lad," said Maria, "you'd be glad today, wouldn't you, to see Mr Caleb done right by after all."

"And Sam," added Sally. "He loved Mr Caleb right well. But he'll know wherever he is. And where we're gone." She shifted the baby to her hip. She loved little Jim in a way she thought she never could. But, sometimes, when she was feeding him, his extraordinary blue eyes made her shiver.

She cheered wildly with the rest as the young master and mistress came out of church. Like the rest of the salters, she gasped at the beauty of the new Mrs Vyne in her wedding dress. But, unlike the rest of the town girls, she was not thinking of Mr Caleb Vyne on his wedding night. Instead, she was remembering the kindly way he held her hand and comforted her on the day she gave birth to his half-brother's baby.

As Mr and Mrs Vyne drove away in their shining carriage to Annesley House and their wedding feast, Sally Shrike wished with all her heart that they would enjoy a wondrous life together.

* * *

Later that day, Albert Younger and Maria collected all their baggage, which was waiting ready on a small hand cart, and walked to Upwych station together with the Shrike children and Sally and her baby.

The stationmaster's eyes were wide with surprise as they waited for the afternoon train to Birmingham. The fare had cost a great deal, and the Shrikes were not folk with money. But Albert Younger had drawn out his pocket book like a gentleman and placed the tickets inside. The master of Stretton and Annesley had been a generous man and, from what he'd seen in Upwych, salt men were gentlemen.

He beamed at Maria and his new family as he put his pocket book back carefully, wishing Mr Caleb Vyne and his pretty young wife, good health, wealth and happiness for the future.

* * *

Chapter 16

The carriage, bringing Lydia and Caleb from their wedding feast, came to a halt at the head of the valley that led to Raven's Mill. There, two grooms were waiting with lanterns, holding Sophie and Caleb's bay. Her new husband helped Lydia mount in the darkness, and his eyes, reflected in the lantern's light, were full of love.

As Lydia waited for the men to mount as well, she looked up to the frosty sky, full of stars. In a few hours it would be New Year, and she was celebrating it as she'd never imagined. On her wedding day.

How different that ride seemed from the ones she had taken with Blanchard. Caleb led the way on the sure-footed bay with Sophie following on the leading rein. Lydia was content. She liked to think this was how it would be in the future, but she also knew that with such a husband, she could lead too if she wished.

They passed that dark and silent place where she'd first seen Sally Shrike leaning against Caleb's chest. What a fool she'd been to mistrust him. Then, watching the lanterns shine on the water, Lydia determined not to think of being swept away under the timber bridge, only of coming to with Caleb whispering words of sweetness in her ears.

The horses picked their way through the darkness of

the wild valley and, except for Caleb's fond solicitudes, Lydia could hear no sounds but the distant bark of dogs and owls crying eerily.

And, soon, she could see a light. Caleb broke into a trot as the path by the river widened. Raven's Mill was close by. Lydia's heart beat in time with Sophie's hoofs as she thought of what was to come.

She gasped as they halted at the timber bridge. On the opposite side, the windows of the once-dark house were full of lighted candles. And a boy was running across to help take the horses. As he and the grooms continued, Caleb looked down at his wife.

"My darling," he said, pulling her close. "Welcome to Raven's Mill." They walked across the bridge together. And Lydia didn't notice the dark water, only leaned on his strong arm.

* * *

How had Lydia ever thought Raven's Mill sinister? She stood inside looking round the stone-floored hall, dressed in its Christmas finery.

The ornate wooden fireplace, decorated with carved classical scenes, held a blazing log fire, while above it, Lydia caught sight of her own un-familiar reflection in the mirror. Then the maid was helping untie her riding bonnet and unfasten her cloak.

"This is Hannah, Lydia. She will wait on you until Sarah comes here after our wedding journey."

The girl bobbed and obediently took their cloaks away.

"How fine everything is, Caleb," Lydia exclaimed.

"You like it then, Liddy?"

She nodded, her eyes wide with wonder. Then, taking

her arm, Caleb led her through to the drawing-room. The sumptuous carpet was as bright as the family silver displayed in an array of tall glass cupboards. The furniture had been bought from the finest maker, and the oil paintings Caleb had loved as a child now had a sharp and brilliant clarity. All that the Sheridans had soiled was gone for ever. Caleb had gone to the most extraordinary amount of trouble to see to that. But he could not replace his mother, whose portrait stood over the mantelpiece, clad in the green gown his father had bought her from Birmingham when they had been first married.

But Lydia's delighted eyes were only drawn to the magnificent spruce standing in the corner of the room, its height towering up to the gallery above.

"A Christmas tree!" she cried, looking at Caleb. They had been the fashion for some time now, and she had seen several in London, but this was the best of all. Its branches gave off twinkling lights where the candles had been set, and upon it hung a variety of packages.

Eyes full of love, Caleb went over, reached out, plucked one and handed it to Lydia. Then, stooping beneath the tree, he held out a second.

"But you have given me presents already, Caleb," she cried, thinking of his Christmas generosity.

"And I will give you many more," he murmured, kissing her.

After they had embraced, he helped her open both. The small box was a joy; a brooch worked in the finest silver. Lydia had never seen anything like it before.

"Snowdrops, Caleb?" Her eyes questioned him. The jewelled flower-heads were mother-of-pearl, with delicate yellow diamond eyes.

"A feature of Raven's Mill, Liddy," he answered. "And now. . ."

Her fingers were probing into the second package excitedly. She saw first its colour, then drew out the garment carefully.

"Oh, Caleb, it's exquisite!" It was the most wondrous robe of brilliant green silk, which matched her eyes. "Where did you get it?"

He smiled at her pleasure. "A secret for now, Liddy." He put a finger to his lips.

"But I have nothing for you," she said, still staring at the brooch and the gown. Then, looking up into his eyes, she blushed.

"You have something for me more precious than any money can buy," he said directly, his face full of love. He held her to him tenderly and, then, her head close against his shoulder, taking the small candelabra in his hand, he drew her towards the staircase.

* * *

Caleb was only just awake when he heard the distant bells of Upwych.

"Happy New Year, my darling Liddy," he said, as she lay, her auburn hair streaming across his naked chest. He stroked its brightness tenderly.

He could scarcely believe his good fortune, having everything he desired in the world. He had always been maligned, but his life had turned into a miracle. He had no great ambitions, except to be a good husband and a fair brinemaster. In that order.

And the bells kept ringing. . .

"Can you hear me, Liddy. It's New Year's Day."

But Lydia didn't stir.

302

He bent and kissed her cheek. "Asleep already?"

She didn't answer. She was far away from Upwych, still dreaming of Raven's Mill and Mr Caleb Vyne.

The End

Eve's Daughter

Michael Taylor

'A fascinating read. This highly enjoyable novel conveys vividly the flavour of life at the turn of the century.'
The Rt. Hon. Dr. John Gilbert, MP.

Lizzie Bishop, full of romantic dreams, finds fulfilment when she marries Ben Kite. But two former rivals for her affection, Stanley Dando, her enigmatic second cousin, and Jesse Clancey, the likeable and handsome son of a prosperous neighbour, remain secretly in love with her. Then Ben, with the noblest of intentions, makes the biggest mistake of his life, and everybody is caught up in the spiralling consequences.

Sensual, riveting, poignantly tender, and often hilariously funny, Eve's Daughter draws the reader into an enthralling saga of obsessive desire and deceit. Set in a Black Country community in the early 20th century, the characters are engaging and vividly true to life. A brilliant debut novel.

'Michael Taylor comes into that small group of male writers able to achieve a warm empathy with the heroine.'
Dr. Hilary Johnson.

'From the first sentence it grips your attention . . . an absorbing read.'
Leigh Rowley - The Dudley News

ISBN 0-9525404-5-2

A DRIVING PASSION

Michael Taylor

Lovely Henzey Kite is wary of allowing herself to fall in love again after her first heady affair with prosperous man-about-town, Billy Witts. But men find her beauty and her talent as an artist irresistible. Then, deeply drawn to handsome engineer Will Parish, a widower, Henzey finds another man vying for her love; wealthy motor manufacturer Dudley Worthington, a married man. Only Dudley is aware of the astonishing links between these three men; links that are enough to turn all their lives upside-down. . .

Set within the external glamour and internal graft of the burgeoning Midlands' motor industry in the 20s and 30s, *A Driving Passion* is a spellbinding saga of obsession, agonising love and restless guilt.

A sequel to *Eve's Daughter*, this compulsive tale confirms Michael Taylor as one of the few male writers able to achieve a warm empathy with the heroine.

Due out Spring 1998

ISBN 0-9525404-6-0

Two for a Lie

Helen McCabe

'An epic saga blending historical fact, fiction and fantasy - a stunning read. I couldn't put it down!'
Susan Sallis

Mary Willcocks, aged eighteen, is returning home across the moor when she is waylaid and almost raped by the brutal Humphrey Moon, the wild young son of her former master.

She is saved by her hero, Jem Farr, the half-French ward of the local squire. And Mary's love remains his throughout the many tragedies she has to face before her dreams come true.

Passion, intrigue, murder and revenge are the ingredients of this rich adventure set in the early 1800s. How Mary, the servant girl was transformed into the exotic PRINCESS CARABOO has puzzled scholars and her admirers for two hundred years.

At last, her secrets are revealed in *Two for a Lie,* which is itself based on a dream as rich as Mary's own.

'*Two for a Lie* is more than a novel. Helen McCabe is a master storyteller with the unique gift of making history come alive in the astonishing adventures of her heroine. When I came away, I had a firsthand knowledge of early nineteenth-century life, and also found myself missing Mary . . .'
Shahrukh Husain

ISBN 0-9525404-0-1